Praise for Thomas Hauser

"Hauser unfolds a story that is complex and speedy."

—*Rocky Mountain News*
on *The Beethoven Conspiracy*

"A suspense thriller of the first order. Very exciting."

—*Library Journal*
on *The Beethoven Conspiracy*

"*The Hawthorne Group*, filled with fine touches and a multitude of surprises, rushes to a dramatic and shocking conclusion."

—*Romantic Times*

The best kind of thriller—the sort that you tend to read in one sitting."

—*United Press International*
on *Dear Hannah*

"A first-rate gripper of a tale of espionage and intrigue. Different and very exciting, *The Hawthorne Group* is a classy thriller."

—*Slidell Sentry News*

"A riveting storyline that will keep readers turning the pages. The ending is spellbinding. Hauser sustains his chilling tempo right to the end."

—*South Bend Tribune*
on *Dear Hannah*

Tor Books by Thomas Hauser

Agatha's Friends
The Beethoven Conspiracy
Dear Hannah
The Hawthorne Group

THE HAWTHORNE GROUP

THOMAS HAUSER

TOR
A TOM DOHERTY ASSOCIATES BOOK
NEW YORK

This is a work of fiction. All the characters and events portrayed in this book are fictitious, and any resemblance to real people or events is purely coincidental.

THE HAWTHORNE GROUP

Copyright © 1991 by Thomas Hauser

Cover art by Paul Stinson

A Tor Book
Published by Tom Doherty Associates, Inc.
175 fifth Avenue
New York, N.Y. 10010

Tor ® is a registered trademark of Tom Doherty Associates, Inc.

ISBN: 0-812-51342-8
Library of Congress Catalog Card Number: 90-26941

First edition: May 1991
First mass market printing: February 1993

Printed in the United States of America

0 9 8 7 6 5 4 3 2 1

For Chelli and Gita

PART ONE

Millie Lloyd was walking down the street one afternoon when she found a locket. She thought of turning it in to the police, but in New York City the odds were far better that it would be stolen at the precinct house than returned to its owner. And besides, Millie feared the authorities might consider her odd if she reported her find. So she kept it. The locket was the size of a penny, eighteen-karat gold with a delicate floral pattern etched on both sides. Its hinge was small enough to be unnoticed when snapped shut and, although the inside had room for small photos, Millie kept it bare.

All of this happened in 1891. Millie's daughter, Sarah, inherited the locket when Millie died and always considered it slightly tarnished because of its origins. But Sarah's daughter, Eleanor, regarded it as "something wonderful that belonged to my grandmother." And by the time the locket passed to Millie's great-granddaughter, Anne Rhodes, it was a family heirloom of the highest order, its mixed pedigree long since forgotten.

Chapter 1

Anne Rhodes had always thought of herself as self-confident and secure. Maybe someday if she stopped to consider the fact that she'd never had a good-looking woman friend, if she asked herself why resentment (she refused to use the word "jealousy") toward other women surfaced as often as it did, she'd reevaluate her view. But for the moment, self-analysis was low on her agenda. What mattered was getting the job. That meant arriving on time for her interview and making a good impression. And one thing more—leaving behind twenty years of a career she loved, because her run as an actress was at an end. She'd been Desdemona, Ophelia, Nora, and Eliza; played lovers, beggars, muses, and queens. She'd been a working actress, albeit mostly in regional theater and Off Broadway, without having to wait on tables in restaurants or do temp secretarial work to get by. She'd been on stage on her own terms, with integrity, without sleeping with anyone or flirting her way into roles. Except now she was thirty-nine years old, walking down Fifth Avenue toward Trump Tower, abandoning two decades of dreams, telling herself that acting interfaced poorly with a normal life. The hours on stage were crazy; it was too emotionally demanding. She'd loved the highs, experiencing roles she'd always wanted to play. But she'd been worn down by the lows, the struggle of every audition, facing rejection at every turn. She was burned out, tired of being "out" or "in," liked or not liked, and often not even knowing why. "It takes twenty years to become an actress," her first drama teacher had told her. Well, Anne's twenty years were up, and she was leaving, saying goodbye; forsaking theater for corporate America—if corporate America would have her.

Part of her was crying; and part of her was just plain mad. Angry that too often her fate had been in other people's hands. Angry that the fairy tales she'd read growing up hadn't warned her about aging princesses who were on the cusp of being too old to have children. Angry at her father, for sleeping with too many women; and at her mother for letting him. And angry at David, whom she'd loved. David, who had taken three years of her life, not when she was young and could afford it, but the last three years when time mattered. She wouldn't miss him. "I refuse to miss him." Then she realized she was thinking about David again, which she'd promised herself she wouldn't do. Eighty years; that's how long she'd live if she were lucky. Eighty years

4

of reasonably sharp intellect and good health to enjoy before she got sick and died. And Part Two, the second half of her life, was about to begin. Leave acting; leave David; put everything that reminded her of that part of her existence behind.

The temperature was warm for late April in Manhattan, the sky an uncharacteristically perfect blue. Fingering the locket and gold chain around her neck, Anne gave a small thank-you for the weather. Getting around New York in the rain was a hassle. If she got the job, probably she'd walk each day from her West Side apartment to Trump Tower. None of the subway lines connected properly. The buses would get her there, but walking would be just as fast given the traffic at rush hour.

If she got the job; if she wanted the job once she got it. She'd thought about leaving acting for a year, but considered herself an unlikely candidate for the job market by virtue of her theater-only résumé. Finally, a month ago, she'd mentioned it to Howard Otis, who bore the dual titles of "sweetest man alive" and "Amanda's husband"—Amanda being Anne's best friend. Howard had put Anne in touch with an acquaintance who ran a job placement agency. Thirty thousand dollars a year was her salary demand. "I know I don't have readily identifiable skills," she'd admitted. "But I'm smart, I'm good, and that's what I make acting."

Yesterday, Howard's friend had called. "If you're serious about quitting theater," he'd told her, "something good just came in."

Directly ahead, sharing the east side of Fifth Avenue between 56th and 57th Streets with Tiffany & Co., Anne saw Trump Tower with its reflective bronze glass exterior. A black-and-white-uniformed doorman stood outside, his primary job to discourage entry by undesirables. Aware that her anger was giving way to anxiety, Anne glanced at her watch. It was 9:50 A.M. Her appointment was for ten. Moving past the doorman, through the huge bronze entranceway, she entered the lobby. Up ahead, she could see the atrium with its hanging gardens and eighty-foot waterfall. Marble, brass, and glass were everywhere. Whether or not she got the job, someday she'd have to come back to explore.

To the left, a directory board read 725 FIFTH AVENUE OFFICES. Anne knew the number of the suite she was visiting, but decided to check anyway. The directory was arranged by floor, not alphabetically. The Trump Organization occupied all of twenty-four and twenty-six, with Meshulam Riklis on twenty-five. Twenty-seven and above were probably residences. Below fourteen, the lowest floor listed, she wasn't sure.

There it was—"The Hawthorne Group," listed with two other companies on the twenty-third floor. There were four elevators just beyond the directory board. Anne approached the elevator closest to her, and a man in a navy blue suit moved to her side.

"Can I help you, ma'am?"

It was less an offer of assistance than an order to halt.

"I have a ten o'clock appointment with Leo Muller at The Hawthorne Group."

"Your name?"

"Rhodes; Anne Rhodes."

"One moment, please."

The guard reached for a service phone, and Anne

realized that three other men, similarly dressed, were standing nearby. Four elevators; four security guards.

"Go ahead," the guard told her. "Twenty-third floor."

The elevator was large, with maroon carpet underfoot and recessed lighting above. The walls and sliding door were polished brass, creating a fun house hall-of-mirrors effect. Anne pushed the button marked "23," and watched as the door silently closed. One of her contact lenses was bothering her, and she blinked, creating a tear as the car moved upward. On the twenty-third floor, the elevator opened and she stepped out into the corridor. The glass and brass entranceway nearby bore an unfamiliar corporate logo, so she passed it by. Midway down the corridor, she came to another door, plain gray metal that looked like a closet, with small black letters that read THE HAWTHORNE GROUP.

Anne tried turning the doorknob, but it held firm. Probably a fire exit, she decided. Moving farther down the corridor, she searched for a second entrance but found none and returned to the gray metal door. Just above the frame, a video surveillance camera pointed down. A small slot the size of a credit card was cut into the doorjamb to the left of the knob. Beside that, Anne saw a button embedded in the wall. She pushed it, expecting either a chime or a buzz, but heard neither. The camera rotated. Then a buzzer sounded.

"You're on stage," Anne told herself.

She opened the door and walked inside.

The reception area, just inside the door, was sleek and modern, with a desk, sofa, and several blue contoured chairs. The receptionist was a man of medium height and build, in his midforties, pleasant enough with well-trimmed gray hair. At his request, Anne took a pen and entered her name in the visitors' log.

> Anne Rhodes
> Time—9:56 A.M.
> Person to see—Leo Muller

"Please, have a seat. I'll tell Mr. Muller you're here."

At precisely ten o'clock, a man Anne presumed was Muller entered the reception area. He was in his late forties, conservatively dressed, rather austere-looking.

"Miss Rhodes?"

"Yes."

"I'm Leo Muller. It was good of you to come."

After the pleasantries, he guided her down a row of offices and secretarial cubicles to a small conference room. Like the rest of the office, the room was spotless. There was no street noise; only the faint hum of air-circulating machinery and the sound of office equipment down the hall.

Muller closed the door, and they were alone.

"I have your résumé," he said, speaking with the trace of a European accent, possibly Dutch. "Obviously, you're new to business, but that does not preclude your hiring. The position we are about to fill is part administrative and part clerical. It involves light typing, some filing, and filling in for members of the office staff. More important, though, it entails some common-sense duties which shall be assigned on a day-by-day basis. My colleagues and I are of the view that, with proper supervisions, intelligent people do most things well, just as incompetent people, no matter how well supervised, do most things poorly. The purpose of this interview is to judge whether you are an intelligent woman who can be trusted to perform properly.''

All right, Anne told herself. I'll play the interview game.

''The Hawthorne Group,'' Muller continued, ''is a multinational corporation with headquarters in Belgium and field offices around the world. We are an energy commodities company with a particular expertise in oil. We are privately held. In other words, there is no public ownership of company stock. And we are fully controlled by one man. Christoph Matthes has built The Hawthorne Group into a much-respected organization and, should you meet him, I'm certain you will be suitably impressed. Now, if I may turn to your résumé. Your professional experience consists of acting only. Is that correct?''

''Yes.''

''Have you performed any other work assignments?''

''No.''

''I mentioned a moment ago the need to type occasional notes and letters. Would that be a problem?''

''I don't think so.''

''Have you any computer experience?''

''No.''

The interview progressed, with Muller remaining formal but growing somewhat friendlier and more relaxed. Not that he was a barrel of laughs, but there was a certain charm about him when he set his mind to it. He was well read and versed in the arts; qualities revealed by his questions. And like a good director, he was adept at drawing out his subject. Before long, Anne was speaking freely about the decision to change her life, her likes and dislikes, even her apartment ("From my bedroom window, I can see the park"). They talked for an hour. Then Muller leaned back, apparently satisfied that he had learned whatever it was he deemed important to know about her.

"I'd like to thank you for coming in," he said. "The position we have open pays thirty-two thousand dollars a year, which we are willing to pay because we want someone who takes the job seriously. Office hours are nine to five-thirty, and punctuality is required. Your lack of familiarity with computers should not be a problem. If you are offered the position, we will teach you what you need to know. There is no smoking in the office. Proper dress is encouraged. Employees receive full medical benefits and three weeks paid vacation each year. Have you any questions?"

Anne shook her head.

"Very well, then. I will discuss the matter with Mr. Matthes, and give you our response within the next few days."

It struck Anne that Muller was assuming she'd take the job if it were offered. Probably he was right. The pay was good; it was a chance to learn something about business. And working at The Hawthorne Group would help reshape her life.

Muller walked her to the reception area, and they

shook hands goodbye. Minutes later, Anne was on Fifth Avenue, retracing her steps north toward Central Park West. It had gone well. She felt good. Hey; compared to a Broadway audition, the job interview had been a piece of cake.

♦ ♦ ♦

Four men sat in a room on the top floor of a fortress-like structure in Fort Meade, Maryland. Three of them wore color-coded security badges with magnetic strips on chains around their necks. The fourth did not. They had been together for four hours this morning, and would be together for at least ten hours more before leaving for the night.

Silently, the man without a badge looked out the window at the grounds surrounding the complex—a ten-foot-high cyclone fence topped by barbed wire; then open space broken by high-voltage strands strung between wooden posts, followed by more barbed wire. The others waited for him to speak. He was their leader; forty-six years old, although he seemed younger; rugged-looking, bordering on handsome. His most noticeable mannerism was the tendency to stare right into people when they were talking. Not past them or through them, but into their soul, as if trying to gauge who they were and what they were truly thinking. First-time acquaintances were unnerved by the habit, but those who worked regularly with him had complete trust in his ability and professionalism. When he spoke at last, it was with a faint accent, North Carolina or Virginia.

"What do we know so far about the woman?"

"Not much," one of the others answered. "Her name is Anne Rhodes. She's an actress, thirty-nine years old, married for a few years when she was in her twenties. Now she's single."

"That's all?"

The subordinate shrugged. "Her name only came in this morning."

"How about Matthes. Do we know where he is today?"

Another of the men reached for a computer print-out that had been brought into the room a few minutes earlier. "Here it is," he said, pointing to an entry:

TWOA.MAR.RI.VEI.NPA.RI.S

The leader shook his head. "With a hundred million dollars worth of equipment on each floor," he grumbled, "when we break a code, you'd think the computer would put dots in the right places." Then he fell silent, mentally rearranging spaces:

TWO.AM.ARRIVE.IN.PARIS

"All right," he said. "Let's find out what we can about Anne Rhodes. We might need her."

♦ ♦ ♦

The doorman at 221 Central Park West was new on the job, and hadn't learned most of the tenants' names yet. But he had an eye for women, so when a nicely dressed man came by with an envelope for Anne Rhodes, he knew who she was.

Miss Rhodes lived on the fourth floor, and was a looker. Five foot five, maybe a shade shorter, with green eyes and shoulder-length auburn hair. The lines on her face suggested she was in her late thirties. What caught the doorman's attention, though, was her body, which anyone would notice. The clothes she wore weren't provocative or particularly tight, but they always clung just right. Anne Rhodes might not be cover-girl pretty, but she was one sensuous lady; the way she talked, the way she carried herself, everything about her.

The man with the envelope was good-looking too. Tall, slender, about forty, with a pleasant smile and dark brown hair. The doorman thought that he and Miss Rhodes would make a nice couple together.

"Your name?"

"Akers . . . A-K-E-R-S."

"First name?"

"David."

Across the street, two children were playing on a stone wall abutting Central Park. A middle-aged woman sat on a green slatted bench, watching.

The doorman entered David Akers's name in the building log, next to "Envelope—Anne Rhodes." Then he checked his watch to record the time of delivery.

Akers seemed nervous.

"All right, sir," the doorman told him. "I'll see to it that Miss Rhodes gets this."

◆ ◆ ◆

Walking home from Trump Tower, Anne spent the first few blocks thinking about Leo Muller. He looked like Thomas Mann, she decided. And that got her thinking about all the great books she wished she'd read but hadn't. *War and Peace*, *Of Human Bondage*, most of Dickens. Her sins of omission were near endless. She enjoyed reading when she put her mind to it, not in ten-minute spurts, but for an entire afternoon or evening. Still, for whatever reasons, she seldom did it. Just past the Plaza Hotel she turned west, and asked herself what it would be like to die without having read *Oliver Twist*. Then she caught herself and chided, Stop moping, you could have been born in Bangladesh.

At Columbus Circle, she turned north and, as her mood grew better, she began daydreaming about Paris. On Broadway, she stopped twice. Once at a cheese store, where the man behind the counter overcut so she wound up buying ten ounces of Roquefort instead of eight; then at a vegetable stand, where she squeezed four avocados before finding one that was right. Probably, no one ever bought the first avocado, she decided, ruminating on the fact that she always squeezed at least three before she was satisfied.

At 71st and Central Park West, her favorite stretch of Manhattan landmarks started. The Majestic and Dakota apartments, the San Remo and New-York Historical Society, the American Museum of Natural History and the Beresford. Then the neighborhood turned less elegant, and she came to her home of fifteen years, 221 Central Park West.

It was a nice building, twelve stories high, dating from the 1920s. Anne and her husband had moved in right after they were married, before the West Side became "in." The rent had been modest, well within the range of a working actor and actress. Then, two years later, the marriage went sour, just about the time 221 Central Park West was going co-op. Anne wanted the apartment. Her husband wanted to move to California, but that didn't keep him from claiming half the tenant "insider rights." So they wound up fighting, and Anne wound up giving him ten thousand dollars so she could buy the apartment from the sponsor at the prospectus price of twenty thousand dollars. And of course, in the end, the last laugh was hers because, almost immediately afterward, New York real estate prices skyrocketed and suddenly the apartment was worth a quarter of a million dollars. Not that she could sell it. If she did, the taxes would kill her. And besides, there was no place else to live. But her mortgage was fully paid, she owned the one-bedroom apartment outright, and it was nice to know that, even though her bank account was low, her financial net worth was well above zero.

The doorman was new. Anne had seen him perhaps a dozen times before and didn't like him. He hadn't done anything out of line, but she had the feeling of being mentally undressed each time he looked at her. Charlie, the doorman's predecessor, had been a gem. Polite, reliable, nice, friendly. He'd even looked like a doorman, with erect posture, bushy eyebrows, and thick gray hair. On rainy days, Charlie had always been in the vestibule, waiting with an umbrella to escort people in and out of cabs. On sunny days, he'd stood on the sidewalk, just beneath the awning. For almost two decades, he'd watched as tenants married, divorced, had children, grew older. And none of the tenants had noticed that he was growing older too until he retired.

Now the new doorman was speaking.

"Miss Rhodes."

"Yes?"

"I have an envelope for you."

Anne followed him to the package room just beyond the vestibule, where he handed her a plain white envelope with her name and apartment number written on the front.

It was David's handwriting. She recognized it immediately.

And something inside her dropped. How long had it been since their final blowup, when she'd rejected his pleading and told him to "get out of my life forever."

Four weeks, and it still hurt just as much.

Aware that the doorman was watching, Anne tried hard not to show emotion as she walked to the elevator. David Akers, attorney-at-law. That's how she'd think of him when she opened the envelope. And that was appropriate, because David was far more reliable as a lawyer than a lover. She liked him as a lawyer. Not that he'd represented her; he hadn't. But in their years together, she'd gotten to know his law firm and his partners. There were three of them—David, Mark Dunlap, and Sheldon Levinson, which is what they called the firm—Akers, Dunlap & Levinson. They were refugees from Wall Street; attorneys who'd left giant offices to set up shop in a loft building near Foley Square in lower Manhattan. And after eight years, their practice was flourishing. Mostly, they represented plaintiffs in environmental pollution litigation. The bulk of their cases were on a contingency fee basis, so in a very direct way, each win counted and each loss hurt. But they were good lawyers, winning far more often than they lost. And it appealed to Anne that David had walked away from the comfort and security of Wall Street to start the firm and then, as his reputation grew, resisted appeals from industrial giants to represent their side. That David and his partners made good money was secondary in her view.

The elevator stopped on the fourth floor, and Anne got off. She wasn't sure she wanted to open the letter. Reading it would be like going to the hospital and being opened up. Inside her apartment, she put her keys on the foyer table, and glanced out the bedroom window toward Central Park.

Her hands were shaking.

It doesn't matter what he says, she told herself. The water flows on and doesn't flow back. It's over; we're through.

Goddammit, David; I believed in you.

Opening the envelope, she took a deep breath and read the letter through:

Dear Anne,

Part of me says that writing now is like banging my head against a stone wall. You've said it's over between us, and that everything that went wrong was my fault. But I love you. You changed my life and changed me in very important ways, and I care about you. So even though you might be past listening, I'm writing in the hope that I can still get through to you. I guess inside, I think you're too

17

smart to believe everything you've said about me. And I think you still love me.

Things have been going pretty well lately, but I miss you terribly and not being with you casts a pall over everything. I've spent I don't know how many hours going over our relationship, and I want to explain to you, or at least try to explain, what happened from my point of view.

You and I met three years ago, thirty-nine months to be precise. We went out a couple of times and I was very taken by you, but you said you didn't want to get involved. I took you at your word. You went out with other people. So did I. Then you fell in love with me, before I realized I was in love with you. We spent a lot of time together after that, but important things were left unspoken. You never opened up about your feelings toward me. You never said you wanted to marry me or live with me or have a child together. After it was too late, I heard a lot of "would haves" and "dids"—"I would have married you, David," "I did want to have a child with you, David." But the truth is, a lot of what you say you felt was never said. Maybe I should have inferred it, but I didn't. Eventually, you stopped going out with other people. I didn't. I don't know why not. Some of the women I saw were old friends. Others, admittedly, were romantic pursuits. Finally, you went off to spend three months doing regional theater in Michigan, and I had an affair with another woman.

Yeah, I knew it was wrong. And I hid it from you. We'd never spelled out what we owed each other and what we were or weren't going to do. But not telling you, seeing someone else behind your back,

18

was a lie of omission. And what bothers me now more than the lie is that I did it at all, but at the time I didn't realize I was in love with you. You found out about it. And although we hung on together for another six months, not much worked right between us after the blowup.

I don't think you understand how rejecting you were those last six months. All you did was tell me how untrustworthy I was, and how I'd better be careful, and what was wrong with me. No one can live like that. It was as though, as soon as I realized how much I cared about you and started trying to make things between us work, you stopped trying and began doing things to hurt me. I'm sorry for the unhappiness we caused each other. I hurt you a lot; I know that. I won't even try to defend some of the things I did. I took too much and gave too little. I don't like the way I was with you, and I'd do things differently if I could do them over again. But no one can rewrite the past. I can't change what I had for lunch yesterday, let alone what happened six months ago. All I can tell you is, I never acted out of malice or tried to hurt you.

I wish, just for a moment, that you could let go of your anger. That you could realize we loused things up; not just me; we. We blew it together. It's been very painful for me to lose your trust and love, and to realize that I'm in part responsible for that loss. But I honestly feel that part of you would rather hold on to grievances than resolve them; that you collect injustices, and won't let go of them.

Losing you has been like a death in the family for me, and it's forced me to do a lot of thinking. There are times when life seems very complicated. But when you sort things out, it gets simple again. What matters is spending every day, day by day, as much of each day as possible with someone you love. I love you. I want the things you want, and I'd like to be there for you. Every day, I hope you'll realize that we're both capable of growing and changing and doing whatever we have to do to be together. When things were good between us, it was impossible to imagine them being better between two people. There was an excitement and chemistry that spoke for itself. Very few couples are excitedly happy together. We could have been. We still can be.

We belong together.

If I could choose one person to go with into the unknown, it would be you.

Love,
David

Anne stared at the letter a long time. Her hands were trembling. She'd heard it before, of course; all of it. She'd heard it from David, when he begged forgiveness for fucking around behind her back, and then kept right on seeing his women friends. And she'd heard it from her parents; her mother saying to her father, "You can do what you want with other women, but if you spend time with someone else, don't come home to me." And then her father would lie, and her mother would weaken and take him back again.

Goddammit, David. I loved you, and you hurt me.

She began to read the letter again: "You changed my life . . . I care about you . . . I think you still love me . . . I've spent I don't know how many hours going over our relationship . . . Maybe I should have inferred . . ."

Maybe I should have inferred! Inferred! It was a brief. Not a love letter; not an apology. It was a goddamn lawyer's brief!

Just leave me alone, David. Please, let the scars heal. Just leave me alone.

Executive offices reflect their occupants far more than they mirror the taste and character of the city in which they're found. This one was located in Paris, but it could just as easily have been London, Tokyo, or any other city serving as a Hawthorne Group outpost around the world. Christoph Matthes had an executive office in each of them, and wherever he traveled, that place was instantly transformed into headquarters for global operations.

Matthes had been sitting for hours. Most of that time had been spent talking on the telephone or staring at the computer monitors on the desk in front of him. On occasion, he rose, paced back and forth across the room, and returned to his chair. Subordinates entered and left at his call. Just outside the door, three men stood guard. Wherever he was, wherever he went, it was with a security detail adequate to protect against abduction, although an assassin willing to make the ultimate sacrifice would probably be able to pierce their guard.

Matthes was handsome in a dark melancholy way, with intense eyes and closely cropped black hair showing only a few streaks of gray. Every word, every motion he made, was measured for economy.

His body was lean, the suit covering it impeccably tailored. He was one of the wealthiest men in the world and determined to grow wealthier.

Now he was on the telephone.

"Follow your instincts," he told Leo Muller. "If you think she's safe, hire her."

Chapter 2

Anne got the job at The Hawthorne Group. She figured she would. Three days after the interview, Leo Muller telephoned and asked if she could start work the following Monday, May 1. She said yes, and he told her to be at the office by nine A.M.

Deciding what to wear preoccupied her for much of Sunday night. A suit might be pretentious given the essentially "clerical" nature of her duties, but pants were out. Finally, she settled on a blue linen skirt and white tailored blouse. Monday morning, she considered sandals but remembered that, during the interview, Muller had spoken of "proper dress," and decided to wear low heels instead.

The weather was sunny, and she walked to work. Muller met her in the reception area at nine o'clock, and she spent several minutes filling out forms—

name, address, social security number, and the like. The receptionist, whose name was Harry Ragin, asked if she wanted coffee. She didn't. Then Muller took her on a tour of the office.

"The Hawthorne Group is highly computerized," he explained as they walked. "Each employee has a computer access card and electronic control number. Some equipment requires only the number. For example, to use the photocopying machine, you press the appropriate buttons on the keypad to enter your number. Certain other equipment requires insertion of a computer card, your electronic signature, so to speak. The card is plastic with an embedded integrated-circuit digital code, and each employee's card is programmed differently. For example, Mr. Matthes has a card which gives him access to every piece of equipment and every area of the office at any hour. Your card offers no computer access at present, but will allow you to enter the main office door between the hours of nine A.M. and five-thirty, Monday through Friday, excluding holidays. The entire electronic access system is controlled by a central processing unit, which records the identity of any person using equipment or gaining access to a given area. Video cameras selectively record certain use. This security might strike you as extreme, but the protection of proprietary information is crucial to the company's competitive position."

One by one, Muller explained the various office computer systems: "Information comes into our New York office in many ways—by telephone, Telex, faxogram, and regular mail. However, in this day and age, electronic mail is far more useful. Each employee has a computer monitor and keyboard at his or her desk. At any given time, you can type your electronic control number into the system and get a listing of your electronic mail. Then you can summon each document onto your computer screen. Employees are able to read only the electronic mail designated specifically for them, since each recipient knows only his or her own electronic control number.''

Anne was starting to feel a little over her head. When it came to computers, the world had passed her by. But at her interview, Muller had told her not to worry; they'd teach her what she needed to know.

''The second office computer system concerns files,'' Muller continued. ''There is very little paper here. Most of our data is electronically stored. Partly, this is to guard against the theft of proprietary information. And partly, it is done to save space with regard to files.'' He paused for a moment, then said with a smile, ''I read recently that there are two trillion paper-based documents stored at present in the United States. Every day, American businesses generate eighty million letters and three hundred million photocopies. We prefer an integrated imaging system for our files. Every document we wish to save is fed into a scanner, much like paper is fed into a photocopier. The paper document is then destroyed, and its contents stored on a computer cartridge which holds the equivalent of a quarter-million pages. Once a day, all data stored in the cartridge is copied onto a backup disk. When a document is entered, it can be categorized in any way the enterer chooses by using the keyboard. Thereafter, each document is recallable by reference to its particular categorization or any word or number in the document. To enter our file system, one needs an appropriately coded computer card, and an approved electronic access code number.''

Muller asked again if Anne wanted coffee, and she did. They drank it in his office; then the tour resumed.

The north wing of The Hawthorne Group's office space consisted of eight executive offices, each of which had a secretarial cubicle outside. The corner office belonged to Christoph Matthes, who, Muller told her, spent several days a month in New York. Beyond Matthes's office, the west wing consisted of two conference rooms, a computer center, the equipment room (photocopying, Telexes, etc.), a kitchen area, and four more secretarial cubicles. All totaled, twenty-three people worked in the office—Matthes, Muller, six more executive-level personnel, eight secretaries, a day and a night receptionist, the equipment room operator, two messengers, Anne, and one other administrative/clerical assistant.

''Because of the importance placed on proprietary data,'' Muller told her, ''we take extra precautions regarding the disposal of waste paper. All such material is shredded in the equipment room and chemically reduced to pulp before being discarded. Telephone conversations, of course, are not monitored, and no effort is made to interfere with the personal life of employees. However, it is of the utmost importance that any approach to you by any outsider seeking information about company operations be reported immediately. Failure to observe this rule shall be grounds for dismissal. All employees, including executive-level personnel, indeed especially executive-level personnel, are encouraged to remain in the office for lunch daily, so as to be available for trading emergencies. Lunches are catered and offered free of charge in conference room B from noon until two P.M. I believe you will find them most satisfactory. That is everything for the moment, except that I wish to give you your computer access card and electronic control number.''

Following his lead, Anne returned with Muller to the reception area, where he reached into an inside jacket pocket and drew out a two-by-three-inch piece of navy blue plastic with ridges of varying width and length and a tiny black arrow on one side pointing toward the edge. "This card," Muller said, "will give you access to the office during normal working hours. At present, it has no other coded function although, as your duties expand, that will change. Come with me, please."

Anne took the card and followed him out into the corridor, where the gray metal door to The Hawthorne Group offices closed behind them.

"You insert the card arrow-first into the slot, with the arrow facing toward the doorknob," Muller instructed.

Anne did as ordered, and a click sounded.

"Remove the card," Muller told her. "The door will be unlocked for ten seconds."

Glancing toward the surveillance camera above, Anne followed his instruction, then turned the doorknob. The door opened. Muller gestured for her to enter, and they returned to the reception area.

"Please, safeguard your computer access card carefully," he cautioned. "Now, if I may give you your electronic control number; in checking your credentials prior to hiring, we learned, quite by accident of course, that you were previously married. Because it is important that electronic control numbers be easily memorized by the employees, I have chosen the date of your marriage—ten twelve seventy-five—as your number. I hope this is acceptable to you.''

''I can live with it.''

''Good. Then perhaps we should try it out on the photocopy machine.''

Leading her back along the L-shaped trail of offices, Muller stopped at the door to the equipment room and ushered her inside. A young man in his twenties, blond with pockmarked skin, was working the faxogram machine.

''Kurt,'' Muller began, by way of introduction; ''this is Anne Rhodes. Anne will be with us at The Hawthorne Group for the foreseeable future. Anne, this is Kurt Weber, who is in charge of the equipment room and will handle photocopying for you. However, in the event he is unavailable, you should know how the machine works.''

Reaching for a piece of paper, Muller gestured toward the keypad. Following his cue, Anne punched in ''101275.''

''I believe the rest of the copying process is self-explanatory,'' Muller told her.

Anne took the paper, inserted it into the machine, and made one copy.

''Well done,'' Muller complimented. ''Kurt will explain multiple copying and collating to you at a later date should that prove necessary. But now, let me show you your own office space.''

Retracing their steps, they moved back toward the reception area, stopping at a cubicle just beyond the first executive office. It was a small area, six by eight feet; large enough for a desk, two chairs, a shelf, and not much more.

"Welcome to your new home," Muller told her. "Of course, much of your time will be spent in other areas of the office." Before Anne could respond, he glanced at his watch. "Later in the day, you will be given your first assignment. But now, since it is twelve o'clock, perhaps you would enjoy joining some of your colleagues for lunch."

Conference room B, which Anne had visited earlier in the morning, had been transformed into a buffet area. The centerpiece was a platter of chicken salad surrounded by rye bread and croissants. Various fruits, cheeses, and soft drinks were also on display. Three men and two women, several of whom Anne had seen in the corridor earlier in the morning, were seated at the table, conversing and eating.

Muller introduced them: "Eric Winslow, our tax specialist; Michael Harney, our computer expert; Ernst Neumann, who monitors changes in the spot price of oil; Emily Lynch and Cassandra Sanger, two of our finest secretaries."

The employees were cordial, and the lunchroom pleasantly egalitarian, although it appeared all the executives were men. Muller left, citing other obligations, and Anne made a chicken salad sandwich. A half-dozen chairs were empty, and she chose one next to Harney.

He was handsome; slightly under six feet tall, conservatively dressed and trim, with a welcoming smile and receding brown hair. "Welcome to The Hawthorne Group," he said, moving his plate slightly to the right to make more room for hers. "I hope Leo wasn't too intimidating this morning."

Anne smiled, thankful that not everyone in corporate America emulated Leo Muller's style.

"Actually, he was rather agreeable," she said.

"Spoken like a diplomat. What line of work were you in before joining The Hawthorne Group?"

They talked about theater, what Anne had liked and disliked about it, and her reasons for leaving. Harney told a story about a goat that ate a book and a reel of film. After digesting both, the goat opined, "I liked the book better." Eventually, the conversation shifted to family. Harney was married with a wife and two children who lived in Delaware. "I have an apartment in Manhattan and commute home on weekends," he explained between mouthfuls of chicken salad. "It's not ideal, but executive-level salaries at The Hawthorne Group are a powerful incentive."

"How long have you worked here?"

"Four years. Two or three more and I hope to retire."

As the hour passed, various employees entered and left the conference room. Most were friendly, although Harney seemed warmer than the others, drawing Anne out and telling her both about himself and the office.

"The Hawthorne Group is a remarkable organization," he explained, nearing the end of his sandwich. "Corporate headquarters are located in Brussels. That's where Christoph Matthes lives, although at least half his time is spent traveling. There's a five-member Executive Council, also in

Brussels, and regional offices like this one around the world."

"What's your job?"

"I'm into computers. The energy market, and particularly oil, operates twenty-four hours a day around the globe. When New York is sleeping, people are trading in Tokyo. When it's night in Buenos Aires, offices in Paris are open. To make money in that environment, you need a constant flow of new data. If someone hears on the radio that the spot price of oil has jumped fifty cents a barrel or the Iraqis have bombed an oil field in Iran, it's too late to act. That information will already have impacted on the market. Split seconds are crucial. Instant data is the lifeblood of the energy commodities business, and we get that data from high-speed computer transmission systems. That's what all the security here is about. It's not the office equipment we're worried about someone stealing. It's the data."

Muller returned after forty-five minutes, and joined them for dessert. He was director of the New York office, Anne learned, "but titles mean little," he told her modestly.

Harney said he'd noticed the locket Anne was wearing, and that it was very pretty. She liked Michael Harney, her first "friend" in the office. And by the close of lunch, largely because of him, she felt reasonably good about The Hawthorne Group.

The afternoon was spent learning a little more about the office and getting her feet wet with various clerical duties. At one point, Anne sat in for Harry Ragin at the receptionist's desk, and discovered that his job entailed doubling as office telephone operator.

There were cameras everywhere, she realized; not just outside the front door, but throughout the office. By midafternoon, Anne had seen a half dozen of them, placed in ceiling recesses like monitors in a Las Vegas casino pit. The employees she met—two more executives, three secretaries, and a woman with administrative/clerical duties similar to her own—ranged from cold to cordial. The least pleasant was her office counterpart—a fortyish woman named Madeline Bouchard, whose expressionless smile suggested a bad face-lift.

There were a lot of closed doors, including the door to Christoph Matthes's office. At various times, Anne heard people speaking Spanish, German, Italian, French, and several languages she didn't recognize. Numbers, names of places, and references to oil prices filled the air. At one point, she walked past the equipment room, looked in, and saw Kurt Weber at the paper shredder.

Late in the day, she telephoned Amanda Otis to confirm an earlier-arranged dinner planned to honor her first day on the job. Amanda had promised to cook; Howard had promised to eat. "I'll be leaving work around five-thirty," Anne told her. "Give me time to go home, change clothes; you know the routine. Anytime after seven would be good."

They settled on seven-thirty. Then Anne went back to sorting invoices, her job of the moment. Once her thoughts wandered to David. She wondered what he'd think if he saw her in the office. Then she chastised herself for thinking about him at all. Life was a puzzle and, as far as her life was concerned, David Akers was a piece that didn't fit.

At five-thirty, Leo Muller came by and suggested

she go home for the night. "Henceforth," he advised, "you may leave at this hour without prompting." She wanted to say good night to Michael Harney, but his door was shut, so she decided against it. Most of the executives were still at their desks. On the way out of the office, the night receptionist introduced himself.

"My name is Mort Gordon. Anything you need, Monday through Friday between five P.M. and two in the morning, I'm the guy to ask."

Gordon, like Harney, struck her as friendly, although Harney was clearly several rungs higher on the socioeconomic ladder.

"I'm Anne Rhodes. I started here this morning."

They chatted for a few minutes; Anne wanting to leave but not wanting to seem impolite. Gordon obviously liked to talk, which was odd for someone whose job was essentially that of a night watchman. Just before leaving, she decided that he looked a little like Paul Sorvino.

Downstairs, even at the peak of the evening rush hour, the Trump Tower lobby was spotless. Attendants were everywhere, cleaning, picking up paper, and polishing fingerprints off brass and glass. Anne passed through the revolving door, out onto Fifth Avenue, and began walking north toward Central Park. Overall, her first day at The Hawthorne Group had been a success; at least that was how she viewed it. The one thing she didn't like was her electronic access code number: 10-12-75. She didn't know how Leo Muller learned she'd been married, let alone her wedding date. Still, he'd been honest about it; he'd told her he knew. And he had a point; she wouldn't forget her code number.

Midway through the walk home, she thought again about David. Their breaking up was like a death; that's what he'd said in his letter. But it was over now; their future had ended. Tomorrow has a way of turning into yesterday, she told herself. Then it becomes a long time ago, and nothing can change it. By the time she reached Central Park West, she'd succeeded moderately well in exorcising David from her consciousness, and was thinking about Mozart. Maybe she'd buy a Sony Walkman, so she could listen to tapes going to and from work.

In the lobby of her building, Anne checked for mail, then took the elevator upstairs to her apartment. She had an hour to change clothes and relax a bit before going to Amanda and Howard's for dinner. Turning her key in the Medeco lock, she opened the door and stepped inside. It was good to be home. Everything in her apartment was just as she'd left it.

That was an odd observation, she told herself. Why would she notice that everything in the apartment was just as she'd left it?

Maybe it was her imagination, but the apartment *felt* different.

Slowly, not quite sure what she was looking for, not even sure if she was looking for something, Anne went to the living room. Everything was in place—her television and VCR, the silver candy dish on the coffee table, her china and crystal in the breakfront. Nothing was missing.

The kitchen was next. There too, everything was as it should be, including her Cuisinart, which had broken two years ago and been relegated to use as a begonia planter.

Anne laughed at herself. This was crazy. Still, part of her was afraid to go to the bedroom, because her jewelry might be missing.

For chrissake, Rhodes. Get it together.

Like the rest of her apartment, the bedroom was just as she'd left it. Except—and again, maybe it was her imagination—it seemed different. The papers on her desk were piled a little too symmetrically. Ridges of dust were where they shouldn't be. She was compulsive about order, but when she opened the top drawer of her bureau, the bras and panties seemed arranged a little too neatly.

Her jewelry was untouched, in the closet where it was supposed to be.

Back to the living room.

What am I looking for? This is crazy. It's only my imagination.

But if I were paranoid, I'd think that someone had been in my apartment.

Chapter 3

Anne stood in the center of the living room, chiding herself for her imagination. She still had the feeling that her apartment had been violated, but a childhood rhyme was cutting away at her fears:

> As I was going up the stair
> I met a man who wasn't there.
> He wasn't there again today,
> I wish, I wish he'd stay away.

It was all in her mind; that's what she told herself. She'd been under a lot of pressure lately; giving up acting, starting a new job, leaving David. Any person would be disoriented with that many major life changes going on.

Just to make sure, she went to the kitchen, picked

up the intercom, and buzzed the doorman to ask if anyone had been in her apartment. Maybe there'd been a leak in the bathroom or some other maintenance problem. The doorman connected her to the superintendent, who said no one had been there.

"I guess it's my imagination," Anne told him. "Nothing is missing."

She changed clothes, listened to the radio for a bit, and thumbed through the newspaper. At seven-fifteen, she left to go to Amanda and Howard's for dinner. Howard—with Jessica, age two, perched on his shoulders—answered the door when Anne arrived. There were hugs; then Jessica ordered them into the kitchen, where Amanda was brushing a striped bass with butter.

Of all Anne's friends, Amanda was the one she felt closest to with the fewest conflicts. They'd met ten years earlier when Amanda was in the throes of an ugly divorce. Her soon-to-be ex-husband wanted out of the marriage, but was resisting alimony and child support. That was when Amanda, who played life by the rules and tried to be fair, learned the unfortunate nuances of the New York State judicial system.

"I'm thinking about marketing a board game called Divorce," she'd told Anne over dinner one night when the legal battle was raging. "The way I envision it, there'll be five players—a wife, a husband, a judge, and two lawyers—who move around a board laid out like Monopoly. The point of the game from the lawyers' point of view will be to extort as much money as possible from their own clients. Every time the wife wants to move, she'll have to throw double sixes with the dice to get out of the court clerk's office. Meanwhile, the husband will try to cut off the wife's income, so she can't buy food or clothing without sacrificing two turns. The game ends when a majority of the players get exhausted and quit.''

After the divorce, Amanda's ex moved to Texas, leaving her with two infant daughters. Soon, despite court orders, all alimony and child support payments stopped, ushering in a seven-year struggle. ''I felt sorry for myself; I felt sorry for the kids; I did a lot of complaining,'' Amanda recalled later. ''Finally, I decided to stop feeling sorry because it wasn't doing any good. Then I met Howard.''

Howard was a financial analyst, shy and awkward around women, two years older than Amanda. They went out together, fell in love, got married, and Jessica was born ten months later. Now Amanda's older daughters—Susan, fourteen, and Ellen, twelve—regarded Howard as their father; Jessica was appropriately precocious; and Amanda and Howard were easing comfortably into their midforties together.

In the kitchen, there were more hugs. Jessica showed off the cookies she and Amanda had baked that afternoon. Howard told a story he swore was true about an arbitrager who had just been reprimanded by Merrill Lynch for telephoning a sex-line service and putting the resulting conversation, moans and all, over the speaker phone in his office. Susan wandered in to pick at the bass before it was ready. Ellen shouted from the living room that someone, preferably not Jessica, should come and help with her French homework.

Dinner was served a little before eight, with Anne's first day of work the primary topic of table conversation. Susan and Ellen opined that The Hawthorne Group sounded creepy. Amanda concurred to a degree, but adopted a wait-and-see attitude. Howard, who worked on Wall Street, said the atmosphere "sounded normal."

Afterward, Anne and Amanda did the dishes, while Howard read Jessica a bedtime story. Amanda had put on weight, Anne noticed. Five or ten pounds, although it hadn't really changed her appearance.

"Howard's mother is coming to visit next week," Amanda reported as they worked. "She comes up from Miami once a year for a week, but it seems like once a week for a year."

"You're exaggerating."

"No, I'm not. Ask Howard. All she does is complain. Last time, it was the weather. Every day was too hot or too cold or too humid or too windy. Finally, we had a perfect day. We were right here in the kitchen, drinking coffee together, and I said to her, 'Mother Otis, look out the window. The sky is blue; there are no clouds; the temperature is in the midseventies; there's a gentle breeze.' Do you know what she told me? 'The window is dirty.' "

When the dishes were done, they returned to the living room and joined Howard for a glass of cognac. He confirmed the dirty-window story, and admitted that, all things being equal, he'd be just as happy if his mother stayed in Florida.

Then Amanda asked Anne if she'd heard from David.

"Last week; he sent me a letter."

"And?"

There was an awkward silence.

"I know you and Howard are fond of David," Anne said finally, "but it's over between us. I feel like I've been through a long illness, and I'd rather you not mention him to me anymore."

Whereupon Howard deftly shifted subjects to the previous day's lunch. "I was at an Italian restaurant called Resignato's," he reported. "Just before dessert, I had to go to the men's room, and there were doors marked 'Bello' and 'Bella.' I don't speak Italian so, needless to say, I was afraid I'd choose the wrong door and wind up in the ladies' room. Then I remembered Bella Abzug and figured 'Bella' probably meant woman. Fortunately, I was right."

Around ten-thirty, Anne said good night and went home to bed. The next morning, walking to work, she reflected on the difference between acting hours and a nine-to-five job, and came down in favor of the latter. She arrived at Trump Tower ten minutes early, took the elevator upstairs, inserted her computer access card into the office door slot, and discovered it didn't work. Then she remembered that Leo Muller had told her the card was programmed to allow entry during "normal working hours," which in her case was nine to five-thirty. She could buzz to get in, but out of curiosity she waited in the corridor until nine. Then she reinserted the card, and a click sounded.

Glancing at the surveillance camera above as she'd done a day earlier, Anne removed the card and entered the reception area. Harry Ragin was at the reception desk. He smiled—it was a plastic smile—and told her that Muller was waiting for her in his office. Muller greeted her with his usual formality, and explained that at The Hawthorne Group non-executive-level personnel took turns setting up lunch. Then he handed her a slip of paper with the caterer's name and telephone number, and advised, "Today is your day. Order what you wish; cost is no object."

After she telephoned in the lunch order, Anne spent the better part of the morning working on a clerical assignment for Ernst Neumann. Then Muller asked her to make several calls to the New York Public Library and United States Council for Energy Awareness. Just before noon, the food arrived, and she set up lunch. During the meal, she again sat next to Michael Harney, who introduced her to Graham Hayes (an expert on commodities trading procedures) and Diane Altschuler (Hayes's secretary). Eventually, they were joined by Muller, who complimented Anne on her choice of seafood salad and outlined her afternoon assignments.

Thus it went for the rest of the week. Most of her chores fell into the secretarial-clerical category. She learned how to work the electronic mail system, grew more familiar with office protocol, and met a half dozen more Hawthorne Group employees.

Thursday afternoon, Howard telephoned and invited her to a party one of his partners was giving the following night. "There'll be twenty-five, maybe thirty people," he told her. "Amanda says you might meet someone you like, and if the party's a bust, you can always talk with me and Amanda."

Friday, at work, Anne had lunch for the third time with Michael Harney. This time, he sought her out. At least, that's what she thought. Muller had given her an assignment that kept her busy until one-thirty and, when she went into the conference room for a bite to eat, Harney followed.

"Jewish deli," he observed, evaluating a platter of assorted cold cuts.

Anne fashioned a pastrami on rye with mustard; Harney, roast beef on a roll with cole slaw. For several minutes, he tried to explain the computer project he'd been working on all morning, but gave up when Anne confessed to not understanding a word he said. Then they talked about the structure of the company, with Harney explaining that it had been an empty shell and not much more when Christoph Matthes had taken it over twenty years earlier.

"The name predates Matthes's involvement," he elaborated. "Nigel Hawthorne was a British financier who structured The Hawthorne Group to allow for maximum flexibility with a minimum of government regulation. He wasn't particularly successful, though, and when he died, Matthes bought the company's assets and restructured its business. The rest is history."

"Why is Matthes so successful?"

"Oil," Harney answered. "In the energy business, fortunes are determined by monetary exchange rates, tax laws, specialized lawyers, and accountants. But the bottom line is, you have to have the commodity, and Matthes has it. The way things stand at present, The Hawthorne Group is divided into five divisions—exploration, marketing, finance, administration, and political action. Exploration locates the oil. The people in marketing buy and sell it. The money for deals comes from finance, and administration runs the operation."

"And political action?"

Harney shrugged. "Dealing with oil, you do business with a lot of third-world countries. Within The Hawthorne Group, everyone is apolitical. The last thing you want in an organization like this is a political ideologue; they're impossible to control. But someone has to explain to the Nigerian government why we buy their oil and sell it in South Africa. Iran and Iraq have to be placated when we do business with both of them. That is what's meant by political action."

One of the executives Anne had met earlier—Hans Werner, an accounting specialist—came into the room for a cup of coffee. For whatever reason, his presence seemed to make Harney uncomfortable, and they shifted subjects.

"I'm curious about something," Anne asked, addressing neither of them in particular. "Every morning when I get here, you people are already at your desks. And when I leave at night, you're still working. What hours do you keep?"

"Eight to eight," Werner told her. "Sometimes longer."

"Same here," Harney answered. Then, responding to the look in her eyes, he held his wrists up in front of him, close together. "Golden handcuffs," he said. "But the truth is, except for weekends when I'm with my wife and children, it doesn't matter. Whether I'm alone in my apartment or here at the office makes no difference."

At day's end, Leo Muller stopped by Anne's cubicle with her first paycheck. Minus deductions for income tax withholding, social security, and disability compensation, it came to $430.76. Feeling wealthy, she took a cab home, stopping on the way to buy herself flowers. Then she changed clothes, and went to the party with Howard and Amanda.

The party was a disaster. Not as bad as Bhopal or Chernobyl, but certainly it ranked with a killer tornado. Howard's partner lived in a duplex apartment on Park Avenue in the eighties, and most of the guests were business related. There was a lot of shoptalk, with wives staying close to their husbands, and, more than once, Anne thought about David. The only other single woman was a municipal-bond analyst, who smoked a pipe and seemed intent on blowing smoke in Anne's face whenever they were in close proximity to one another. Several single men came and went during the course of the evening, the last of them being a stockbroker named Alex Hilliard.

"If Alex were a football play," Howard acknowledged later, "he'd be a fumble." Be that as it may, he latched on to Anne and wouldn't let go. When Anne excused herself to go to the bathroom, on her return Alex was waiting. When she walked away to get another drink, Alex dutifully followed. She tried talking with other people, and he simply stood there, inserting himself into every conversation. Finally, she abandoned hope of evasive action and resigned herself to talking with him for the rest of the evening, but all she could think to ask was, "Do you have any hobbies?" That led to a twenty-minute summary of Alex's coin collection.

"It was nice meeting you," she lied at the end of the evening.

"Could I see you again?"

"I don't think so. I appreciate your asking, but I'm involved with somebody."

44

"Maybe we could get together for a drink or something."

"I'm afraid not, but thank you for the thought."

In the cab going home, Howard apologized for the evening. Anne protested that it wasn't his fault, adding, "Maybe I'm just not ready yet to go partying."

In the lobby of her building, she passed the night doorman, then went upstairs to get ready for bed.

She missed David.

If the telephone were to ring now, if it were David—

No!

A thousand times, no.

Never.

She brushed her teeth, put on her nightgown, and turned back the bedcovers. It wasn't that late: eleven-thirty on a Friday night.

Leaving David is the hardest thing I'll ever do.

Not really. Getting over him will be.

◆ ◆ ◆

Fort Meade, Maryland. The men were tired. The demanding pace of too many hours for too many days over too many weeks was taking its toll. Outside the building, barbed-wire fences and high-voltage barriers lit by floodlights exuded a garish otherworldly glow. Inside, on the top floor, the men sat watching as file references and numbers flashed across a computer monitor:

XBL-PAR
624-93107286
STANDARD-4
FRSCHOL

Then the letters and numbers stopped.

One of the men rubbed his eyes.

"God, the world has changed," he said, a faint southern accent audible in his voice. "When I was young, the president of the United States could ride in an open limousine through any city in the country. At least we thought he could. And now . . ."

His voice trailed off, then picked up again as the image of an attractive auburn-haired woman appeared on the screen. "That's Anne Rhodes. As best we can tell, she's what she claims to be. A former actress; no political connections or business background. Michael Harney says she's bright, friendly, and that what she knows about computers would fit in a thimble. He thinks she's honest."

"Nice body," the man to the speaker's left offered.

"Thank you, Gottlieb. It's good to know that, with the fate of the world hanging in the balance, you've managed to keep a sense of perspective."

Refocusing his attention on the monitor, the speaker continued. "Anyway, as far as Anne Rhodes is concerned, our assumption is, she's not one of them. I don't know what else there is to do right now, except keep an eye on her."

Chapter 4

Week number two at The Hawthorne Group was a lot like week number one. On Monday, Anne brought several Degas reproductions into the office to brighten her cubicle. Leo Muller expanded her duties to include sorting mail that came in via the United States Postal Service, and Kurt Weber taught her to operate the paper shredder. Late in the morning, Muller asked her to copy a two-page memorandum. Following his instructions, she brought it to the equipment room, entered her electronic control number on the copymachine keypad, pressed the copy button, and fed both pages into the machine. It whirred, a light flashed, but only the original and two blank sheets of paper came out. She tried again with the same result, then looked up and saw Muller beside her.

"How careless of me," he said with a smile. "Certain of our memoranda are prepared on specially processed paper to prevent unauthorized reproduction.''

He'd known all along what he was doing, Anne decided later. And he'd done it to remind her that, whatever she did in the office, someone or some system would always be watching.

Tuesday saw more clerical-administrative work. While sorting mail, Anne came across an envelope addressed to the XBL Travel Agency, and brought it to Kurt Weber's attention.

''This was delivered by mistake. What should I do with it?''

''XBL is one of our subsidiaries,'' Weber answered. ''Give it to Hans Werner.''

During lunch, Anne mentioned the envelope to Muller, adding, ''I didn't realize we had a travel subsidiary. Maybe XBL could book my vacation if I go to Europe next summer.''

''Most unlikely,'' Muller told her. ''XBL handles only private jets and accommodations at luxury villas. I doubt you could afford it.''

After lunch, Ernst Neumann sent her to Citibank to deposit a check drawn on a Japanese bank, made out to The Hawthorne Group in the amount of $200 million. Later in the day, when a repairman was summoned to the office to fix a broken watercooler, Muller called Anne away from her cubicle and instructed, ''Keep an eye on him. Make certain he does what he's supposed to do and nothing more.''

Tuesday night, Anne had dinner with Amanda and Howard. Mostly, she talked about the office. ''Every day, I feel more uncomfortable,'' she acknowledged. ''All my life, I've been trusted, and now at work I'm in an environment where no one seems to trust anybody. I'm surrounded by mixed messages. One minute, Leo Muller plays games with me about photocopying confidential memoranda. Then someone sends me out of the office with a check large enough to balance the budget of a small country. Everyone is polite, but there's something sterile, almost intimidating, in the air. The executives are all like Stepford husbands. Office security reminds me of a foreign embassy or military installation. I don't know. They pay me well. Overall, I'm treated nicely. But sometimes I think they're doing things at The Hawthorne Group that I don't want to be involved with.''

Wednesday, Muller left New York to visit European headquarters. In his absence, the office functioned as before. Thursday, Anne lunched again with Michael Harney, who explained that, like most energy-related companies, The Hawthorne Group registered its oil tankers in Panama, Liberia, and the Cayman Islands. ''Liberia,'' he offered, ''is in western Africa between the Ivory Coast and Sierra Leone.''

''And the Cayman Islands?''

''In the middle of the Caribbean, a hundred and fifty miles south of Cuba.''

One of the secretaries came into the lunchroom, and Harney ended the geography lesson to ask how her daughter with the measles was doing. That turned the conversation to children, and allowed him to reminisce about how, at eighteen months, his own daughter Debbie wouldn't eat anything on her plate that touched other food. ''Now she's two,'' he added, "and insists on mashing everything together."

Harney was a nice man, Anne decided, the human side of The Hawthorne Group; a balance to Muller and the others. What didn't make sense, though, was why he spent so much time away from his family. He genuinely seemed to care about them, particularly the children. Whenever he talked about his son and daughter, humor and warmth were evident in his voice: "Debbie's at the age where, if she can't eat it or break it, she's not interested in it. Marc is four now, and each night at dinner, he tells us the part of his stomach that likes vegetables is full, but the part that likes dessert is hungry."

"How can you spend so much time in New York?" Anne wanted to know.

Harney shrugged. "It's my job."

After work, Anne had dinner with a friend from theater; then went home, and polished a pair of shoes while watching television. When that was done, she skimmed the *New Yorker*—mostly Talk of the Town and the cartoons—and readied for bed.

The telephone rang while she was turning down the covers, and she picked up the receiver.

"Hello?"

There was no response. Only silence.

"Hello? . . ."

Still no voice. Just dull static and someone listening on the other end of the line.

She hung up.

Three hours later, at 2:00 A.M., it happened again.

The next day at work, Friday, passed slowly. One of the secretaries called in sick, and Anne was relegated to typing and running errands. Eric Winslow sent her across the street to buy a book at Double-day. Ernst Neumann asked her to pick out a watch for his brother at Tiffany. In Muller's absence, Hans Werner gave out the paychecks and suggested Anne leave a half-hour early. TGIF. After two weeks of work, the novelty of a regular job was wearing thin.

A little after five, Anne rode the elevator down to the lobby, and with no better plan for the evening, decided to explore the Trump Tower shopping mall.

Up the escalator to the second level.

The first shop was Galeries Lafayette, and she passed it by. Then came Arras, Harry Winston, and Asprey Gallery, where she went inside. Asprey was like a museum, with china, crystal, and antique wares. A George III mahogany desk, circa 1760, was on display for $22,000; a china tea service for twelve, unforgivably expensive at $9,750.

After Asprey, she window-shopped her way past Boehm Porcelain and Kenneth Jay Lane; then took the escalator to the third level. There was Fred Leighton (jewelry), followed by Botticelli (shoes), Martha (women's clothing), and Napoleon (men's fashions)—none of them as interesting as the floor below. Growing bored with window-shopping, Anne changed course and rode the escalator down to the atrium waterfall.

The atrium was sunny and bright, with terraced walkways, hanging plants, and a huge skylight above. Marble, glass, and brass were in abundance, but the waterfall dominated; eighty feet tall, dizzy-ing in its height, cascading down through pools and streams on its way to the floor. Two dozen tables were geometrically arranged on the marble patio. A sandwich shop and bar stood just to the right. Anne bought a glass of white wine, cast about for a place to sit, and chose a small round table facing the waterfall.

Most of the people nearby looked like tourists. There was an elderly couple studying what appeared to be a travel brochure; a fat man in Bermuda shorts sitting with an equally overweight woman and two pudgy children; two businessmen in Brooks Brothers suits; several fashionably dressed women; a young man with a camera.

One of the businessmen glanced toward Anne. I'm checking you out, his look said. She wasn't sure how to respond. She could look back, smile, turn her head away; use body language as she chose to encourage or deter him. There was something arrogant in the way he was posing.

Anne took a sip of wine and ignored him.

Gentle music sounded in the background. The waterfall beat a constant refrain. So here I am, Anne told herself. In the Trump Tower atrium, with a new job, a new life, thirty-nine years old.

Life got harder as she got older; at least that's how it seemed. After college, it had been easy. She'd come to New York, found a place to live, put together head shots and a résumé, and gone to her first audition. That audition would remain emblazoned in memory until the day she died.

She'd arrived at the theater at eight in the morning and waited for nine hours while all the Equity actors and actresses were called. Finally, at five P.M., the union people had been heard and it was time to go home, but the casting director decided to stay fifteen minutes more to look at the first five non-union people there. Anne was number four. She wasn't nervous. Looking back, that surprised her but, after nine hours of waiting, she'd been too tired to care. She went on stage, did what she had to do, earned a callback, and got the job. Her first audition, her first New York role, Off Broadway. Then the play hit, moved to a larger theater, and the entire cast got Equity cards.

The businessman in the conservative suit was looking at her again. Anne was used to attention, onstage and off, but this time it made her uncomfortable. Rising from her chair, she circled the table and sat in a seat opposite the one she'd been in. Now her back was to him, but she couldn't see the waterfall anymore. And suddenly, the atrium's magic spell was broken. The aura was gone. People on their way home from work were streaming by. She saw glitzy shops, pay telephones, congestion, and heard noise. It wasn't like being in a European garden anymore. It was like Grand Central Station, the World Trade Center, or the post office at noon.

Anne finished her wine, stood up, and walked out of Trump Tower to go home.

Avenue of the Americas . . . Broadway . . . The streets passed one by one . . . Columbus Circle . . . up Central Park West . . .

A homeless man had taken up residence on a bench across the street from her apartment at the edge of the park. Noticing but refusing to acknowledge his presence, she entered her building and checked for mail. There was a bill from Bloomingdale's, her monthly American Express statement, a dance company promotional flyer. And a plain white envelope.

Looking at the envelope, she recognized the handwriting.

Goddammit, David. Leave me alone.

On the elevator going up, she opened her other mail.

Inside the apartment, she turned on some lights and went to the kitchen for a glass of water. She wondered if David had timed it this way; mailed the letter so she'd get it on Friday, just before the weekend. Probably not. Mail delivery in Manhattan wasn't that reliable.

Moving to her bedroom, she wasn't sure what to do.

Get it over with, she told herself. Open it and read it.

The letter was short:

Dear Anne,

It's been three weeks since I wrote, and I guess at this point it would be foolish for me to expect a response. Still, I wish you'd reconsider.

We only live once that we know of, and I don't know if I'm going to catch up with you in another world or not, so I'd like to be with you now.

Please think about it.

Love,
David

Love, David. Why did he have to send her letters? Why was he forcing her to end the relationship slowly, peeling the Band-Aid away bit by bit instead of letting her rip it off? Maybe she should have answered his last letter. But why? It was over between them. She'd made up her mind, and all she wanted now was to distance herself from the past.

Outside the bedroom window, Central Park was bathed in early evening light. The setting sun reflected off Fifth Avenue buildings. Joggers and bike riders were vying for space on overcrowded paths.

She could call David; pick up the telephone and dial his number; tell him to stop sending letters and leave her alone. Except, if she did call and heard David's voice, she might give in to the part of her that still loved him.

"We only live once that we know of . . . I'd like to be with you now . . . Please think about it . . ."

Cursing softly, Anne moved to the kitchen, took a glass from the cabinet, and filled it with ice; then crossed to the living room and poured three inches of scotch.

Back to the kitchen for a splash of water.

I'm not sure this is a good idea, she told herself. Liquor, anger, and depression don't mix. What am I now—angry or depressed? Both, I guess.

Goddammit, David, why did I have to fall in love with you? Why couldn't I have fallen in love with someone who knew how to trust and give and love?

Raising the glass to her lips, Anne took a sip.

David, you're history.

The telephone rang.

She picked up the receiver.

Nothing. Only silence.

"Hello? . . ."

Still nothing.

Returning to the living room, scotch in hand, Anne moved to the stereo, and gazed at the row of albums on her record shelf. Maybe music would help.

Mozart? No.

Caruso? No.

The Beatles? No.

Lerner and Loewe. *My Fair Lady.* Yes.

Often she'd thought, if she were marooned on a desert island, forced to listen to one cast album over and over, *My Fair Lady* would be the one.

"Oh, shit!"

The curse came out loud; not softly or to herself. She couldn't listen to *My Fair Lady*; not now. Because four years ago at the Equity Library Theatre, she'd played Eliza Doolittle in *Pygmalion*. And two weeks after the show ended, she'd been walking down Broadway when a man approached and asked, "Excuse me; didn't you just play Eliza Doolittle?"

And the man was David. That was how they'd met.

When did she fall in love with him?

Probably a year later, when she'd been in a show with a New Year's Eve performance that didn't end until one in the morning. David was waiting for her when she got home that night; that had been arranged. And he'd brought champagne, which had been arranged too. But what he'd also done—and it was wonderful—was tape the ball coming down the pole in Times Square on her VCR, so they could share the moment. That night, they went to bed together for the first time, and the chemistry was extraordinary. "We're sexually compatible," she'd told him, but it was more than that. David Akers turned her on. He satisfied her completely, and she'd thought it was mutual. And then David had to fuck around.

Forget *My Fair Lady*. Choose another record— Mozart, Symphony No. 39. And as long as she was leaving David behind, she might as well clean up some other debris. Now was a good time to clean up her apartment, starting with twenty years of theater memorabilia. A lot of what she'd kept was dated, and there was no reason to keep it anymore. She'd never be on stage again.

Back to the bedroom. Where to begin? The file cabinet. Opening the top drawer, Anne saw twenty or so folders, neatly arranged, lifted them up and dumped them on the floor.

She couldn't hear the Mozart; it wasn't loud enough.

Into the living room to turn up the volume.

Back to the bedroom again.

Take a gulp of scotch.

Two piles is how I should do it. One pile for everything I want to keep; one pile for everything that gets thrown out.

File number one—Actor's Equity Pension Fund statements. Those I keep. I'm entitled to money when I'm sixty years old.

File number two—lists of casting directors and agents in New York. Out.

File number three—union dues receipts. Out.

Actor's Equity newsletters. Out.

A list of theater companies in New York. Out.

Pay stubs from each of my salary checks. Keep the last five years for the IRS.

The Actor's Equity union rulebook. Anne flipped through the pages, then took another sip of scotch.

If I could figure this crazy rulebook out, there's no reason I can't learn to work the computers at The Hawthorne Group.

Her college transcript. Northwestern School of Drama; B.A., 1972. "You have talent," the best of her professors had told her. "You can make it in theater, but I want to warn you, most actors and actresses who stay in the business do so ultimately because there's nothing else they can do. They have no other skills, no other way to earn a livelihood."

Anne put the transcript on her "keep" pile, and turned to the next file folder.

Contracts. One for every show she'd done since coming to New York. There was no reason to keep them, but also no way she could throw them out. Her whole career, each show, began with those contracts. They stood for the proposition that, yes, she'd been a working actress. People paid her to go on stage.

Side one of the Mozart symphony ended. Anne went to the living room, turned the record over, and returned to work.

Twenty years of résumés. She kept one copy of each.

A letter from Sandy Meisner, her first acting coach in New York: "Keep working all the time. Do all kinds of plays whether they're right for you or not, because eventually time and you will catch up with each other."

Playbills from every show she'd ever been involved with. Broadway, Off Broadway, national tours, regional theater, industrials, showcases, dinner clubs, Shakespeare in the Park. She'd avoided musicals. "I'm an actress, not a performer," she told a producer once. "I want to do legitimate theater; not musicals, commercials, television, or film."

Had she wanted to be a star? Of course she had; that's why people were in the business. But there was more to theater than being on top. There was standing before a live audience, that exhilarating feeling, riding the crest of a wave. There was the camaraderie backstage, incredibly intense, like being war buddies and lovers at the same time. And there'd been the oppressive side; the competition and envy. I'm better than she is. Why did she get the job? Getting each role had been a crapshoot, like winning the lottery. And theater was a personal business, up and down the line. Casting directors, producers, they always said it was strictly business but that wasn't true. A lot of decisions were personal—who you were friends with; who was sleeping with who. Looks were important, not to performance but almost always to getting a role. "If you want someone to play Charlie's Angels," Anne had told a producer who wanted to see her in a tight sweater for a nonsexy role, "get Shelly Hack or Farrah Fawcett."

She wouldn't play the game. She'd had too much integrity or was too afraid to leave herself vulnerable. And she'd hated not having control, being at the mercy of other people's whims. She'd survived as an actress because she was good, but she hadn't succeeded at the level she wanted.

And time went by. Actresses lose time.

She'd understudied on Broadway for a lead and never went on. That was a year out of her life. Then she did the national tour of the same show as lead with a "name" male star; another year gone. Somewhere along the line, she fell into "the crack"—the point in her career where she was too old for young roles and too young for old ones.

"If you haven't made it to the top as an actress by the time you're forty," her agent once told her, "you won't make it. You'll be relegated to character roles and Off Broadway all your life. As many actresses reach star status after forty as baseball players suddenly become stars after forty."

Anne took another gulp of scotch, and stared at the playbills spread in front of her on the floor. *King Lear, Our Town, Elephant Man, Equus, Of Mice and Men, Romeo and Juliet, The Glass Menagerie, Amadeus.* There were fifty in all; each show with its own memories. Her first starring role; her favorite performance; the time her father saw her on Broadway, two months before he died. It bothered her that her parents would never see her children—if she had children. Each period in life was meant to be special, but there had to be continuity for life to be right.

The scotch was gone, leaving a sour burning taste in her mouth.

She decided to keep the playbills and the critics' reviews in the next file folder. Time now for the photo albums. Stage shots; publicity shots; candid photos of cast members, in costume and out. Twenty years worth of head shots; eight-by-ten glossy photos that were the staff of life. Her face had changed over the years. She was older now; she knew that. But seeing the photos, side by side, spread out on the floor, shook her up. It was like one of those photo sequences where, in the first photo, a healthy middle-aged man is holding an infant boy in his arms; and in each succeeding photo, the child gets bigger and stronger as he grows to adulthood, while the man gets older and more decrepit until, looking at the last photo, you know he's ready to die.

Stop it, Anne told herself. Your face is a little thinner now; there are more lines around your eyes. That's all.

Mozart's Symphony No. 39 was over. It was time for Brahms.

Remembering is lonely if you do it alone.

A little more scotch might be all right.

I want someone to share the flowers.

My emotional immune system doesn't work anymore.

Her makeup case was in the closet. Maybe she'd take a break from sorting through files and see what was there, because that was the direction her mind was floating in and the makeup case was an old friend. Acting was uprooting. An actress traveled from place to place, and whatever happened, the makeup case was there. Even in strange dressing rooms, especially in strange dressing rooms, there was something calming about opening it up and seeing the familiar inside.

The telephone rang.

Anne picked up the receiver.

Nothing.

Maybe it was David, playing games.

''Hello? . . . Hello? . . .''

Still no one.

Back to the makeup case. God, what a mess inside. Sponges, powder, sparkle powder, makeup remover, brushes, blushes, eye shadow, eyeliner, eyelashes, glue, eyelash combs, eyelash curlers, lipstick, bobby pins, hair elastics, mascara, chopsticks for Chinese food ordered in.

She laughed at the chopsticks; then looked back toward the file folders, twenty years of her life spread out on the floor. No way could she throw those files out. They were the story of her life. Peaks and valleys, too few plateaus, far too much jagged terrain. But they were her soul.

◆ ◆ ◆

Settling behind the leather-topped desk, Christoph Matthes stared across the room. The hour was late. Both men were tired; particularly Leo Muller, who had flown into Brussels only an hour before. Under different circumstances, Matthes would have offered him the opportunity to freshen up at the hotel before appearing at headquarters, but the matter at hand was too urgent for small courtesies.

"Thank you for coming," Matthes began. "I thought it best that we meet in person because of the gravity of my present concern. Unfortunately, it appears as though there has been a breach of security in the New York office."

"In what form?"

"An infiltrator."

"Who?"

"Michael Harney."

Muller leaned forward, caressing his chin with the edge of his hand. "Do we know who he's working for?"

"No."

"Perhaps he is just an industrial spy?"

"Perhaps, but I doubt it." Rising from his chair,

Matthes crossed to a table by the far wall, where an elaborately enameled chess set lay beneath a glass dome. "This set was given to me by the Sultan of Brunei," he said, raising the glass dome on its hinge. "Inferior players seek to reduce chess to the level of mathematics: sixty-four squares, a prescribed number of moves. However, no one has been able to program a computer to play competitively at the grandmaster level. That is because chess, like music, depends on creativity. The parallel is quite remarkable, actually. Music consists of a handful of notes, several octaves, and time; yet no one suggests reducing music to mathematics. There are as many chess games as there are melodies."

Reaching down, Matthes fingered a pawn. "This set depicts the forces of Christianity versus the Muslim world as they did battle in the First Crusade. Each piece has been hand-cast with a twenty-two-karat gold overlay. The board is made of silver and gold. The rubies, sapphires, and emeralds which adorn each piece are, of course, real." Speaking in a quiet controlled voice, he went on. "The blue pieces represent the army of Pope Urban the Second. *Deus vult*—God wills it—was their rallying cry. Opposite them, in red, stand the forces of the Mohammedan East as they defeated Syria and Asia Minor. But let us return to Michael Harney. I believe that certain precautionary measures must be taken."

"What do you suggest?"

"Kill him."

"When?"

"Not this moment, but reasonably soon."

Chapter 5

Week number three at The Hawthorne Group.

Monday, before work, Anne went to the ophthalmologist for her annual checkup. As always, it was a nuisance. She wasn't supposed to wear contact lenses during the hours preceding her appointment, and her regular glasses were fifteen years old, which left her half blind as she journeyed to the ophthalmologist's office. There were no cabs; the bus she took was uncomfortably crowded. Although Anne had reserved the day's first appointment, when she arrived at eight A.M., several patients were ahead of her. Then came the assembly line. Drops in her eyes; preliminary tests by a medical assistant; waiting in one room, reading eye-charts in another. Finally, the real doctor came in to see her. Then it was over, and she took a cab to work, arriving late. For most of the morning, the drops in her eyes rendered her useless. Then full vision returned, she was able to read the computer monitors, and Muller gave her a job indexing fluctuations in the price of Saudi Arabian oil.

Tuesday and Wednesday were equally prosaic. Energy traders live constantly at the edge of a precipice, so there was always a measure of tension in the office, but Anne's chores were mundane. Summarizing invoices, rerouting electronic mail. Thursday, Muller gave her a new computer access card, saying he was pleased with her progress and that she'd been cleared for "expanded duties." However, her new "smart card" varied little from its predecessor. The main difference was, she was now able to store data in the firm's master computer file, but still unauthorized to retrieve it.

Friday, she committed her first faux pas. Not major, but enough to draw Muller's attention. Rather than eat in conference room B, she went out for lunch; the first time she'd done so since starting at The Hawthorne Group.

"I would prefer it if you remain in the office during normal working hours," Muller told her afterward. "That might seem demanding, but we compensate our employees quite well and provide a more than adequate lunch in return for your undivided attention."

It wasn't an unreasonable request, she decided. After all, factory workers, schoolteachers, most employees were tied to their job for a given number of hours. Not having the freedom to leave at noon was an imposition of sorts, but The Hawthorne Group was paying well.

The weekend was uneventful. Friday night, Anne read. Saturday she was supposed to have dinner with a blind date, but he canceled at the last minute.

"I hope it doesn't foul up your evening," he told her.

"It does change my plans," she answered sweetly.

Sunday she went to the Museum of Natural History, and had dinner with Amanda, Howard, and family. Monday, it was back to the office for her second faux pas in as many workdays. This one, like its predecessor, seemed harmless enough. The office reception area overlooked midtown Manhattan, and Anne brought in her camera to take pictures. Hans Werner happened by while she was in the act, and minutes later, she was summoned to Muller's office.

"Under no circumstances are cameras or unauthorized recording devices allowed in the office."

"I'm sorry. I just—"

"They are not permitted," Muller interrupted. "That is all; thank you."

It shook her up, the anger in his voice. And at lunch, she made a point of seeking out the person she felt most comfortable with at The Hawthorne Group—Michael Harney.

"Don't worry about it," he told her. "It takes a while to learn the ropes; everyone makes mistakes."

"But the way Muller reacted; he jumped down my throat."

"I know; but The Hawthorne Group has certain rules, and each of those rules has to be followed. You were taking a picture of the New York skyline, but someone else might photograph the inside of the office and inadvertently reveal security data. Leo gets excited about that sort of thing. It's his job. Probably, he should have told you when you started work not to take photos, but he took it for granted that you understood.''

She liked Michael Harney; his warmth, his way of easing tension. In some ways, he reminded her of Howard Otis—except she couldn't imagine Howard taking a job that kept him away from Amanda and the children five nights a week.

"How are your kids?" she asked, keeping the conversation flowing.

"The usual chaos. Last weekend, Marc held goldfish races in the bathtub.''

As they talked, co-workers came and went. Sometimes they incorporated new arrivals into their conversation, sometimes not. Graham Hayes was the most persistent in seeking inclusion, and lunchroom ethics required that they oblige him. Several secretaries also joined in but eventually departed, and when Hayes followed suit, Anne and Harney were alone again.

He was an interesting person. All the executives at The Hawthorne Group were smart, but Harney alone had a human side to him. He seemed caring, with a sense of humor. And unlike the others, he was on Anne's wavelength.

"Acting is crazy," she told him over coffee, "and auditions are the craziest part of all. Once, my agent booked me into an eleven A.M. audition for the role of a hooker, and told me to go in looking as slutty as possible—clothes, hair, makeup, everything. Then, he called and said he'd scheduled a second audition for the same day at noon—for the role of a nun in *Agnes of God*.''

Harney laughed.

Muller wouldn't have. Muller would have stared or smirked or grimaced, or smiled politely. But he wouldn't have laughed because, like virtually everyone else in the office, Leo Muller had no sense of humor at all.

"Which role did you get?"

"The hooker. And it was wonderful. Theater is alive. It's the only place you can take a character from beginning to end and develop her fully in a matter of hours. Films are different; they're shot piecemeal. Outside of fantasizing about a movie with Woody Allen, I never wanted to do film. But to be on stage—every audience is different; the energy changes each night. You have up days, down days, tired days, days when you're particularly alive. And each time, you re-experience the role." Smiling wistfully, Anne leaned back in her chair. "I was a good actress."

"I'm sure you were."

There was something special in the moment. Anne wasn't sure what it was, but she and Harney seemed to be crossing a boundary.

"I guess we'd better get back to work," he told her.

The afternoon passed. Tuesday, Muller apologized for snapping at her the previous day about the camera. Wednesday, Anne got her first look at the inside of Christoph Matthes's office, when Eric Winslow sent her in to find a book on oil platform drilling. "Leo Muller's computer access card will get you into the room," he advised her.

The last thing in the world Anne expected was for Muller to hand over his access card, but he did, albeit with the warning, "Bring this back in sixty seconds or else."

Anne took the card, went to Matthes's office, inserted it in the appropriate slot, and a click sounded. Probably Muller wouldn't hold her to sixty seconds, but he wouldn't expect her to operate leisurely either. She gave herself two minutes; just enough time to find the right book and survey Matthes's office. It was slightly larger than the others but not markedly so, with a large oak desk, black leather chairs, and a small conference table by the south wall. She wondered if she'd ever get to meet Christoph Matthes, or for that matter, if he existed at all.

Then it was back to the monotony of routine. Sorting mail, preparing indexes, covering for Harry Ragin at the reception desk while Harry went to the men's room. In midafternoon, she took a short break and telephoned Amanda.

"Hello. Oh, Christ! Hold on a second," was how Amanda answered the phone. "Sorry," she added, coming back on the line. "There was peanut butter on the earpiece."

"The earpiece?"

"Yeah! The mouthpiece would make sense. The earpiece, I don't understand . . . Jessica, did you put peanut butter on the telephone?"

"No," a voice in the background answered.

"Then who put peanut butter on the telephone?"
Again from the background—"Me."

They made plans to get together for dinner alone on Friday ("Howard will babysit"). Then Anne went back to sorting invoices, and worked until five-thirty when it was time to quit.

On the way out of the office, she stopped to chat

with the night receptionist, Mort Gordon. Outside of Harney, Mort was the friendliest person around. And he was different. Thank God for someone who didn't fit The Hawthorne Group mold. Every other man in the office was "imperially slim," as Edward Arlington Robinson once said of Richard Cory. At first that had appealed to Anne. Middle-aged men got fat in an unattractive way, with blubber hanging over their belt like their pants fit wrong. But after three and a half weeks of tight-assed formality, it was reassuring to know that someone at The Hawthorne Group was spontaneous enough to eat more than his diet chart called for. In Gordon's case, the added pounds were part fat, part muscle. More than anything else, he looked like a retired cop.

"Good day? Bad day?" Gordon asked when he saw Anne coming.

"In between. And you?"

"I'll let you know at two in the morning."

Each night, Gordon was responsible for watching the cleaning woman do her job and making sure nothing was out of order. Beyond that, he sat at the reception desk, more as a guard than a receptionist or telephone operator. Like Anne, he'd gotten his position through an employment agency. Before that, "I traveled a lot; did all sorts of stuff." Anne didn't know much else about him, other than he'd been with The Hawthorne Group for three years. "And I like it here," he told her once. "It's a strange place, but they pay me well so I don't ask questions. Some jobs, you ask questions; some jobs, you don't."

"Good night, Paul Sorvino," she said on her way out the door.

"Good night, beautiful."

The next two days were business as usual, except that Anne got her period, which was annoying. Friday, because of the impending Memorial Day weekend, the office shut down at three o'clock. Just before she left, Anne went to say goodbye to Michael Harney, but his secretary said he wasn't in.

"I don't know where Mr. Harney is today. Mr. Muller asked the same question earlier this morning. It's quite odd, really. He was expected in."

The rest of the day was taken up by errands. The dry cleaner; the bank; the supermarket, where checkout lines were aggravatingly long. Twice, Anne was stopped by panhandlers on the sidewalk, who stood in front of her, blocking her path. Both times, she said "sorry," changed direction, and passed them by. Once she wondered what David would be doing over the weekend. But that didn't matter; not anymore.

Howard was home and in a jovial mood when Anne arrived to pick up Amanda. "How's Auschwitz on Fifth Avenue?" he asked about the office.

Ellen was dressing for a major date with a high school sophomore. Susan was in the bathroom, giving Jessica a bath.

"I'll be home by ten," Amanda promised, kissing Howard as she went out the door.

The night was warm, and Anne suggested they eat outdoors, at the Boathouse Cafe in Central Park. Walking over, they talked mostly about Ellen and Susan; what kind of children they were, and how they were growing. "It's a constant challenge," Amanda offered. "Susan is fourteen; she just started dating, so now I wonder if I've taught her enough

71

about birth control and AIDS. Ellen is twelve and studies harder in school than any child I know, but her grades fall short of Susan's so what do I do? How do I keep her working hard and, at the same time, make sure she understands that grades aren't the most important measure in determining how good people are?''

At the cafe, the maître d' gave them a table at the edge of the lake. They ordered drinks. Amanda reported on her plans for the weekend—''Taking Jessica to a birthday party, taking Jessica to a puppet show, taking Jessica to an exercise class; and if the weather is good, taking Jessica to a barbecue on Long Island.''

The waiter returned and interrupted to ask if they were ready to order dinner.

They weren't.

''I'm planning what we'll call a quiet weekend,'' Anne said, picking up the conversation after he'd gone. ''It's strange. I used to feel supremely confident about men. I had dates all the time. Now, every morning, I look in the mirror and think maybe I'm doomed to grow old alone.''

''You're not.''

''I hope not; but it's getting late. I'm thirty-nine, and I'm tired of going through each day alone. I look at you, and even before you met Howard, I was a little jealous. That might sound crazy because I know how you struggled; but at least you had children. Does that make sense to you at all?''

''Yes and no,'' Amanda answered. ''The kids were a blessing. Even when times were bad, I was thankful I had them, but don't overromanticize what I went through. After the divorce, I felt like I'd been raped. Then, day after week after month went by, and instead of enjoying life, I felt like it was passing me by. I can't tell you how many times I found myself making lists of things to do—laundry, go to the supermarket, work eight hours, spend some quality time with the kids. And every time, at the bottom of the list, I'd pencil in, 'Figure out what to do with my life.' I'd go to parties, and maybe I'd meet a man I liked; and if he said he liked long hair, I'd tell myself, only half joking, maybe I should grow my hair down to my ankles so he'll marry me. And all the while, the years went by. Thanksgiving, Christmas, New Year's Eve. Every holiday season, I had to put on a good face for the children. Then I'd slog through January and February and, just when I thought the worst part of the year was over, the *New Yorker* anniversary issue would come in the mail with Eustace Tilley on the cover to remind me that another year had gone by."

The waiter returned, and this time they ordered. Spinach salad for Anne; cold pasta for Amanda. Out on the lake, a small boat was gliding through the water. Amanda watched, counting ripples as they spread; then turned back toward Anne and, with a trace of uncertainty, asked, "Do you want some unsolicited advice?"

"All right."

Amanda spoke softly, choosing her words with care. "When I met Howard, he wasn't perfect. He still isn't; neither am I. But we had two very important things going for us. First, there was chemistry. And second, we fell in love with each other. I know, right now, you're furious at David. You've excised him from your life and don't want to see him anymore. But you loved him once, and I think the chemistry is still there. Howard and I have talked about it. Both of us are fond of David; you know that. And you also know that our loyalty lies with you. I just feel, we feel, that if you could bring yourself to let go of your anger, things between you and David could still work out.''

The waiter returned with spinach salad and cold pasta. "Will there be anything else?"

Anne looked up and shook her head; then turned back to Amanda. "It won't work. Even if I still loved David, I couldn't trust him. Too many bad things happened between us. Put yourself in my place. How would you feel if you found out that Howard was fucking around?''

"I'd be devastated; I'd be furious. It would break my heart. But Howard and I are married. We've made certain commitments and know what to expect from each other. You and David never had an understanding like that, and I don't recall your telling him you wanted one.''

"He knew.''

"How? By osmosis? Look, I'm not minimizing what happened between you. But by the same token, you were on tour for five or six months. You knew David was going out with other women. Maybe you thought they were platonic friends, but you never sat down and had the talk with him that could have clarified everything. In a way, it seems like you're mad at David for not figuring out on his own what you wanted from him before you knew.''

"Whose side are you on?''

"Yours.''

"How can you say I should go back to David?''

"Because that's what I feel."

"Then you don't understand what happened between us. I was in the most incestuous business in the world, where everybody fucks everybody, and I didn't fuck around. I had every opportunity to do it. I lost jobs because I wouldn't do it. And then, not only did David do it; he lied to me."

"In a manner of speaking."

"It was a lie of omission. He lied like a lawyer."

Amanda shrugged. "I'm not going to sit here and defend everything David did. What's more important is whether you can forgive him."

"I tried. For six months after I found out, I tried. And there were always too many women around. This one's a friend; that one's a neighbor. Her? She's an old classmate from college who flew into town. How would you like it if, every time you turned around, Howard was having lunch with another woman friend?"

"I guess that would depend on the friend."

"Bullshit, Amanda. It wouldn't depend on the friend. You were single between marriages for eight years. How many of the men you knew then do you see now? Howard was forty-one when the two of you got married. How many of his old women friends are hanging around?"

"I don't think David is a womanizer."

"He sure was."

"Maybe once, but not anymore. Falling in love with you changed him."

"It's too late," Anne said, bringing the conversation to an end. "People fall in love and they fall out of love. I'm not in love with David anymore."

After dinner, they walked home.

"I love you," Anne said, when they parted at Amanda's door. "You're my best friend."

Saturday morning, Anne slept until ten. The weather was lousy; hot and humid with intervals of rain. Finally, the sun made a brief appearance and she went out to the shoe-repair shop, stopping on her way home to pick up a copy of *The New York Times*.

Back in her apartment, the telephone rang. It was a friend, and they talked for the better part of an hour. Then she went to the kitchen, made a sandwich, and cast about for something to read, settling on the *Times*.

She read the theater section first; after that, international and local news. America's balance of payments deficit had widened. A dozen real estate developers had been indicted for systematically bribing city housing department officials.

Then, suddenly, there was a queasy feeling in the pit of her stomach. It paralyzed her body and worked its way through her entire insides.

Please, God! Don't let it be true!

OIL EXECUTIVE, BATTLING CANCER, CHOOSES SUICIDE

Michael Harney, a computer specialist with The Hawthorne Group, died Thursday night from self-inflicted gunshot wounds. He was forty-six years old, and maintained residences in Delaware and Manhattan.

Harney joined the European-based energy commodities firm in 1985. Family members confirmed that he had been treated for leukemia during the past year. Authorities were summoned to Harney's Manhattan residence late Friday afternoon after he failed to appear at work. A suicide note citing illness was found at the site, but police would not otherwise divulge its contents.

Leo Muller, director of The Hawthorne Group's New York office, termed the death ''a horrible tragedy.''

Harney is survived by his wife, Madeline, and two children.

Chapter 6

Memorial Day notwithstanding, it was a lousy weekend. Anne spent a lot of time reading as an escape mechanism, but her thoughts kept coming back to one simple reality. Michael Harney was dead. She hadn't known him long. Four weeks; just enough time to grow fond of him, to like him. Maybe that's the way life was. You think you're important, and then you realize that you and everyone you care about and love are statistics, probabilities on some medical chart or insurance actuarial table.

Sunday afternoon she went out for a walk. The streets were strewn with holiday-weekend garbage. The homeless man who'd taken up residence across the street from her apartment seemed dirtier than before, less transient and more deranged. Now he had two shopping bags filled with belongings instead of one. She wondered if there'd be a funeral for Harney. Probably not; or if there were, it would be in Delaware. She wasn't sure she could bring herself to go back to The Hawthorne Group on Tuesday. But looking rationally at her situation, the job paid well and, outside of acting, there wasn't much else to do.

So she went back, arriving at the office Tuesday morning at nine, just like she was supposed to. When she got there, Harry Ragin told her that Leo Muller wanted to meet with the staff in conference room B at 9:15 A.M. It was the first time since Anne had been at The Hawthorne Group that the entire New York staff was present in one room. Even Mort Gordon, who normally worked evening hours, had been called in.

Muller began precisely at nine-fifteen. "I would like to thank each of you for being here," he said. "As all of you know, The Hawthorne Group has suffered a terrible tragedy. Mr. Matthes feels that each of you is entitled to know accurately what happened, and has asked that I report fully to you on the death of Michael Harney.

"Eleven months ago," Muller continued, "Michael learned that he was suffering from leukemia. That information was shared with his wife, Mr. Matthes, and myself but, at Michael's request, was divulged to no one else. Leukemia is an insidious disease; a cancer of the blood which, in Michael's case, was fought with chemotherapy. Unfortunately, it was a losing battle and, rather than subject his wife and children to the agony of watching him die slowly, Michael chose to end his life. Last Friday, some of you will recall, Michael did not appear at the office. This was highly unusual, indeed unprecedented, and late in the day, I telephoned the management office at the building where he lived. At my request, the superintendent entered Michael's apartment, where the suicide weapon, a note, and Michael's body were discovered. At that point, the police were notified. The note itself is personal in nature, and I believe it would be improper for me or anyone other than Michael's wife to reveal its contents. It is possible that the New York City police will investigate the matter further and, of course, each of you should cooperate fully with all appropriate inquiries. I believe there is nothing more to say other than this is a tremendous personal loss, but our work must continue. The world goes ahead because each of us builds on the success of our predecessors. So shall it be with ourselves and Michael Harney.''

One of the secretaries asked if there would be a funeral, and Muller said that services would be held in Delaware but that they would be private. Hans Werner had the poor taste to inquire who would take over Harney's computer duties and was told, ''That will wait.'' Then it was back to work, with the computers and paper shredder and everything else operating as before.

''I'm not sure how much longer I can take it,'' Anne told Amanda when they talked by telephone that night.

''Let me put Howard on,'' Amanda offered.

On request, Howard picked up the receiver, and did his best to assure Anne that better days would follow. ''Ride this storm out; give it another month.

Then, if you're still unhappy, I'll help you find another job.''

That made sense, of course. Accentuate the positive. But the next day was worse, because now it was starting to sink in that Michael Harney was dead, which was a bitch for Michael and, as far as Anne was concerned, left her with no one else at work to talk with. People in the office were superficially friendly, but she was emotionally alone. The only person with any semblance of soul was Mort Gordon, and he didn't come in until five in the evening.

At lunch on Wednesday, Anne sat with several of the secretaries, but couldn't get into their conversation at all. All day long, she felt as though she was dealing with human automatons. The only time she sensed contact with anyone was when she stopped to say good night to Gordon on her way home.

"Harney was a nice guy," he said. "I mean, most people here are pretty stiff. They pay my salary so I shouldn't complain, but let's face it, the atmosphere here isn't what I'd call relaxed or friendly.''

"You've noticed."

"Yeah. I might not be the most sensitive guy in the world, but hit me on the head with a hammer and I feel it. Good night, beautiful.''

"Good night, Paul Sorvino.''

Somehow their ritual farewell made her feel better, but the next day at the office she felt as alone as before. There had been too many losses lately. David; giving up theater; now Michael Harney. It was too much. Everything was going wrong. She couldn't concentrate. All she could do was sit at her desk, stare blankly at pieces of paper, and periodically rest her head in her hands, until late in the morning, tears started to fall.

And then she looked up to see Leo Muller standing over her with something surprisingly akin to sympathy in his eyes.

"Are you all right?"

"I'm fine," she answered. "I'm sorry. I've been through a lot lately."

"I understand. This has been a difficult time for all of us, but perhaps more difficult for you because of other changes in your life."

Fumbling through her purse, Anne found a tissue. What she really wanted was to blow her nose, but somehow that seemed unladylike, so she wiped her eyes instead.

"I would like a favor," Muller said. "For your benefit, as well as ours, take the remainder of today and tomorrow off. Then, with the weekend, you'll have adequate time to rest and relax."

"I'm fine, really."

"Perhaps the strain on your emotions is more evident to me than to yourself. Regardless, I insist that you take this afternoon and tomorrow off—with pay, of course."

Anne protested, but Muller held firm, reminding her that this was The Hawthorne Group and, where the New York office was concerned, he was in charge. Finally, she succumbed and, instead of going to lunch, left the office at noon. Walking up Fifth Avenue, she came to the Plaza Hotel, where normally she veered west, and decided to continue north instead.

A day and a half off from work. Maybe Muller wasn't so bad after all.

Yes he is.

And what about The Hawthorne Group?

It's not that bad. I just wish Trump Tower would burn down so I didn't have to go back again.

Not a bad fantasy, but in all likelihood, the building had a superefficient sprinkler system.

So what should she do with her afternoon off? Nothing Muller had said required her to lie in bed at home like an invalid.

The zoo? No.

Shopping? No.

The Metropolitan Museum of Art? Yes.

The prospect of the museum boosted her spirits, and walking up Fifth Avenue, Anne let her mind wander. As a child, she'd liked painting, but eventually shifted her allegiance to theater. And what she'd wanted was what she eventually got—the chance to play Lady Macbeth, Portia, Electra. Whatever else happened in life, no one could take those memories away from her.

Oblivious to passersby, Anne closed her eyes, just for a moment, and was transported back to the Renaissance in Verona:

Come, gentle night, come loving black-browed
   night,
Give me my Romeo; and when he shall die,
Take him and cut him out in little stars,
And he will make the face of heaven so fine
That all the world will be in love with night
And pay no worship to the garish sun.

83

Suspended in time, Anne continued up Fifth Avenue beneath an arc of tree limbs reaching toward the sky.

> What's here? A cup closed in my true love's
>   hand?
> Poison, I see, hath been his timeless end.
> O churl! Drunk all, and left no friendly drop to
>   help me after?
> I will kiss thy lips;
> Haply some poison yet doth hang on them. . . .

Just about the time Juliet stabbed herself, fell upon Romeo's body, and died, Anne came to the Metropolitan Museum of Art. It was an imposing structure, stretching from 80th to 84th Street, with a long row of granite steps leading to the lobby.

Suggested admission was five dollars. Anne paid, was given a bright blue button with the letters "MMA" to pin to her blouse, and decided to visit the Egyptian collection at the north end of the floor. She was impatient with museums. As an actress, sometimes that made her feel guilty, giving short shrift to someone else's art. Nonetheless, she moved quickly, almost restlessly, past centuries of antiquities—jewelry, pottery, wall paintings, reliefs—inhaling what she saw, until she came to a rectangular wood coffin painted brown with turquoise markings. Beside it lay a smaller anthropoid coffin, with a young androgynous face in gold, white, and bronze. The smaller coffin was partially open. Inside, the shriveled mummified remains of Nephthys were visible, wrapped in parched brown cloth. Nephthys, who had lived during Egypt's Twelfth Dynasty, four thousand years before. A real person, who had walked, talked, lived, and loved, and now was on display in a museum in New York.

In the next room, she saw the coffin and mummy of Khnumhotpe. After that, the coffin and mummy of Ukhhotpe. More coffins; more mummies. Anne wanted to get away from death, but now she was trapped in a maze of corridors lined with glass cases and funerary boats. Each room led to another, which led back to the first, until she began to think she might never get out.

There was one last door. Anne pushed through it into a cavernous glass-enclosed room. Water flowed gently in a reflecting pool. In front of her rose the Temple of Dendur, transported block by block from Egypt to the Americas before the rising waters of the Nile could submerge it for all time. The temple stood as it had two thousand years before. Simple, beautiful. A vestibule, antechamber, and sanctuary. Anne could only begin to imagine what dramas had transpired inside.

It must have been wonderful, she thought to herself.

Maybe, centuries before, she had been in Egypt. Maybe Michael Harney was there now.

And he died.

So will we all.

Anne turned. It was time to go. But before she left she reached into her pocket for a coin; a shiny one so it would glow. Then, walking past the reflecting pool, she threw it out as far as she could, watched it settle beneath the ripples, and said a prayer for Michael's soul.

Back in the lobby, Anne felt more at peace with

herself than before. There was so much to see; she wanted to go to the museum's second floor.

Up the stairs. Past the Farnese Table, built in sixteenth-century Rome, an inlay of marble, alabaster, and semiprecious stones; six feet wide, twelve feet long, with a "PLEASE DO NOT TOUCH" cardboard marker on top. Anne touched it, of course. The table was hard, smooth, and cold. Then she moved to an adjacent gallery, where five El Grecos graced the walls.

Each succeeding gallery was as remarkable as the one before.

Titian.

Van Dyck.

Velázquez.

Raphael.

Then Rembrandt; Gallery 15; her favorite room.

Except, just inside the gallery entrance, Anne realized that someone was watching her. She'd seen him before, in the Velázquez room, but it hadn't registered. Like everyone else, he'd been looking at the paintings. Now he was looking at her.

Pretending he wasn't there, she moved past the first Rembrandt—*Portrait of a Lady*—to the companion *Portrait of a Man*. Both paintings were signed and dated 1632.

The man stood behind her, positioned between the two portraits, just off her shoulder.

"They make a nice couple," he said.

Anne ignored him, and moved to the next painting.

The man dropped back, accepting the rebuff, and turned his attention to portraits on the opposite wall.

Maybe I was too brusque, Anne told herself.

But she resented the presumption that she could be picked up on demand, and she preferred not having someone loom over her shoulder.

Moving past *The Noble Slav*, *Bellona*, and *Flora*, Anne stopped at *Christ and the Woman of Samaria*. Next came *Aristotle with a Bust of Homer*, and she smiled, recalling the fuss over its acquisition by the museum three decades earlier for 2.3 million dollars. Times had changed. Now 2.3 million would buy ten percent of a Van Gogh sunflower.

Across the room, the man who'd followed her was moving from *Hendrickje Stoffels* to *The Standard-Bearer*. He was attractive, actually. Six feet tall, about forty years old; rugged-looking bordering on handsome was how Anne would describe him. Not Paul Newman, but better-looking than Richard Dreyfuss or Jack Nicholson.

The Rape of Europa was next on the wall.

Okay; he wants to meet me. He's nice-looking. He's wearing a suit. And he's cultured enough to be at the museum.

Another Rembrandt portrait; then two by Frans Hals.

Anne looked at the man again. No wedding ring. Now they were playing the same game, casting glances across the room.

Their paths converged at the exit from Gallery 15.

"Let me try again," he offered. "My name is Ned Connor."

"Hi. I'm Anne Rhodes."

"Do you come here often?"

"Two or three times a year. And you?"

"About the same."

The next gallery had seven more Rembrandts and

four portraits by Vermeer. Connor asked what Anne did for a living, and she answered that she worked for an energy commodities firm. There was no reason to tell him more. He reciprocated with the information that he worked in Maryland, and was in New York on business. That was a downer, because she was starting to like him, and working in Maryland made him less of a social prospect. Still, there was a certain chemistry, attraction, whatever, between them.

More galleries; lesser-known artists. Pompeo Batoni, Sebastiano Ricci, Jacopo Amigoni, Francesco Guardi.

Connor divulged that he was forty-six years old (which surprised Anne because he looked younger) and that he worked in the communications industry.

Eventually, they came to Pieter Bruegel's *The Harvesters*; after that, a roomful of paintings by artists Anne had never heard of.

"Would you like some coffee?" Connor asked. "There's a cafeteria downstairs."

"Sure," she answered.

The cafeteria was on the main floor, just beyond a model of the Parthenon.

"How about something to eat?" Connor asked when they reached the serving area.

Actually, she was hungry. It was midafternoon, and she'd left work before lunch, so she ordered a turkey sandwich, which came with lettuce, tomato, and a pickle.

Connor opted for coffee, and reached for his wallet as they neared the cash register.

"Dutch treat," Anne said.

After they'd paid, he steered her to a table in the

corner, and took the chair facing out for himself. That meant he could see everyone and everything in the cafeteria, while Anne was left with a view of the wall.

Bad manners, she thought. But then she remembered the chocolate cake joke that Howard Otis had once told her. A young boy and his father were eating dinner, and there were two pieces of chocolate cake—a big one and a small one—on the table for dessert. The boy helped himself to the larger piece, whereupon his father launched into a sermon on manners, closing with, "You were very rude. If I'd chosen first, I would have taken the smaller piece."

"So what are you complaining about," the boy countered. "You got it, didn't you?"

So I shouldn't complain, Anne told herself. Being polite, I would have taken the seat facing the wall, and I got it.

She picked up her sandwich and began to eat.

Connor went back to the cafeteria line for some milk to go with his coffee.

"I'd like to ask you something," Anne said when he returned to the table.

"All right."

"Upstairs, on the second floor, you were following me, weren't you?"

"Yes."

"Why?"

"Because I wanted to meet you."

That was honest enough. Instead of being on the defensive, he'd knocked the ball back into her court.

There was an awkward moment.

"That's a nice locket," he said, nodding toward the chain around her neck.

"Thank you. It belonged to my great-grandmother."

And then Anne stopped, because suddenly Connor was staring at her; not sexually, but with more intensity than she'd ever felt, as if he were looking into her soul.

"I have to tell you why I'm here," he said.

"I don't understand."

"I need your help. I have to be honest with you. But first you have to promise me that everything I say will be kept absolutely confidential."

"You're being silly."

"To the contrary, I'm deadly serious."

"Is this a game?"

"Hardly."

Anne was starting to get nervous. "I don't want to talk to you anymore."

"You have no choice."

She started to stand up.

"Don't go," he told her.

That was all. Just two words, but something in his voice bound her to her chair.

"I'd like to tell you more, but first I need your pledge of absolute secrecy."

"Who are you?"

"I've already told you. My name is Ned Connor. Promise me you'll keep what I say in absolute confidence, and I'll tell you more."

"And if I don't promise?"

"You will; you have to. There are more lives at stake than you can possibly imagine."

"I think you're a nut. And on the chance you're not, I don't want that responsibility."

"Neither do I. Neither did Michael Harney."

Anne sat still, locked in place as though her entire body had been cast in lead.

"Michael was murdered," Connor said.

"I don't believe you."

"Yes you do."

"Who are you?"

"First, you promise."

"How can I believe you?"

"By listening to what I have to say."

There was a pause.

"All right; I'll listen. But if I want, you have to stop."

"Fair enough."

"What happened to Michael?"

"He was shot to death and his murder made to look like suicide."

"Why?"

"Because Christoph Matthes wanted him dead."

"I don't understand."

"There's no reason you should. Have you ever heard of the National Security Agency?"

Anne shook her head.

"Then that's a good place to start. The NSA is a branch of the Defense Department, with twenty-five thousand employees in Fort Meade, Maryland, and a hundred thousand more overseas. I've been with the NSA for twenty years. We make codes; we break codes; we intercept communications from foreign powers, and we secure our own government's electronic transmissions. We don't make policy; that's up to the president and his advisers. We don't implement policy; that's the State Department, the military, and the CIA. All we do is handle the flow of information. Are you with me so far?"

Anne nodded.

"Then let's take things a bit further. Every United States intelligence agency has desk men and field operatives. And each agency has deep-cover agents—operatives who have been on the payroll for years while developing parallel careers. You can go into any multinational corporation in the world, and someone employed there will be working for the NSA or CIA. And someone else will be working for the KGB; that's the way things are. Michael Harney was one of us. From the time he graduated from college, he worked for the NSA. At every job, from Bechtel Corporation to Occidental Petroleum, his mission was to keep his eyes and ears open. Moving to The Hawthorne Group was a natural career switch for him. Apart from intelligence community considerations, the job represented an enormous increase in salary. And from our point of view, having someone inside the world's largest private energy commodities firm was a phenomenal coup. Most of what we got from Michael at The Hawthorne Group involved market manipulation, games Christoph Matthes plays with the supply and price of oil. Then, eight months ago, we heard an extraordinarily disturbing rumor. Michael backdoored into The Hawthorne Group's computer system, confirmed the story, and began gathering data as best he could. Our guess is that someone, probably Matthes, learned what he was doing and ordered him killed. I can tell you for certain that Michael Harney didn't commit suicide."

"How can you be sure?"

"Because that's not the sort of person Michael was. Forget that he loved life. Forget that he was battling leukemia and would have fought it to the end. Forget that he never would have abandoned this project. Look at it in terms of his wife and children. Michael loved them more than anyone and anything in the world, and he had a life insurance policy designed to pay them a million dollars but, like all life insurance policies, it doesn't pay a penny for suicide."

"And his suicide note?"

"It was typed on a word processor in his apartment. Obviously, that makes handwriting analysis impossible."

Anne had heard enough. "This is too strange. I don't want to get involved."

"You have to. We need your help."

"Why? Why me? There are twenty other people who work for The Hawthorne Group in New York."

"There's no way of knowing which of them we can trust."

"And what makes you think you can trust me?"

"We trust you because Michael said we could. He said you were decent, honest, and smart; that you were less invested in The Hawthorne Group than any of the others; that you have a conscience; that whatever else is going on in your life, you aren't working for the other side."

"This is crazy."

"Anne, we have twelve weeks to break this plot. There are people working in every major city in the world, but we desperately need someone inside The Hawthorne Group in New York."

"You're not making sense. What am I supposed to do? I have minimum security clearance inside the office. I don't even understand computers."

"There's no doubt we'd be better off if you were more skilled and positioned at a higher level, but there's no one else."

"How can you say that? What about Hans Werner? What about Ernst Neumann?"

"Would you trust Werner or Neumann?"

"There are eight secretaries in the office."

"You're smarter than all of them."

Anne's shoulders sagged. "I won't do it."

"You have to."

"That's what you think."

"We'll pay you; any amount you want."

"I don't want to hear any more."

"I'm not prepared to take no for an answer."

"Ned, the conversation is over. You promised, anytime I wanted, you'd stop."

"Name your price."

"A million dollars."

"Fair enough."

Then something happened; a circuit inside Anne's head overloaded and it was like an electrical shock. Because the reason she'd said a million dollars was to end the conversation. It was a silly amount and she wanted out, but Connor had just accepted the number without blinking, and something about him said he was serious.

Anne stared. "You mean it, don't you?"

"Yes."

"I don't understand. What could I possibly do that would be worth a million dollars over the next twelve weeks?"

"We don't know. But we want you there in case we need you."

Things were happening too fast. Anne's head was spinning. A million dollars.

"I don't want to get involved."

"You're already involved."

"But not in the way you want me to be. And from what you've said, from what happened to Michael . . ." Her voice trailed off.

"Look, Anne; I can't tell you there isn't any risk. I can promise we'll do everything possible to protect you, that you'll be compensated financially beyond your wildest dreams, and that you'll be helping to avert a frightening disaster."

"That doesn't make sense."

"Maybe not now; but it will later."

"When?"

"I can tell you more once you're on board."

"A million dollars?"

"That's what I said."

"Tax free."

Connor's face took on the look of James Bond suddenly turned government bureaucrat. "I'm sorry. I can't do that."

"What do you mean, you can't do that?"

"Taxes are taxes. I pay taxes; the people I work with pay taxes. You have to pay taxes too."

"If I'm paying taxes, I want two million dollars."

This time, the response was slower in coming.

"I can't do that. Two million dollars is too much."

And then Anne was laughing because, really, the whole thing was absurd. I mean, here was this guy who'd picked her up in the museum and started talking about government plots and promised her a million dollars and it was ludicrous.

Except for one thing—Michael Harney was dead,

and this guy knew about Michael Harney. And more important, every instinct in Anne's body told her that Ned Connor could be trusted.

"I want to ask you something," she said. "How do I know your story is legitimate—that you really work for the government; that this isn't some kind of industrial espionage or crazy third-world plot? How do I know that what you're telling me is true?"

"What you're saying is, you want verification."

"That's right."

"All right; I'll tell you how we'll handle that."

Anne waited.

Speaking in slow measured tones, Connor looked into her eyes. "The President of the United States is holding a nationally televised press conference tonight. How would you like that press conference to start?"

"What do you mean?"

"What I mean is, you're about to learn how high up this thing goes. At eight P.M., the President will be in the East Room of the White House answering questions from reporters. Obviously, you can't go to the White House to meet the President, but we'll get word to him beforehand to send you a signal. Now how would you like the press conference to start?"

Anne looked down at her hands, flustered. "I don't know."

"Think of something."

"I guess . . . have him call on someone in a blue dress."

Connor stood up. "All right. Have a good evening. I'll be in touch with you tomorrow."

And then he was gone. And Anne was alone in

the Metropolitan Museum of Art cafeteria, thinking probably he was crazy but, God forbid, there was something about him she trusted.

She took the bus home. It was crowded and she had to stand, but that didn't matter because her mind was wandering. It was back in the museum with Ned Connor, in the Rembrandt room where they'd met. Hendrickje Stoffels, Flora, Bellona, all the people Rembrandt had painted. They were dead. Did the fact that Rembrandt had made them immortal make any difference? The bus wound its way through the park, stopping at the corner of Central Park West and 81st Street. Anne got off, walked north to her apartment, and went inside.

Then came the waiting.

Five o'clock . . . 5:30 . . . 5:45 . . . 6:00 . . .

Just before eight, Anne turned on the television. *Wheel of Fortune* was ending. There was an ad for a brokerage house, followed by one for Kellogg's Frosted Flakes. Then the CBS logo flashed on the screen, and Dan Rather was talking.

"Good evening. This is the President's fifth press conference of the year. Among the issues expected to be discussed are last month's economic summit and events in South Africa." The camera moved in for a close-up of Rather. "The President is also expected to face questions concerning environmental protection legislation and recent developments in the war on drugs."

Then Rather's image disappeared from the screen, and was replaced by a throng of reporters in the East Room of the White House.

Anne waited.

"Ladies and gentlemen," a voice intoned, "the President of the United States."

The camera moved again, this time focusing on the President as he strode down a red-carpeted hall-way through the East Room entrance, up to the podium. Behind him, to the left, an American flag was visible. A large blue flag with the presidential seal hung to the right. Nervously (or was it just Anne's imagination?), the President scanned the room, then spoke.

"I have no opening statement, so why don't we get right down to questions. Ms. Stahl, you look very pretty in that nice blue dress. Let's start with you."

PART TWO

No matter how dedicated the enforcers are, there's always the danger, almost a certainty, that plutonium or enriched uranium is going to be sold for vast profits to countries that want that material for explosive capability. In a worst-case scenario—and it frightens me to say this—we might even see a black market in nuclear weapons.

—Jimmy Carter

Chapter 7

After the President's press conference, Anne turned off the television and began working herself toward nervous-wreck status. She'd promised not to tell anyone about Ned Connor's overture, so there was no one to turn to for reassurance or support. Around eleven, she went to bed, anticipating a long sleepless night; but lying beneath the covers, to protect her equilibrium she found herself acting out a role. This wasn't happening; not really. Instead, she was auditioning for the lead in an international drama, and the most important thing for her to do was maintain composure.

In the morning she woke up reasonably rested, and waited at home on the assumption Connor would call.

Nine o'clock . . . ten o'clock . . . At 10:20, the phone rang but it was a telemarketing call.

Eleven o'clock . . . 11:30 . . . Finally at noon, she decided that Connor had found her at the Metropolitan Museum of Art and was capable of finding her again, wherever she was, so she went for a walk.

She liked being outdoors. Usually, it put her mind at ease, but this time, outside her apartment, Anne's thoughts were jumbled. What day was it? Friday. Maybe I should buy a newspaper to see a transcript of the President's remarks: "Ms. Stahl, you look very pretty in that nice blue dress. Let's start with you."

She didn't want to go back to the office on Monday. Michael Harney. Leo Muller. A million dollars. It was all too crazy.

Walking down Columbus Avenue, Anne stopped at a greengrocer and bought a nectarine, which the counterman gave her in a brown paper bag. Then she continued on to Tower Records at Broadway and 66th Street, and went inside.

"Check your bag, please," instructed the guard at the door.

Exchanging her nectarine for a white plastic tag, Anne moved down the aisle, ignoring the rap music blaring in the background. Most of the records and compact disks on display were by groups she didn't know. It made her feel old; contemporary culture had passed her by.

An obese woman in baggy green slacks was blocking the aisle. Maneuvering around her, Anne came to a flight of stairs and walked down to the basement level. There, the music was more familiar—Frank Sinatra, Barbra Streisand, rows of show tunes and classical sounds.

Maybe I should get an Ella Fitzgerald album.

In the Female Vocalist section, she saw *Ella Sings Broadway*, *Ella in Rome*, *Ella and Louis*; then Ella's Songbook series—hundreds of songs by Cole Porter, Johnny Mercer, Duke Ellington, Jerome Kern, Harold Arlen, George and Ira Gershwin, Rodgers and Hart, Irving Berlin—

"Those are nice albums," a voice from behind offered.

Anne turned and saw Ned Connor.

"Let's go someplace where we can talk," he told her.

They went back upstairs, past the obese woman in the baggy green slacks, down the first aisle to the front of the store. Connor looked the same as the day before, except now he seemed more authoritative and in control.

"Don't forget your nectarine," he prompted as they passed the guard.

Snotty bastard. That was what she wanted to tell him, but she didn't. Her heart was pounding.

Outside the store, he turned west onto 66th Street and Anne followed.

"I've always liked Ella Fitzgerald," he told her. "Once, I saw Peggy Lee interviewed on television, and the talk-show host asked who was the greatest jazz singer of all time. Lee got this befuddled look on her face and answered, 'I assume you mean, after Ella.'"

At West End Avenue, they stopped for a red light, then continued west as far as they could, coming to Freedom Place—an isolated four-block stretch of road running north to 70th Street. There was no traffic. The only pedestrian was a hundred yards ahead. On the far side of the road, Anne saw a waist-high concrete wall with a chain-link fence on top. Beyond that was a thirty-foot drop to an abandoned Penn Central railroad yard, which looked like an overgrown pasture crisscrossed by rusting tracks. The yard extended to the West Side Highway, which gave way in turn to rotting piers and the Hudson River. Tall weeds were growing through the sidewalk. The noises of New York seemed far away.

Connor gestured toward the edge of the sidewalk. "How do you feel about sitting on the curb?"

"Whatever you want."

Following his lead, Anne sat.

"All right," he began, looking directly at her. "I assume you saw the President's press conference last night, so you know that this is deadly serious. I'd like to tell you more about what's at stake, but first I want to repeat what I said yesterday about the need for confidentiality. That means you tell absolutely no one; total silence. Understood?"

Anne nodded.

"I can't hear you."

"Yes."

"Thank you. Now if you'd like, I'll fill you in on what's really happening at The Hawthorne Group."

"First, tell me more about Michael Harney."

"Fair enough. You ask the questions, and I'll answer them."

"How do you know it wasn't suicide?"

"Because as I told you yesterday, Michael's personality, how he felt about life, and the job he was doing for us, all point toward murder."

"How was he killed?"

"By a gunshot wound to the side of the head,

The Hawthorne Group

from a weapon he owned and was licensed to
carry.''

''And the suicide note?''

''It said he loved his wife and children, and had
decided to end his life rather than put them through
the torturous end stages of a battle against leukemia.
It also made reference to wanting people to remember him as vibrant and strong rather than a decaying
shell. The language and style are Michael's, and the
fact that it was written on a word processor makes
forgery nondetectable. We checked for fingerprints—not just the letter, every piece of word-
processing equipment in the apartment. All we
found were Michael's prints and the residue of latex
gloves.''

Anne shifted silently on the curb.

''That's it,'' Connor told her. ''That's all we know
about Michael's death, and the next order of business is to put things in perspective. Yesterday, I told
you I work for the National Security Agency. I don't
know how you feel about intelligence gathering, but
I'll tell you flat-out, it's essential for our survival. In
1941, the United States was surprised by Pearl Harbor. A surprise like that would be fatal today. Intelligence gathering is about data and warning. Its
purpose is to provide the president, his advisers, the
military, and Congress with the most reliable information possible. Sometimes the CIA goes beyond
that role to implement policy. The NSA doesn't. I'm
telling you this because I want you to understand,
good intelligence isn't right wing or left wing; it's
devoid of ideological bias. Are you with me so far?''

Anne nodded.

''Good; then let's go on to Christoph Matthes.

Matthes was born in Belgium in 1939. His parents were Nazi sympathizers but not active in the cause. He was educated in Europe, speaks five languages fluently, and has built The Hawthorne Group into an empire that makes most corporations look like a Ma and Pa corner store. He's cold-blooded, ruthless, greedy, and totally amoral. Some entrepreneurs pay for publicity. Matthes, by contrast, takes pains to avoid it. He acquired The Hawthorne Group in 1970 when it was on the verge of bankruptcy, and has turned it into one of the largest privately held companies in the world. At first, there was nothing to distinguish Matthes from a hundred other small competitors in the energy-commodities business, but over time he began to emerge. Partly, that's because he does more than simply trade resources on paper. He moves them back and forth around the globe, and is personally involved. He's crossed the Sahara in search of oil, and inspected uranium mines in the heart of Africa. He meets directly with each foreign contact, and has learned every nuance of the energy trade. Time and time again in the early 1970s, Matthes's bids on transactions came in a fraction of a point ahead of his competitors', in large part because of an elaborate electronic surveillance system he put in place to monitor suppliers, customers, and rivals. Then, in 1973, the Arab oil embargo hit, and he rode it to incredible power. During a single two-month period, OPEC raised the price of oil from three to eleven and a half dollars a barrel—an increase of almost three hundred percent. Matthes had advance notice of the boycott, and made a fortune on oil futures. But more important, he worked out a deal with the Arabs to buy and sell oil outside the structure created by the multinational oil companies. If you needed oil during that period, you dealt with Matthes. In a sense, he financed the oil boycott, and OPEC repaid the favor by selling to him below the official OPEC price once the boycott ended. That gave The Hawthorne Group a major price advantage over its competitors, and made future success all but inevitable. Then, in 1979, the Shah of Iran was overthrown and the Ayatollah Khomeini came to power. Iran was dependent on oil for ninety percent of its export income, but before long it became a criminal offense for American companies to trade with Iran. Once again, Matthes stepped into the void. By the early 1980s, The Hawthorne Group had estimated assets of ten billion dollars, and each success gave Matthes more leverage and more power to reach out on an even greater scale.''

Just for a moment, Connor paused to make sure Anne was following. Then he went on.

''Putting together a complete picture of The Hawthorne Group is an impossible task. It's a montage of corporations, subsidiaries, and holding companies. Most of its business is conducted in third-world countries, where very little that goes on is documented, and even in the United States, it can't be properly monitored. Too much is happening; its business is too widespread and moves too fast for scrutiny. At any given time, Matthes is making deals in twenty countries around the world. He has credit lines of a hundred million dollars or more with banks on five continents. The way The Hawthorne Group is structured, he can take a billion dollars and move it from company to bank to subsidiary to country until it vanishes completely. By keeping money moving, he avoids taxes and virtually all regulatory restrictions. The only thing that matters to him is profit. Dealing with Libya is the same as dealing with Norway. Doing business in South Africa is no different to him from doing business in Panama. He never considers the moral aspects of a deal, only the bottom line. Governments treat him as an equal power, and he in turn treats all governments equally. He never stops working, and has total recall of events, numbers, and places. But like everyone else on this planet, Matthes is fallible and, several years ago, he ran into trouble. In the early 1980s, oil was selling at thirty-five dollars a barrel. Then the price began to fall, and by 1986 it had dropped to ten dollars a barrel. The Hawthorne Group got caught in the squeeze. Matthes owed the radical oil-producing states a fortune for futures at old prices, and his empire was threatened. He began to retrench and finally, to preserve his fortune, he entered into a frightening arrangement.''

Twenty yards away, a middle-aged woman was approaching. Connor broke off and waited for her to pass, then lowered his voice and began again.

''Fourteen months ago, a CIA agent in Algeria was approached by a Libyan contact, who offered to reveal a 'big secret' for ten thousand dollars. Libyan contacts being what they are, the agent figured it was most likely a hoax, but paid the money anyway. He got the secret, still thought it was a hoax, and reported it to CIA headquarters in Langley, where it was disregarded as one of a hundred end-of-the-world scenarios that come our way each year. Then, eight months ago, the unthinkable happened. The story resurfaced, and this time it was confirmed.''

Speaking slowly, Connor went on. "At present, there are nine nuclear powers in the world—the United States, Soviet Union, Britain, France, China, India, Israel, South Africa, and Pakistan. Canada, West Germany, and Japan have the capacity to develop nuclear weapons, but have chosen not to. Brazil and Argentina are on the verge. Obviously, the spread of nuclear weapons is of great concern, but up until now they've been confined to governments we trust not to use them. As early as 1970, Muammar Qaddafi sent an aide to China in an attempt to buy an atomic bomb, but he was turned aside. Then, in the mid-1970s, Libya bankrolled Pakistan's nuclear program, before being rebuffed by President Zia. After that, Qaddafi gave Argentina a hundred million dollars during the Falkland Islands war in the hope of gaining nuclear favors. I could go on, but the message is clear—Libya will pay anything for an atomic bomb, and other countries like Iraq and Iran have similar agendas. Hydrogen bombs are incredibly complex. Setting them off is like keeping a candle lit in the midst of a hurricane. Only four nations have them, and our guess is, only a few hundred physicists have mastered the technology involved. But designing an atomic bomb is relatively simple; thousands of scientists understand the principles. The only real barrier to making an atomic bomb is acquiring weapons-grade uranium or plutonium, and there's far too much of it around. Nuclear power plants produce plutonium as a by-product of generating electricity. Reprocessing plants handle thousands of tons of spent fuel. Theoretically, at every step of the fuel cycle, material is weighed, analyzed, and any discrepancy in quantity found. But the truth is, there's an international black market in nuclear material and everyone knows it. Twenty years ago, enriched uranium was diverted from a nuclear power plant in Pennsylvania to Israel's nuclear weapons program. Israel now has a hundred atomic bombs. Five years ago, fifteen tons of heavy water processed in Norway disappeared and was diverted to India by a West German firm. Black market weapons-grade plutonium sells for ten million dollars a kilo. Less than eight kilos is required to make a bomb. Christoph Matthes is making bombs. He's bought the plutonium. He's hired physicists, engineers, and machinists. We've seen his design plans. His bombs are crude, far less sophisticated than those in superpower arsenals, but they'll do the job."

Anne sat still. Everything she was hearing, the way Connor was speaking—it was so matter-of-fact and impassive, it couldn't be real.

"Ms. Stahl, you look very pretty in that nice blue dress. Let's start with you."

"In Christoph Matthes's world," she heard Connor saying, "everything is for sale. And nothing brings a greater return on investment than an atomic bomb. Libya, Iraq, and Iran will pay in oil. Other governments are offering cash and gold. Matthes is the ultimate arms profiteer, and so far we've been unable to stop him. That's because some of the bombs have already been made, and we don't know where they are. Right now, the United States government has ten thousand men and women in every intelligence-gathering agency working on this matter. At most, two hundred know what's happening. The rest have been given a cover story. All of the information gathered is being processed and analyzed at NSA headquarters. The director of the NSA is working full time on the project. The President is making all ultimate decisions. Congressional leaders from both parties have been advised. We've intercepted literally thousands of communications, using every method at our command. But as soon as we find a way to break Matthes's codes, he seems to change them. For every piece of data we gather, there's something equally important we don't know. There are thirteen bombs—or at least there will be when Matthes is done. Apparently, twelve of them will be shipped, and one left behind. We have a partial list of where the bombs are going. We even know the shipping date. But we don't know where the bombs are. My job, and your job, is to help find the bombs. You're one possible road to a solution; that's all. We've infiltrated Hawthorne Group regional offices around the world, but for a variety of reasons, we think the bombs are being built and stored in or around New York. Assuming the plutonium has already been obtained, construction could take place in a small farmhouse or industrial loft. Matthes has compartmentalized his operation to the point where losing several bombs or several men wouldn't bring him down, and if we strike without total success, there's no way of knowing how he'd retaliate with the remaining bombs. That puts us between a rock and a hard place. Today is June second. We have until August twenty-fourth, shipping date, to find the bombs.''

''You make it sound real.''

''It is real. It's deadly real, and the future of civilization as we know it is involved. Up until now, terrorist organizations have relied primarily on publicity for effect, but with nuclear weapons, any nation or organization could perpetrate unacceptable harm. Look at Libya. It's a fleabag country with three and a half million people. The Libyan army has fifty thousand soldiers and can't even win a border war against Chad, and still Qaddafi drives us up a wall. One atomic bomb makes Libya a superpower. The United States military can't stop an Arab terrorist from driving a truck into an army barracks in Lebanon and killing two hundred of our soldiers. Do you really think we can intercept a freighter carrying a Libyan bomb into New York Harbor? When the bomb went off, we wouldn't even know where it came from or who to blame. And even if we did, what good would it do to obliterate Tripoli if New York were destroyed? Look at Iran. If the ayatollahs ever get nuclear weapons, our only defense will be their own self-restraint. Terrorist groups like the Red Brigade and Baader-Meinhof gang don't have the funds to buy Matthes's bombs, but a purchasing country might give them one. Israel could be destroyed. The likelihood of carnage would increase worldwide. There's no alternative. We have to find the bombs.''

''This is crazy. There's no way I can possibly help.''

''You said that yesterday, and the answer is, you can. Matthes prefers not to take risks. He's obsessed with security, but at heart he's a gambler or he wouldn't be where he is today. The way his nuclear operation is set up, there has to come a time when it's all vulnerable. Maybe that time will be shipping date. I hope it's earlier, because I'd hate to go down to the wire on this one. But whenever it is, we need as many infiltrators as possible in his organization, and the New York office is crucial. There's nothing concrete for you to do now, but in time something will come."

"Why not just arrest Matthes and do whatever you do with people like him until he tells you where to find the bombs?"

"It's been considered, from torture on down. The problem is, as best we can tell from communications intercepts, one of the bombs has been deployed with an automatic detonator. That means, it has to be re-set or it explodes. We don't know where that bomb is or how the timer is reset, whether it's done by radio signal or by hand. And if we arrest Matthes, if we're unable to break him . . ." Connor's voice trailed off, then picked up again. "I don't think you understand what an atomic bomb is capable of doing. Hiroshima and Nagasaki; those were small bombs. One well-placed bomb today could obliterate New York City. Eight million people would die. Communications and financial institutions throughout the United States would be destroyed. It's a scary world. Most people are poor and hungry, desperate and sometimes fanatical. Give those people nuclear weapons, and you're charting a holocaust."

"If all this is true, why would Matthes hire an outsider like me at all?"

"Because he's got an energy-commodities business to run. Someone has to work in the New York office. And my guess is, by hiring at random through an employment agency, he figured he was eliminating the possibility of bringing in a mole."

"How many people in the New York office are involved?"

"You mean, how many are bad guys working for the other side?"

"That's right."

"Leo Muller, for starters. We're not sure exactly what he knows, but clearly it's a lot. Several others know something illegal is going on, but presume it relates to the oil business. The rest of the crew is just doing its job."

"I won't."

"You won't what?"

"It's too scary. I don't want to get involved."

"Anne, you have to."

"That's what you think. I'm quitting The Hawthorne Group now. A million dollars, two million dollars. It doesn't matter. I want out."

"You can't do that."

"Yes, I can."

"Look—"

"No, you look. This is your job. You like this sort of thing, playing hero. But cloak and dagger means there's a dagger involved and, assuming this is for real and you're not an escapee from a lunatic asylum, I have no intention of winding up like Michael Harney. So play your games; follow me around to museums and record stores and anywhere else you want, but I'm getting out."

"Are you done?"

"Yes, I'm done, finished. I'm finished with you, finished with The Hawthorne Group, finished with this whole crazy mess."

"Then calm down and hear me out. You're scared; I know that. Getting involved will mean living with

114

fear every moment of every day for the next twelve weeks, but then it will be over. Hundreds of thousands of American soldiers have lost their lives protecting this country in time of war. Some of them wanted to be heroes, most didn't. Michael Harney didn't want to be a hero; he was doing his job. I don't want to be a hero. My job says I'm a GS-level-twelve government employee. That means I make forty-three thousand dollars with thirteen sick days a year, which is a lot less than your million dollars. I'm doing this because there comes a time when the stakes are so high that you can't say no.''

''And why do I have to be the person you come to?''

''Because of who you are, and the fact that you happen to be in a certain place at a certain time. Now, I've been totally honest with you. I've told you more than I wanted to because I felt you were entitled to know, but in return I need your help. Trust me, and I promise, I'll never betray that trust.''

She trusted him; that was the crazy part. She felt the trust.

''Suppose I say yes. Suppose for a moment that I get involved. What would I tell people? How would I explain my contact with you?''

''You met me at the Metropolitan Museum of Art.''

''And how could I get in touch if I need you? I mean, you follow me around, but I might need you sometime when you're not there.''

''I'll give you the phone number for a company called Collins Communications. That's where I work, if anyone asks.''

''What's Collins Communications?''

"One of our proprietaries; a company owned and operated by the NSA as a commercial cover for intelligence purposes. Its phones are secure, but we can't vouch for terminals other than our own, so use a pay phone when you call. Wherever I am, at any hour, the company will find me. And as far as going back to work is concerned, try not to change your habits at the office. They say the most important thing for a spy is not to be noticed, so don't do anything differently that might draw attention to yourself. That's about all I have to say for the moment except, officially, there are five people at the NSA who will know I'm working with you. If anything happens to me, if for any reason I become unavailable, respond only to a man carrying a handkerchief with the monogram ENC. In case you're wondering, Ned is short for Edwin and N is my middle initial. Is there anything else you'd like to know?"

"I don't think so."

"All right; I'll walk you home."

Both of them were quiet going back to Anne's apartment. Just short of the lobby to her building, Connor stopped and offered his hand to say goodbye.

"You'll be hearing from me," he promised. "Incidentally, your face is wonderful. It shows exactly what's going on in your mind."

The doorman Anne didn't like was on duty. Passing by with a perfunctory hello, she checked for mail, then took the elevator upstairs. She was scared; that was the dominant emotion in her makeup. She was excited; she felt important, and there was anticipation over the money, but mostly she was scared.

If anything happens to me, respond only to a man carrying a handkerchief with the monogram ENC.

And what if something happened to her? Would anyone care?

Inside her apartment, she put her keys on the foyer table, took off her shoes, and performed the other rituals of coming home. Somehow things seemed the way they had after her first day of work at The Hawthorne Group—as though her space had been violated by someone who didn't belong. It was her imagination, of course; that's what she told herself. But now there was reason not to be sure.

Maybe I should look around a bit, and see what's here.

She started in the bedroom. After that, the kitchen and foyer. Everything was the same. Skip the bathroom and closets, she told herself. Go to the living room.

There, on the mantelpiece, she saw the intruder. It had been there for years. David had given it to her for Christmas. He'd come over on a snowy evening two years ago to exchange gifts, and at evening's end he'd given her one last present—a vase; Meissen crystal, handcut with a cobalt blue face, a work of art. It was stunning, but she didn't want it on the mantelpiece anymore because it reminded her of David.

Should I throw it out? No.

Sell it? That wouldn't be right.

But I don't want it here; not where I have to look at it anymore.

There was a shoebox in the bedroom closet. If she wrapped the vase in newspaper, it would fit just right.

Anne went to the closet, took out the box, and set it down on the floor. Then she crossed to the mantelpiece and lifted the vase. All but involuntarily, she flicked a finger against its blue cobalt face to hear the resonant sound.

Ting!

Yesterday's newspaper was still in the apartment. She wrapped the vase, stuffed it in the shoebox, and put it in the closet on a high shelf, way in back.

There.

That was that.

David would grow old, unhappy and alone. At least, that was her fantasy, or fear for herself. What were the words he'd used to end his letter; the one he'd left with the doorman weeks before?

"If I could choose one person to go with into the unknown, it would be you."

Well, David; I'm about to journey into the unknown; but I'm going with Ned Connor, not with you.

Chapter 8

The weekend passed slowly. Anne wasn't sure what to do.

She read, went to the movies, and Saturday evening had dinner with Amanda and Howard. All she told them about Ned Connor was that she'd met a man at the museum, and if he asked her out, she'd probably go. Her instincts told her that Connor was for real. Agent 002; that's what she'd call him. Michael Harney had been 001. And Sean Connery would always be 007, no matter who United Artists cast in the role.

Sunday night, Anne had a dream. Torrential rivers were overflowing their boundaries. A cold wind was blowing; there was driving rain. The sky was gray; the water, black. Spirits were jangling; not resonant peals, but harsh shrill—

Her telephone was ringing.

It was three A.M.

Half asleep, Anne picked up the receiver.

"Hello?"

Nothing.

On the other end of the line, someone was listening.

"Hello?"

Still nothing.

Go back to sleep.

All she remembered in the morning was the image of rivers overflowing.

She thought she might hear from Connor before work on Monday, but no last-minute instructions were forthcoming. She walked to the office, inserted her computer access card in the door slot at nine A.M., and went to her cubicle, where a pile of invoices was waiting. Soon after, Leo Muller dropped by and asked solicitously if she was feeling better.

"Yes, thank you. You've been very kind."

Then it was back to work as usual—indexing documents, running errands, sorting mail. Except things seemed different; bad vibrations were everywhere. It was hard to tell what was real and what was imagined, which people in the office were pawns and who was evil.

Be an actress; maintain composure.

The next few days were more of the same. Computer files, catered lunches, oil statistics. Thursday, a New York City police detective came to the office in conjunction with the department's investigation into the death of Michael Harney. One by one, Hawthorne Group employees were called into conference room A and questioned about Harney's work, personal life, and habits. Anne's turn came in mid-afternoon.

"I apologize if this is difficult for you," the detective began, "but we want to confirm our essential findings. How well did you know Michael Harney?"

"Not that well. I started at The Hawthorne Group six weeks ago. I didn't know him at all before then."

"Did you have any contact with him outside the office?"

"No."

"What about inside; how often did you interact with him?"

The questioning went on for a half-hour, ending with, "Do you have any reason to believe that Michael Harney's death was anything other than suicide?"

"Not at all," Anne answered.

Then it was back to work, with the sound of the paper shredder whirring in the background.

That night, Anne dreamt about rivers again. The next day Muller mentioned that a permanent replacement for Harney wouldn't be hired until after Labor Day weekend. Twelve weeks was a long time. August 24 was clear in her mind.

At the close of work, Anne rode the elevator down to the Trump Tower lobby and walked out onto Fifth Avenue. It had started to rain, not a downpour, but heavily enough so that not having an umbrella mattered. Traffic was moving slowly; there were no cabs available. Probably it made sense to walk over to Sixth Avenue and catch a bus heading uptown. The sidewalk was crowded; too many people struggling in opposite directions. Maybe she should go back inside and have a drink by the waterfall until the traffic or rain, one or the other, subsided.

"Would you like half an umbrella?"

Anne turned, as Ned Connor drew beside her.

"Which way are you going?"

"Home," she answered.

Reaching out, he held the umbrella between them and moved closer. "How are things at the office?"

There wasn't much to tell him. The visit by the New York City police detective; Muller's statement that Harney's replacement wouldn't be hired until Labor Day. At the corner of Fifth Avenue and Central Park South, they turned west.

"The paperwork on your assignment is complete," Connor told her. "You're now officially a consultant to the National Security Agency. Incidentally, you did well yesterday."

"What do you mean, I did well?"

"The police detective who interviewed you was one of our men. We sent him to observe what he could and get a feel for the office. He never suspected you were different from the others."

A dark blue sedan pulled up behind them. Lowering his umbrella, Connor gestured toward the rear door. "Would you like a ride?"

They got in back; Anne first, Connor beside her. "Through the park," he told the driver.

The man behind the wheel stepped on the gas, and they were moving again. All Anne could see of him was the back of his head. The angles were bad, including her sight line to the rearview mirror.

"There's really not much for you to do right now," Connor told her. "I just wanted to touch base and see if you had any questions or problems."

"Your coming and going like this makes me nervous."

"I understand, but right now it's for the best. A lot of thought goes into these contacts. We don't want to tip our hand to the other side. Generally, you can count on my showing up at least once a week; more if we need you for a particular assignment. And you have the number for Collins Communications if there's a problem."

The driver turned west, past the Mall and Bethesda Fountain. Anne gazed out the window, then back at Connor. He looked like an athlete; there was a physical aura about him. She'd never seen him in anything other than a business suit, but he gave the impression of being well-muscled and strong.

"How much time do you spend in New York?"

"It varies," he answered.

"Where do you live?"

"Alone, in Maryland."

Then Anne remembered the nuisance calls.

"I meant to ask you something. Does the NSA fool around with telephones?"

"I wouldn't characterize it in just that fashion, but we've been known to deal with telephone systems."

"What I mean is, ever since I started work at The Hawthorne Group, I've been getting nuisance calls. Whoever it is, calls, stays on the line, and doesn't say anything. I'd like you to find out who's calling."

"I'm not sure we can."

"Why not? You're supposed to be sophisticated enough to save the world from nuclear war. Why can't you trace a nuisance call?"

"It's not that we can't in terms of technology. The problem is, executive guidelines prohibit the NSA from intercepting wholly domestic telephone conversations. If one of the speakers is overseas, we're allowed to do it, but if both parties to a transmission are in the United States, it's outside our jurisdiction."

"Then pretend I'm getting nuisance calls from Syria. I don't believe you. Here I am, risking my life; someone, probably Christoph Matthes, is harassing me by telephone; and you won't help."

"I doubt it's Matthes. In a worst-case scenario, he might tap your phone, but there's no conceivable reason for him to make nuisance calls. Why don't you call the telephone company?"

"Because I don't want to call the telephone company. I want you to help."

Connor shrugged. "All right; give me twenty-four hours, and we'll put a computer trap on your phone. All you have to do is write down the exact time of future calls."

"And then what?"

"We'll check the computer to determine call origin, and nail the perpetrator to the wall."

The sedan pulled up in front of Anne's apartment.

"Take care of yourself," Connor cautioned as she left the car. "And whatever happens, keep your cool. The best asset an undercover operative has is common sense."

"If I had any common sense, I wouldn't be in this to begin with."

The following day, Anne went shopping in the morning, and after lunch, took Jessica to the Central Park Zoo. There were seals and penguins, but no lions, tigers, or giraffes. Jessica liked the polar bear, but was out of sorts because what she really wanted was to see an elephant. Walking home, Anne tried to remedy the problem.

"I have a question, Jessica. How does a cow go?"

"Cow go moo-o-o."

"Right! And how does a duck go?"

"Quack-quack."

"Very good! Now, here's a hard one. How does a lion go?"

"G-r-r-r."

"Right again! Next question: how does an elephant go?"

Jessica wasn't sure.

Anne did her best to imitate an elephant, and promised they'd go to the Bronx Zoo soon. Then, after dropping Jessica off with Amanda and Howard, she walked home and spent the evening wondering what she'd do when August 24 came and she got her million dollars.

The next day was overcast. Early in the afternoon, Anne walked down to a flea market on Columbus Avenue in the seventies. The market was a neighborhood institution, open fifty-two Sundays a year. When the weather was good, three hundred vendors congregated outdoors on a cracked asphalt playground. During winter months, they moved indoors. Most of what they sold was too expensive or junk, but occasionally she found a buy.

Wandering up and down the aisles, Anne scanned what was there. Lamps, vases, dishes, decanters, hats, shoes, dresses, shawls, baskets, clocks, postcards, cookie jars, maps, jewelry; an eclectic mix of old and new. Some of the dealers specialized in oddities. One sold nothing but old war medals. Others had tables piled with everything from lingerie to electric can openers.

Stopping at a table piled high with books, Anne picked up a copy of *Treasure Island*. She'd read it once; at least she thought she had. Maybe her father had read it to her when she was a child. This edition was illustrated by N.C. Wyeth, published in 1911. The price, marked in pencil, was forty dollars, which meant the dealer would sell it for twenty-five.

And then her heart dropped.

Because standing right next to her, she saw David.

He looked the same as he always looked. Tall, handsome; casually dressed, which was his way when he wasn't lawyering. His eyes were brown, piercing and bright.

"Hi," he said.

"Hello."

"How are you?"

"Fine, thank you." Inside, she was shaking. Don't let it show.

"It's nice to see you. You look wonderful."

"David, leave me alone; all right?"

"Can't we talk?"

Anne turned away and began to walk. What was the best way to make her exit? She could stop and examine the antique silver at the end of the aisle; that was better than bolting. Or she could go back and tell David never to speak to her again. But what she really wanted was to get the hell out.

Down the aisle, through the chain-link fence surrounding the flea market, out onto Columbus Avenue.

Don't look back.

You're wrong about us, she imagined David saying to her.

No, I'm not. I'm never wrong; not about people.

This time you're wrong.

David, there are twenty other women who mean as much to you as I do.

Home was the best sanctuary.

Why couldn't Ned Connor have been there to protect her?

Anne's hands were trembling. She could feel her heart beating.

Think about something else, anything. How about counting the restaurants she passed on Columbus Avenue? Or trying to figure out the origin of street names; that was better. On the West Side, the avenues were obvious, but the East Side was more complicated. Had Park Avenue ever really been on a park? And where did Lexington Avenue come from? Probably, once, there had been a Duke of Lexington.

The homeless man was still on the street opposite her apartment. A panhandler was accosting pedestrians farther down the block. Anne went upstairs, put a record on the stereo in her living room, and turned the volume up loud to block out her thoughts.

The telephone rang.

She picked up the receiver.

"Hello?"

Nothing. Just someone listening.

"Fuck you! Whoever you are, stop calling."

And then it hit her. The caller was David; and she wasn't sure what that made her feel—anger, sadness, vindication . . .

Write down the time, she reminded herself. That

way, Connor could check the call against his computer, and together they'd screw David over.

Three-ten P.M.

Eight hours later, there was another call.

In the morning, work at The Hawthorne Group began anew. Leo Muller called Anne into his office, and announced he was upgrading her computer access card again, this time to allow operation of the paper shredder. Another secretary joined the company, replacing Cassandra Sanger, who was moving to California. Like Anne, the new arrival had been referred to The Hawthorne Group by a placement agency; and she was smart. Whatever else one might say about The Hawthorne Group, most of the employees were bright. Anne wondered if Connor knew about the new secretary, and whether it was worth calling Collins Communications to pass along the information. Probably not.

"Agent 002" appeared again on Wednesday evening when she was walking home. By now she was used to his unannounced arrivals, and hardly broke stride when he approached on Central Park South opposite the St. Moritz. He was eating an apple, offered her a bite, and suggested they walk through the park. There wasn't much for Anne to report—the fact that her computer access card had been upgraded; marginal data about the new secretary. Connor asked several questions about office activity during the early part of the week, finished his apple, and tossed the core into a nearby trash basket.

"And one thing more," Anne added. "Sunday afternoon, and again on Sunday night, I got calls from someone who stayed on the line and wouldn't talk. You promised me you'd check it out."

"What time were the calls?"

"Three-ten on Sunday afternoon, and eleven-ten that night."

Connor kept walking.

"Aren't you going to write it down?"

"Anne, trust me. If I can't remember the time of two telephone calls, I'm in the wrong business."

"You don't have to be snotty about it. Maybe you don't think it's important, but it just so happens, I do."

At 72nd Street, they exited from the park. Just across the street, there was a pay telephone booth. Connor stopped, took a quarter from his pocket, inserted it in the phone, and dialed. Almost immediately, someone answered.

"It's Ned. On that computer trap, the times are fifteen ten and twenty-three ten, Sunday June eleventh. Thanks a lot.

"That should do it," he said, hanging up the receiver and turning to face her. "They'll have an answer in an hour. Meanwhile, while we're waiting, maybe you'll let me apologize for being snotty by buying you dinner."

She couldn't think of a reason not to.

"All right."

"It's your neighborhood. Why don't you choose the restaurant?"

They decided on Kea Fong's Pavilion, a Chinese restaurant on Columbus Avenue. Inside, they took seats in the no-smoking section, scanned the menu, and ordered. The restaurant was nearly empty, with no other patrons sitting within earshot. Connor took the sanitary wrapper off a pair of chopsticks. The waiter brought sesame noodles and hot and sour soup for two. The soup was watery. The noodles had too much peanut butter in the sauce. Anne wondered what her soup would taste like if she put some of the noodles in it. Probably it would be better, but she wasn't inclined to play with her food.

"We broke another of Matthes's codes this morning," Connor told her. "The way things work, he uses computers to scramble messages, and we have computers designed to unscramble. Making and breaking codes has gotten complicated lately."

"Wasn't it always?"

"Not really. During World War II, all the United States had to do was put a Navajo Indian in each field unit and let them talk by radio. The Navajo language had no written form and hadn't been closely studied by foreigners. Put a Navajo at each end of a field telephone, let them talk, and the Germans and Japanese were totally befuddled."

"What did you learn when you broke today's code?"

"Nothing we didn't already know. The bombs are being manufactured and stored on the East Coast of the United States. We were hoping today for a better fix on location, but even after breaking the code, we came up empty."

"How can you not find nuclear bombs?"

"You talk like it's easy, and it's not; it's hard. Twenty-five years ago, an American bomber carrying nuclear weapons crashed in Spain near the village of Palomares. Using the best detection equipment available, it took us years to find the bombs. Our detection is more sophisticated now, but today's bombs are smaller, which makes them harder to find. The United States Army has a backpack nuke that one man can carry. It's powerful enough to destroy any bridge in the world. We've developed four-hundred-pound bombs capable of wiping out a medium-size city. Weapons like that can be stored almost anywhere. And most likely, Matthes's bombs have been shielded in lead to prevent the escape of detectable radiation."

The waiter returned, cleared away the soup, and came back with their entrees.

"How do you know the whole thing isn't a hoax?" Anne prodded. "I mean, think about it for a moment. A Libyan informer gives you a bad tip. Then someone sends phony cables, knowing they'll be intercepted. For very little money and virtually no risk, Libya or Iraq could throw the NSA and every other American intelligence agency into turmoil."

"Wishful thinking," Connor answered. "Unfortunately, too much corroborative evidence checks out. We have a pretty good idea of which arms merchants sell what to who for how much money around the world. Christoph Matthes is selling nuclear weapons."

This is crazy, Anne told herself. I mean, here I am, sitting in a Chinese restaurant, pretending to be a secret agent or NSA consultant or whatever they call me.

Maybe she was being set up. But why?

"What are you thinking?" Connor interrupted.

"I'm sorry; I drifted off."

There was an awkward moment. Anne had to say something.

"Why did you go into intelligence work?"

"The challenge, patriotism—I wanted to be a war hero without going to war. The NSA recruited on campus during my senior year of college. They were looking for electrical engineers, mathematicians, and language majors; the more obscure the dialect, the better. I didn't come close to fitting the mold, but they took me anyway. The war in Vietnam was going on, and government agencies weren't very popular so they had to make compromises. Now it's my career."

"Do you ever think about changing jobs?"

"Sure. Working for the NSA is middle-class all the way, and with what I've learned, I could make a fortune in private industry. But somehow, when I think about leaving, it doesn't seem right. So what I do is, I fantasize about what it would be like if the people I'm up against worked for the NSA. I compare myself with personnel on the other side and ask, who would make the better agent, them or me."

"And?"

"I'm good. Usually I come out on top. But I'll tell you something; Christoph Matthes would make a wonderful agent. He's brilliant; he's daring; he has a remarkable memory. What he's learned about oil and geopolitics is extraordinary. I despise him, but sometimes I wish I had his talents."

At the end of dinner, Connor insisted on picking up the check. Anne protested, but not too much. Then they went back out onto the street and began walking north in the direction of her apartment. Columbus Avenue was crowded with pedestrians and panhandlers. In spots, unlicensed street vendors made the sidewalk virtually impassable. Cassette players were blaring. A teenage boy was hawking joints. As they walked, Anne thought of asking about Michael Harney and how his family was doing; but talking about Michael would make her feel more vulnerable than she already did, so she buried the thought.

At 77th Street, they came to a pay telephone and Connor stopped. "Let's find out about your nuisance caller," he told her.

It was David. At least, that's what Anne thought.

Repeating his ritual of an hour earlier, the agent inserted a quarter, dialed, spoke, listened and hung up.

"Both nuisance calls came from the same number," he announced.

"Who is it?"

"The telephone is in an apartment on East 40th Street. It belongs to someone named Alex Hilliard."

"Who?"

"Hilliard; Alex Hilliard. Ever heard of him?"

"I don't—" And then it clicked. The party, six weeks ago, the one she'd gone to with Amanda and Howard. Hilliard was the cretin who'd followed her around all night; the one with the coin collection. Alex Hilliard. Not terrorists; not David. Alex Hilliard.

"I know him. He's an asshole I met at a party last month."

A self-satisfied look was working its way across Connor's face. "Like I said, I knew it wasn't Matthes."

"So what do I do now; complain to the telephone company?"

"That's one option. Or if you prefer, out of the goodness of my heart, I'll handle it."

"You do it."

"Fine. Let's go back to your apartment."

The walk home took five minutes. Going up in the elevator, Anne wondered if she felt comfortable bringing Connor into her apartment, and decided yes. Inside, he asked where the telephone was. Anne showed him. He picked up the receiver, dialed, and on the third ring, Hilliard answered.

"Alex," Connor began, speaking slowly. "Who I am is none of your business, but I have a warning for you. If you make one more nuisance telephone call to anybody, I'll come over to your apartment and cut your balls off with an ax."

Then he hung up, and smiled in Anne's direction. "That should do it. If he calls again, let me know, and I'll bring my ax."

"You sound like you mean it."

"I do."

Just for a moment, their eyes met.

Anne wondered what he'd be like to kiss.

"I've got to catch a plane back to Maryland," he told her. "But I'd like to see you again if I could."

"Business or social?"

"Social, for dinner."

"All right; but if it's social, I'd like to make plans like normal people, in advance, instead of your popping up behind me on the street."

"Fair enough. How about Friday night?"

"It's a date."

◆ ◆ ◆

"Nowhere have I ever beheld such a rich and pleasant land."

Thus wrote Henry Hudson of the region that ultimately bore his name. When America was young,

George Washington directed the Continental Army from a command post at the Hudson River's edge. Robert Fulton piloted the world's first steamship upon its waters. Washington Irving created Rip Van Winkle and Ichabod Crane in the hills nearby.

Even today, in the upper reaches of the Hudson Valley, farms and houses are few and far between. Inhabitants are disinclined to pry into what doesn't concern them. If a problem arises, state troopers are available, but come to the scene only when called. In the heart of the region, people live and work in anonymity, confident that no outsider will intrude where intruders don't belong.

The black car moved slowly on narrow back roads, its headlights piercing the oncoming night. A swarm of mosquitoes hovered nearby. The smell of wet grass filled the air. Ten miles north of Chatham, the driver made one last turn onto a rutted dirt road. Then he stopped, waiting for the unseen guard to beckon him on. Ten seconds passed; slightly longer than usual. A red light flashed twice in the underbrush. In response, the driver dimmed his brights. The red light flashed a third time, and the driver moved forward; past a pigsty and dilapidated well; through a field of invisible electronic sensors; until finally, he halted again by an old dairy barn at the end of the road.

Then he waited, precisely forty-five seconds. Any errant move would bring bursts of machine-gun fire tearing through the car, so he contented himself with looking at the barn. It was a hundred years old, last painted before the Second World War; two stories tall with a hayloft and roof that sagged from the weight of too many snows.

Forty seconds . . . Forty-five . . .

The barn door opened, and the outline of a large bulky man appeared.

The driver unbuckled his seatbelt, and got out of the car.

They stood opposite each other.

The foreman.

And the driver.

The driver was Leo Muller, and these meetings unnerved him. The foreman was a hostile forbidding figure. Six feet tall, in his midforties, balding, well over two hundred pounds with forearms of steel. He was dressed as Muller had always seen him, in muddy boots, a plaid workshirt, and jeans. And although it was dark, Muller imagined the foreman's glass eye—a remnant of Vietnam—glowing in the night.

"Come in," the foreman offered.

Inside, the barn had been remade into an elaborate machine shop. Old railroad tracks converted to crossbeams braced lead-paneled ceilings and walls. The original oak floorboards were still in place. In back, a large wooden crate marked GENERAL ELECTRIC—FROM SCHENECTADY occupied one of several stalls.

Simplicity.

At times like this, Muller marveled at how simple the entire operation was. The first step had been to secure a sufficient quantity of plutonium. That had been costly but, given Matthes's resources, not unduly difficult. Next, several physicists had been recruited to design the bombs. After that, the project had been delivered into the hands of a half dozen engineers and machinists. Their job, essentially, was to place two slugs of plutonium side by side in a container with a trigger capable of crushing them together to cause a chain-reaction explosion. Fashioning the container was simple. Designing the trigger had been the true challenge. Any munitions expert can detonate explosives, but a nuclear trigger must be hand-shaped to blow inward causing the plutonium to implode. Any irregularity in the explosive charge, anything that caused a portion of it to blow outward instead of in, would cause the plutonium to disassemble rather than explode.

To date, eleven bombs had been constructed, each one the size of a beer barrel, weighing one thousand pounds. Encased in lead, packed in wooden crates with General Electric logos, they seemed harmless enough. Looking at the crates, one would think they contained industrial machinery or large household appliances.

The crate Muller was about to examine contained bomb number eleven. The government of Iraq had contracted to buy it for $700 million. Part of Christoph Matthes's genius, Muller realized, was the manner in which he was auctioning the bombs—one at a time. And with each passing sale, the third-world governments with which he did business had come to realize how essential it was to have a bomb. And once they'd bought one, many deemed it desirable to contract for a second, and then a third; always more than their adversaries. And if they bought enough, perhaps there would be no bombs left for their adversaries to buy at all.

All totaled, there would be thirteen bombs. Twelve to be sold; one left behind for Matthes to control as a nuclear insurance policy.

"We have until August twenty-fourth," Muller told the foreman. "I assume there will be no problem with the remaining production."

"None at all."

"Very well, then. The truck will come for number eleven tomorrow. Pursuant to instructions, it will be stored until shipment."

The foreman nodded. Muller was certain his glass eye was glowing in the barn's dim light.

Chapter 9

After Ned Connor left her apartment, Anne found herself contemplating how surreal their involvement was. Nuclear weapons, million-dollar payoffs, high-stakes espionage. All her life, certain things had confused her. Like where did electricity come from? And if the earth was round, why weren't people in China upside down? But confusion regarding human nature was different in tone. She wasn't sure she understood Connor. Even the way he'd said good night was cloaked in ambiguity. There had been no hint of a kiss at the end of the evening; just a touch of hands.

At work the next day, the hours moved slowly. To pass the time while indexing documents, Anne made a mental list of people in the office and separated them into categories—"truly evil," "bad," "livable-withable," and "good." Muller fit in the first category. Hans Werner and Ernst Neumann probably belonged there too, and certainly Christoph Matthes was "truly evil." The rest of the executives qualified as "bad," particularly Eric Winslow, who was a pompous ass. Winslow could be on the ground floor of the building, and if Anne were on the roof, he'd still find a way to look down on her. Most of the support staff was "livable-withable." Mort Gordon was the only person she classified as "good."

Gordon was a strange mix. In some ways, he was a loner, working nights in what was essentially a day office. But he was also the only person at The Hawthorne Group who said what was on his mind and had the balls to be candid. "When someone makes a billion dollars in the oil business," he told Anne one evening, "my guess is, some laws get broken." And unlike the others, Gordon was willing to reveal things human, even embarrassing, about himself. "You see this tooth," he said during one of their five P.M. talk sessions. "Back in high school, thirty years ago, I was French-kissing this girl in the parking lot. Someone threw a snowball and hit me in the head. Our mouths banged together, and the tooth got chipped."

"Good night, Paul Sorvino."

"Good night, beautiful."

On Friday, the day scheduled for dinner with Ned Connor, Anne walked to work wondering how, when, and where their get-together would be orchestrated. Trying to contact him through Collins Communications seemed inappropriate. In all likelihood, he'd pop up somewhere on the street after work. For most of the morning, she fed memoranda into the image-processing file system. At lunch, she sat with Graham Hayes and Kurt Weber. Midway through the afternoon, while she was indexing documents, Harry Ragin buzzed her on the telephone and said Mr. Connor was on the line.

"Hi; it's Ned. Why don't we meet by the entrance to Trump Tower at five-thirty this evening."

So much for cloak-and-dagger tactics. Anne finished indexing the documents and, later in the day, picked up her paycheck from Leo Muller. Just before leaving, she snatched a roll of Scotch tape from the supply room and put it in her purse to take home. At five-thirty, she left the office, rode the elevator downstairs, and scanned the crowd leaving Trump Tower for Connor at the door. He was standing on the sidewalk, just beyond the bronze exitway, with a copy of *Time* magazine under his arm. They waved, drew close, and began walking north up Fifth Avenue.

"How was your day?" Connor asked.

Anne allowed as how it had been boring.

"What would you like to do for dinner?"

"I'm flexible. Why don't we walk for a while and decide later."

The sidewalk was crowded with rush-hour pedestrians. Vehicular traffic was moving slowly.

"There was a marvelous controversy at NBC yesterday," Connor offered, picking up the conversation. "Donald Trump attended a White House conference on urban development, and one of NBC's cameras caught him picking his nose. He'd just reached in, pulled out a huge glob of snot, and was holding it up for a better view when the cameraman zoomed in for a close-up. Finally, after considerable

141

discussion, the network decided not to broadcast the footage. We're getting a copy for our next office party."

"You really do things like that, don't you?"

"Sure; no one gets hurt."

At Central Park South, they entered the park. The air was heavy, hot, and humid. Passing joggers were sweating profusely. A teenage boy lay on the grass next to a cassette player that was booming loudly. For a while, Connor engaged in small talk. Then he switched to energy sufficiency, noting, "The former Soviet states are self-sufficient in oil. Unfortunately, the United States is not."

"Do the Russians know what's happening with Matthes?"

"Probably. At least, we assume they've intercepted enough communications to have a good idea of what's going on."

"Have you thought about asking Moscow for help?"

"Unfortunately that's not the way things work. Most likely, the Soviets are on the fence. They can't be comfortable with the idea of Libya, Iraq, and Iran having nuclear weapons. But at the same time, they know the situation will cause more headaches for us than them. Also, you have to remember, summit meetings aside, we're not on the best of terms with certain hard-line Soviet elements. Years ago, we managed to establish a policy against unnecessary deaths. That is, we don't assassinate KGB agents, and in return, they don't assassinate us. That way, all of us live longer. But some people in Moscow are more than a little suspicious of Washington, and obviously that lack of trust is mutual."

"So we're in this alone?"

"Not exactly. In the Middle East, Israel intelligence has been our eyes and ears for decades. The British and French are involved, and South African intelligence has been enlisted on an unofficial basis. Believe me; we're doing everything we can to stop Matthes, but the ultimate responsibility lies with us."

"Why?"

"Because we're the United States, and in the twentieth century that's our role."

"Do you really believe that?"

"Yes; and so do you, or you wouldn't be helping. I don't think you're doing this just for the money."

Following their route of two days earlier, they exited from the park on West 72nd Street opposite the Dakota. Homeless men and women dotted the benches, while other men and women wearing thousand-dollar suits walked by.

"It's a strange world," Connor said, echoing Anne's unspoken thought. "Coming to New York on the plane today, I was looking out the window. From the air, baseball and football stadiums are the most consistent markings. Someday in the future, if space travelers visit Earth, they'll think sports stadiums were our houses of worship, and goalposts some sort of religious symbol."

"That might be right."

The agent shrugged. "I remember my father complaining once that all the potentially great military leaders of our time were becoming football coaches. But really; think about it! What kind of legacy will we leave on this planet? At first, we were benign. Then we progressed, and started building armies and killing each other. After that, we polluted the earth so badly that the life-support systems we rely on to survive began to decay. And maybe, as the grand finale, we'll blow ourselves up." He paused, wondering what to say for an encore. "What would you like to eat for dinner?"

"How about pizza?"

"That sounds good."

Thirty yards ahead, a black man in his twenties was coming toward them. His clothes were leather; his eyes said he was angry. Anne watched as he brushed against an elderly couple. Stepping to the side, she moved toward the curb to avoid him. The man came closer, changed direction to pass within inches, and swung an elbow, hitting her on the shoulder.

And suddenly, before Anne could react, Connor was in motion.

"Excuse me," he said, calling after the assailant.

The man kept walking. Connor moved quickly after him; then in front of him.

"Excuse me," he repeated. "Are you bumping into people on purpose or by accident?"

"What's the difference?"

"If it's an accident, then everything is cool."

"And if it's on purpose?"

"Then we have a problem."

The black man looked ready to explode at any moment.

Connor stared straight into his eyes.

And the black man folded.

"Hey, man. It was an accident."

"All right; accidents happen, but try to be a little more careful in the future."

"Okay, man. I'm sorry."

And then he was gone. And Anne was staring at Connor.

"Ned, you're absolutely one hundred percent crazy. What would have happened if he'd pulled a knife?"

"I'd have shot him."

"You what?"

"Maybe not shot him, but I'd have pulled my gun."

"Do you do that often? Shoot people who bump into your friends?"

"Not really, but someone has to stand up for people. I work for the government, which means you and that couple he pushed aside pay my salary."

"I still think you're crazy."

"Maybe you're right. Where do you want to go for pizza?"

She wasn't sure. Pizza wasn't uppermost in her thoughts at the moment. What she was aware of now was that, moments ago, she'd been nervous, scared—and very turned on.

"It depends," she answered. "Pizza Joint has the best pizza in the neighborhood, but it's kind of dingy."

"Whatever; it's your choice."

"I'll tell you what. Let's get a pizza there and bring it home."

Inside the Pizza Joint, they ordered a large pie with mushrooms and pepperoni, waited, and when it was ready, took it out on the street and began walking. The night air was muggy. Anne wondered if she'd have to sleep with the air conditioner on. After a few blocks, they crossed over to Central Park

West, walking north along the edge of the park. The homeless man was still in residence on the sidewalk opposite Anne's apartment. His shaggy beard was wet and matted; his long brown hair grimy and unkempt. As they passed, Connor reached into his pocket, pulled out a dollar, and dropped it in the man's lap.

"That's not like you," Anne said.

"Yes, it is. We're walking home with a fifteen-dollar pizza. Somehow, that man has to eat."

Upstairs, in her apartment, Anne led the way to the kitchen. Connor set the pizza down on the butcher-block counter opposite the sink, and waited for instructions.

"What would you like to drink?" she asked.

"What are the choices?"

"Beer, wine, Coke, orange juice, gin, vodka—"

"I'd like a beer."

Anne gave him the beer, and poured a glass of wine for herself. Then they settled in the dining area, with the pizza on the table between them.

"Do you always carry a gun?" she queried, reflecting back on the previous hour.

"Almost always."

"How come?"

"It's not a particularly pleasant subject. Once, years ago when I was overseas, I got picked up by the other side and treated badly. From that point on, I've made it my business to be armed."

"What do you mean, treated badly?"

"I was tortured. After a week, I managed to escape. They chased me for a mile, until I got to a river and dove into the water to get away. That mile took every ounce of strength in me. I started out running as fast as I could, and when my lungs began bursting, I ran even faster. My life was at stake. All I could think was, if I don't run faster, I'll die.''

After dinner, Anne added their dishes to those already in the kitchen sink. Then, wineglass in hand, she offered Connor another beer, and they relocated to the living-room sofa. She liked Ned Connor; and it seemed he liked her. For a while, they talked about acting and drama. Then, gradually, Anne found herself opening up in ways that surprised her.

''My father was a strange man,'' she acknowledged. ''Growing up, I never thought he loved me. Once, I said so to my mother and she told me, 'Don't take it personally; he doesn't love anybody.' People on the outside thought he was wonderful. On the surface, he was outgoing, warm, and friendly; but it was easier for him to give to strangers than to his family.'' A self-conscious look crossed her face. ''I don't know why I'm telling you this, except I feel like talking.''

''That's all right; I like to listen.''

''The biggest problem I had with my father was other women. He liked to screw around, and I don't mean with my mother. I guess what they say about marrying someone like your father is true, because my husband didn't stay faithful for long either. After we'd been married a year and a half, he started having an affair with someone named Muffie.'' Leaning back, Anne took another sip of wine. ''What about you. Have you ever been married?''

Connor paused, then shook his head. ''Once, about five years ago, I came close, but we couldn't get our act together. Now I tell myself I'd like to settle down and have children, but I've stopped thinking it will actually happen.''

''That's sad.''

''Maybe, maybe not. Living with too many fantasies can hurt you.''

She liked his body. How many times had they been together? They'd met at the museum two weeks earlier. And the day after that, Connor had followed her to Tower Records and they'd talked overlooking the Hudson River. The ride in Central Park. Dinner at Kea Fong's Pavilion. In a manner of speaking, this was their fifth date.

''What are you thinking?'' Connor asked.

Actually, she was wondering what he'd be like in bed, but that seemed inappropriate to say at the moment. Get your head together, Anne told herself. He's handsome, he's a protector; but that's not reason enough to go to bed with somebody. Or is it?

How would Connor react if she said what was on her mind?

There was one way to find out.

''I was wondering what you're like in bed.''

His response was measured, not missing a beat. ''Is that an invitation?''

''I think so.''

''All right; I'm interested.''

''Fine, but—Ned; wait a minute. There are things we have to talk about first. What I mean is, it's been a while since I've slept with anyone besides an old boyfriend and—I don't know. What about safe sex?''

''That's a fair question. I'm straight, I'm healthy, I'm not Haitian, I've never been an intravenous drug user.''

''How many women have you slept with lately?''

"That's really not relevant. One bad guess is enough."

"Do you have a condom?"

"Not with me. I didn't plan on this."

She was glad he didn't carry condoms as a matter of course. And it would have offended her if he'd brought one on the assumption they'd be sleeping together.

"There's a drugstore, three blocks away on Broadway. I have a diaphragm, but I'd feel safer if you used a condom."

"Do you have a brand preference?"

"Not really," she answered.

"Is there anything else I can bring you back from the store? Chocolate chip cookies, butter pecan ice cream?"

"Not that I can think of."

"All right; I'm on my way. I trust you'll still be here when I get back."

Armed with his instructions, Connor left. Anne calculated it would be twenty minutes before he came back. How to get ready? There were candles in the foyer. She moved one to the dresser opposite her bed. Should she roll back the covers? Later; that could wait. Probably it made sense to put her diaphragm in now.

This is crazy. I don't even know whether or not he likes me.

She wasn't sure she wanted to do it.

Ten minutes left.

There isn't any love or passion involved.

Five minutes and counting.

There's still time to change my mind. I don't have to do this.

People do what they have to do.

Then Connor returned, and everything seemed blurry. All Anne could think of was, David, you're part of my past now; not my present or future. Watch me, David. I'm getting laid, just like you used to do.

Avenue architecture. She wondered if Connor could

Chapter 10

The morning after.

Anne sat at the kitchen table, drinking coffee. Connor was spreading butter on his toast. He'd picked up a razor and toothbrush at the drugstore with his condoms, and after making love, had spent the night. Anne hadn't been sure she wanted him to stay, but acceded in order to be polite. Now, sitting opposite him at the breakfast table, she wished he'd leave. Maybe, in a few days, she'd be ready to see him again, but for the moment she felt she needed space.

"Your apartment has a nice view of the park," he offered.

The observation was filler, designed to keep the conversation going. Anne responded with an appropriate thank-you, follo̶w̶i̶n̶g̶ ̶i̶t̶ ̶u̶p̶ ̶w̶i̶t̶h̶ ̶ ̶Fifth see through her facade. Most likely, he knew how uncomfortable she was; maybe he felt equally awkward. He's more impressive when he's playing secret agent, Anne thought; when he's in control and talking about international espionage. Eating toast after a night of okay but not great lovemaking, Ned Connor was just another guy.

Did that disappoint her?

If she was being honest, yes.

"What are your plans for the weekend?" Connor asked.

"Nothing much. Tonight, I'm invited to a party in Tribeca. Tomorrow, I'm seeing a friend, Amanda Otis."

"Tell Amanda I said hello to Howard."

Anne's heart skipped a beat.

"How do you know about Amanda and Howard?"

"They're in your dossier. We had to investigate you before making contact. Don't worry," he added. "None of your friends knew they were being checked out."

Probably it wasn't worth fighting over. They finished breakfast, and passed another ten minutes in forced conversation. Then Connor stood up. "I guess it's time for me to go," he announced. "I'll be in touch early next week."

Anne walked him to the door; they exchanged a perfunctory kiss; and the day seemed brighter after he left. She took a walk, vacuumed the apartment, wrote some letters, and decided against going to the party in Tribeca. Instead, she read, slogging her way through two hundred pages of Edith Wharton, and

Sunday, she telephoned Amanda to arrange for brunch.

It was early afternoon when they finally met. Anne recounted spending Friday night with Connor, and acknowledged in retrospect that she'd been largely going through the motions. Revealing Matthes's bomb plot would have made things clearer, but she was pledged to silence. For most of the meal, they talked about Amanda's children—particularly Ellen who, at age twelve, was torn between loyalty to Howard and allegiance to her natural father, who rarely visited, telephoned, or wrote. After brunch, they walked up West End Avenue. Traffic was light. Elegant prewar apartments dominated. At the corner of West End and 84th, they passed the building where David lived.

What were the chances of his walking by, Anne wondered.

Not very good, she assured herself.

There was a lull in the conversation. A low-flying pigeon fluttered overhead.

"Howard and I ran into David the other night," Amanda offered.

"That's nice."

"It was at the movies. He asked how you were, and we told him about your job at The Hawthorne Group."

"Was that necessary?"

"Probably not, but I don't think it did any harm either. Obviously, he still cares about you."

Anne could feel her temperature rising. "I wish you hadn't told him I'd given up acting."

"Why not?"

"Because I don't want David to know anything about me."

"I think that's being awfully unforgiving."

"I don't."

Amanda shrugged. "I've told you before, my loyalty lies with you, not David. But I'm fond of him, and I wish you'd consider what you might have contributed to the breakdown of the relationship."

"The relationship broke down because David kept fucking me over."

"I know that's your view of it. But it's one thing to tell someone you love that you're furious at them for hurting you, and quite another to say, 'You're awful; I hate you.' Sometimes I think you were so angry at David that you wanted to hurt him more than you wanted things to work out between you."

"That's not true. I loved David."

"And what hurts him most now is your refusal to accept how much he loves you. The other night, at the movies, he admitted making a lot of mistakes. He came down pretty hard on himself; harder even than I thought he should. But he also made the point, and I think it's a good one, that you always focused on what he did wrong and rarely on what was right between you."

"Amanda, that's bullshit."

Up ahead, a man in his forties was walking toward them. For a fraction of a second, Anne thought it was David. Then the man passed, and again, Amanda was talking.

"I don't want to belabor the point, but life is about maturing and growing. I can look back on the way I was ten years ago and say, 'God, I was naive and foolish then.' Right now, things are pretty good. But there's no doubt·in my mind that, ten years from now, you and I will be looking back at today and saying, 'God, we were naive and foolish.' Think about it. It's not too late."

They spent the rest of the afternoon walking, talking, stopping once for coffee. Afterward, Anne went home alone and passed the evening listening to Mozart. On occasion, she let her mind wander. What was it David had told her once—that she was the type of person who would go back and write down the license-plate number of any car that hit her. Well, goddammit, if someone was driving recklessly enough, they deserved to be apprehended, put on trial, and punished.

Work the next day was a carbon copy of the previous week. The only difference was that, on a whim, one of the secretaries ordered Chinese food for lunch. Eric Winslow told a story about the time his wife caught him smoking cigarettes after he promised he'd quit. "It was as though she'd discovered me in bed with another woman," he reported. Late in the day, Anne found herself thinking about Connor. In a way, she was glad he'd spent the night. She'd have resented it like hell if he'd screwed her and left. Also, thanks to him, her nuisance telephone calls had stopped. Still, it annoyed her that she didn't have his home telephone number. Not that she'd use it, but his cloak-and-dagger tactics were a way of controlling her.

The following day, she spent seven hours indexing testimony from a congressional hearing on oil imports. At one point, Muller asked her to contact the Department of Energy to get copies of Reporting

Form XS-2. Anne telephoned, but was stymied by a busy signal on her first three attempts. Finally, she got through, only to have a tape recorder answer and put her on hold. Five minutes later, an operator came on the line, said she'd transfer Anne to the appropriate party, and proceeded to disconnect her. When Anne called back, all lines were busy.

She left the office a little after five-thirty. Walking home along the edge of Central Park, she crossed to the west side of the street just north of Columbus Circle, and peeked into the lobby of an ornate apartment building. The floor was marble, dotted with Old English furniture. An Art Deco mirror hung on the wall.

"Can I help you, madam?" asked a voice from behind.

Anne turned, expecting the doorman, and instead saw Connor.

The fact that he'd popped up again without warning pissed her off.

"Can I buy you a drink?"

"How do you know I'm not busy this evening?"

"If you are, I'll come back another night, but I have to talk with you for a moment about Matthes."

Under those circumstances, she needed a drink.

"Tavern on the Green would be nice," she said.

They began walking north, the direction they usually traveled in together.

"How are things at the office?" the agent asked.

"Pretty much the same."

"I understand that yesterday you had Chinese food for lunch."

He was showing off.

They stepped off the curb. Suddenly, Connor's arm shot out.

"Look out!"

Anne felt herself being violently yanked back, as a man on a bicycle whizzed over the spot she'd been standing on a split-second earlier. Then the bike rider was gone, and there was nothing to do except breathe deeply and mutter, "Fucking messengers!"

The rest of the walk passed without incident. At Tavern on the Green, they sat outdoors. A waiter came and took their orders—"Club soda for the gentleman; a Bloody Mary for the lady." The drinks were served. They bantered a bit. Connor told a joke about an organization called DAM—"Mothers Against Dyslexia." Then he turned serious.

"What do you know about eavesdropping equipment?"

"Nothing," Anne answered.

"All right. I'm about to give you your first lesson. Telephones are the most commonly used eavesdropping device, but at The Hawthorne Group, the phones are secure. That means, to penetrate the office, we've had to rely on more sophisticated equipment. Six months ago, Michael Harney planted a bug in the telex printer. By analyzing the sound of keys when they hit, we were able to reconstruct every incoming Telex. Michael also planted a transmitter the size of a pin in Leo Muller's desk chair. Some transmitters turn on and off by remote control. Others are activated by voice or heat. This particular transmitter responds to pressure, and activates whenever anyone sits in Muller's chair. Are you with me so far?"

Anne nodded.

"Good; then I'll go on. The bug Michael planted sent signals in microsecond bursts to a relay antenna in the Trump Tower air-conditioning duct. After Michael was murdered, Matthes's security personnel found the antenna and discovered the Telex bug, but they missed the transmitter in Muller's office. That means it's still operative, and we need a new antenna to relay signals to our listening post." Reaching into a jacket pocket, Connor drew out what appeared to be a plastic coffee stirrer, identical to those in cafeterias across the country. "Put this in your purse."

"Why?"

"Just do what I tell you to do."

Anne complied.

"Thank you. You now have in your purse a fifty-thousand-dollar relay antenna. Sometime in the next forty-eight hours, I want you to leave it near a window in The Hawthorne Group. Don't put it in with the coffee stirrers, because with our luck, someone will use it to stir their coffee. Don't leave it in the open, because the evening cleaning crew will throw it out. Use your best judgment. Drop it someplace where it won't be noticed."

"Why forty-eight hours?"

"Because we're running out of time. Today is June twentieth."

Anne didn't feel like finishing her Bloody Mary.

"Any more questions?" the agent queried.

"Yes; why did you sleep with me the other night?"

"Pardon?"

"Why did you go to bed with me last Friday? Was it because you cared, or to lock me into the project?"

158

"That's a bitchy thing to say."

"Maybe, but I'm feeling used at the moment."

"And I felt used last Friday night." Pushing his chair away from the table, Connor stood up. "And in case you're wondering, you weren't exactly overflowing with warmth on Saturday morning either. Now, unless you have any more questions, I'm going back to Maryland. I'll be in touch sometime Thursday."

The rest of the evening passed without note. Anne walked home alone from Tavern on the Green, made a salad for dinner, and turned on the radio. WCBS-FM was playing golden oldies—"Runaway," "Mr. Blue," "Take Good Care of My Baby." Listening to the music, it seemed to her that time could be suspended. Ten years, twenty years. It was as though she could go back to whenever it was she'd first heard the sounds and, if she chose, live her life over again.

Memory lane was interrupted by a commercial for auto insurance, and after that, five minutes of news. Then the music came on again. Muffled drums, an electric guitar. The beat picked up, and a long-forgotten voice was singing:

Don't you understand what I'm trying to say?
Can't you feel the fears I'm feeling today?
If the button is pushed,
    there's no running away,
There'll be no one to save
    with the world in a grave.

Barry McGuire: "Eve of Destruction."

Take a look around you boy,
It's bound to scare you, boy.
And you tell me over and over
    and over again my friend,
You don't believe
    we're on the eve of destruction.

An omen?

People imagine, and events follow.

A little before midnight, Anne went to bed, and after a restless sleep, awoke in the morning. Connor had said there'd be two days to plant the antenna, which meant it made sense to decide on a hiding place first. Then she could bring her "coffee-stirrer" into the office.

Close to a window: those were her instructions.

At lunch, she realized that conference room B, where everyone ate, was the best location. She had access to the area; there was a window overlooking Fifth Avenue; and the bookcase against the far wall was tall enough that no one could see the antenna if she laid it flat on top.

The decision made, Anne spent the rest of the day filing documents in the computer image-processing system. Muller was out of town on business, but otherwise everything in the office was normal. Late in the afternoon, just before leaving, she stopped at the reception desk to chat with Mort Gordon, who was marveling at the vagaries of contemporary American style.

"Why do women wear diamonds in their nose?" he wondered. "Is it like pierced ears? Do they think it's pretty? Is it harder to blow your nose with a diamond in it? I mean, I had a flat-top haircut when

I was a kid and my father hated it, but at least I never mutilated my nose.''

That night, Anne dreamt about roasted chestnuts. She liked the way they smelled, but not the taste. In the morning, she put the antenna in her purse and walked to work, arriving at nine o'clock. Muller was back from wherever he'd been, and sent her to the bank to make a deposit. It was close to ten when she returned to the office.

Down to the kitchen for a cup of coffee. Passing conference room B, she looked inside. The room was empty. If she went in and anyone saw her, she could say she was curious about the books.

Anne slipped through the doorway.

She felt her heart beating.

This is insane. Why am I doing this?

She stopped, listening for footsteps in the corridor.

Nothing.

Pull yourself together. You've been in this room a hundred times. Maybe she should look at some of the books on the shelves. *Production of Crude Petroleum 1985–1990; Energy Conversion Factors; Petroleum and Allied Products in Iran.*

She reached into her purse, and fumbled for the antenna.

There it was.

Hide it, quickly.

The top of the bookcase was just beyond reach.

Stretch!

Even on tiptoe, she was six inches too short.

Do something.

The antenna was covered by a thin layer of plastic. If she threw it on top, would anything break?

There was one way to find out.

Clink.

The antenna landed on top of the bookcase, out of sight, exactly where she'd wanted.

Now get out of here.

Walking down the corridor, she passed Hans Werner, who smiled and said nothing. Then it was back to work; sorting mail, indexing documents. She wondered if the antenna was working properly, but there'd be no way to know until she heard from Connor.

At lunch, Anne sat with Graham Hayes. Be cool; and whatever you do, don't look at the bookcase. Afterward, Muller sent her back to the bank; this time to convert dollars into Japanese currency. The errand took longer than Anne expected, and by the time she returned, it was after two-thirty. Upstairs, the office glowed with excitement. One of the messengers was straightening his tie. Ernst Neumann hurried by and nodded. Anne brought the currency to Muller's secretary, and went back to her cubicle adjacent to the reception area.

"He's coming," Harry Ragin told her.

"Who's coming?"

"The boss; Matthes."

"Oh my God! If—"

Before she had time to finish the thought, the outer door opened and four men swept into the reception area. Three of them looked like security guards—strong, well dressed, with a tough hard edge. The fourth, surrounded by the others, was handsome in a dark melancholy way, with intense brown eyes and closely cropped black hair.

162

That's him, Anne realized. That's Christoph Matthes.

The entourage moved quickly by, like a Secret Service presidential escort. Leo Muller came out of his office and walked down the corridor, joining them as they turned a corner. Anne heard a door open, then close. The palace guard was now in Matthes's office.

Back to work. The show was over.

A pile of invoices lay on her desk. Leaning forward, Anne picked one up. Saudi Arabian crude oil production. The Hawthorne Group had purchased nine million barrels from the Saudis last week. Two hundred thousand had been shipped through a broker. The rest had come without paying a commission. Concentrating on the invoices as best she could, she stayed with the job until five o'clock. Then she looked up and saw Muller standing over her.

"Mr. Matthes would like to see you," he said.

"I don't understand."

"I believe my words are plain enough. Mr. Matthes enjoys meeting new employees. He has requested that you come with me to his office."

Anne's nerves began to tingle. The walk down the corridor was ominously silent. Michael Harney flashed through her thoughts. Remember, you're an actress. Voice control and bodily grace; maintain your composure.

The security guards were posted outside Matthes's door. Muller stepped to the side, and gestured for Anne to enter first. The office looked as she'd remembered it from before. A leather-topped desk,

163

black leather chairs, a small conference table and beige rug.

Matthes was standing behind the desk. He was five foot nine, shorter than she'd imagined; conservatively dressed in a tailored gray suit, patterned tie, and white silk shirt.

Muller made the introductions.

"It's a pleasure to meet you," Matthes said. "I hope you're enjoying The Hawthorne Group."

"Yes, very much," Anne answered.

"Leo tells me that you were an actress. I admire your craft."

"Do you?"

"Absolutely. During my life, I have accumulated a great deal of money. You, on the other hand, have experienced life the way Shakespeare wrote it. Who is to say which of us has lived more wisely."

It wasn't at all what she'd expected.

"Now, if you'll excuse me; perhaps we'll have time to speak again someday."

Muller stepped back to open the door, and Anne realized the meeting was over. Fifty seconds was all it had taken. She hadn't had time even to begin assimilating Matthes. Was he an avenging angel? A merchant of death? He looked evil; was that her imagination? In some ways he seemed surprisingly ordinary. No; that was wrong. He was far from ordinary. He'd controlled her completely. He'd studied her, learned whatever it was he'd wanted to know, and dismissed her, all in less than a minute.

Anne could feel her fear ebb and flow.

Back to her cubicle.

More summaries of invoices.

Then five-thirty came, and it was time to go home.

On Fifth Avenue, outside Trump Tower, she looked for Connor but he wasn't there.

What would she do if Matthes's people came after her?

Don't get paranoid, she told herself. No one is coming after you. You're safe and secure.

Right! And no one was coming after Michael Harney either.

Maybe she'd walk in a different direction—down Fifth Avenue instead of up. Then she'd take the subway home instead of walking.

Where was Connor? He said he'd be in touch today about the antenna.

Probably it was her imagination—but someone was following her. She wasn't sure why, but she was sure, she was sure—

Pull yourself together.

But, pulling herself together, she was still sure she was being followed. It wasn't her imagination. He'd been behind her for three blocks now. Stocky, with a broad forehead, sallow complexion, and flat chin.

Turning east at St. Patrick's Cathedral, Anne looked back over her shoulder.

The man stayed behind her.

At Madison Avenue, she changed direction again, heading back north.

The man was still there.

A storefront sign read WEISMAN ELECTRONICS. It was crowded inside. Anne stepped in. The merchandise was mostly miniaturized audio equipment. A rack of tapes stood on the far end of the floor. Anne walked to the rear and examined what was there. Whitney Houston, the Pointer Sisters, Polly Gilbert. Each cassette was wrapped in plastic, with an antitheft tag coded to an electronic beeper at the door.

The man was in the store now, looking in her direction.

Taking a cassette off the shelf, Anne retraced her steps toward the front of the store.

The man pretended not to see her, which was fine because that meant she could bump into him.

Here goes.

"Oops!"

"Sorry."

Anne kept walking toward the door.

The man followed.

She stepped out onto Madison Avenue.

And then she ran.

The man reached the door.

Beep!

"Hold it right there," a security guard ordered.

The man took another step, and the guard grabbed him. "I said hold it, mister. No one walks out of here without paying."

The man played it cool. "I don't have anything to pay for."

"Oh yeah? Well, something set off the beeper at the door. So empty your pockets and we'll see what's there."

Connor was sitting on a bench across the street from Anne's apartment when she arrived home. Crossing against traffic, he met her at the awning and cut her off with, "Let's go upstairs to talk."

On the elevator, they both were silent. Anne was churning with excitement and fear. Meeting Matthes, planting the antenna, being followed from Trump Tower to the electronics store.

Upstairs, she unlocked the door to her apartment. They went inside and stood in the foyer.

"Congratulations," Connor told her. "You just got one of our agents arrested for shoplifting."

"What?"

"The man who was following you—the one you set up by putting a cassette in his pocket; he was one of our people."

"I'm sorry. I didn't know."

"What you knew was irrelevant. It would have been worse if he'd been working for Matthes. Anne, use your head. Matthes is supposed to think you're innocent. If he wants to follow you, let him."

"I said I'm sorry."

"Next time, that might not be enough. I told you once, common sense is the most important asset an agent has. Be sensible! We're trying to protect you. Don't make our job harder than it already is."

The sound of a siren pierced the air; an ambulance crossing Central Park. Anne waited. Then Connor was talking again.

"Follow the script the way we wrote it for you. Trust us; rely on your support system. That's the best way to protect yourself."

Anne nodded, but too much had gone wrong for her to feel secure. Michael Harney was dead; he hadn't been protected by the support system. And the agent assigned to follow her this evening had wound up not knowing where she was.

"I know you're scared," Connor continued, responding to the look of fear in her eyes. "In real life, everyone is scared; some people just don't realize they are. But believe me, this will turn out all right. And you're helping; you're important. The antenna you left in the office this morning is working beautifully."

Anne smiled to force back tears. "How did you know I left it this morning?"

"Because that's when our monitor began getting signals. And in case you're wondering, Muller has indigestion. All afternoon long, he was farting in his chair."

"Ned, you're sick."

"I'll take that as a compliment. Now get some sleep. Everything will seem better in the morning."

Sleeping well was easier said than done.

Anne went to bed at eleven o'clock, but tossed and turned for most of the night. Part of that time, she thought about Matthes, imagining him on a beach surrounded by children. They were building sand castles. Matthes was fashioning a palace; larger, gaudier, more extravagant than the others. And then he crushed the children's castles. Living with fear; that was her reality. What would happen if Matthes found the antenna? Would he know she'd done it? Who would protect her?

In the morning, Anne went back to work. Matthes was gone. Muller sent her to the bank again, this time to exchange Brazilian currency. Graham Hayes asked her to choose an anniversary gift for his wife at Cartier. When she returned from that errand, Ernst Neumann needed a new battery for his watch.

At lunch, Eric Winslow told a story about his six-year-old son, who'd brought a friend's turtle home for the night. "Sometime during the evening,"

Winslow reported, "I'm not sure when, the turtle died. I gather that happens to turtles on occasion, but in this case my child has been scarred for life."

After lunch, Anne went back to indexing documents. Harry Ragin asked her to cover for him at the reception desk while he cashed his paycheck. At Muller's request, she helped Kurt Weber feed a stack of memoranda into the paper shredder. Hans Werner sent her downstairs for a newspaper.

The newsstand was on the ground floor, catty-corner to the indoor garden area. Anne reached ground level, then realized she'd forgotten to bring her purse. For a moment, she considered taking thirty-five cents out of the pool at the base of the waterfall. After all, the money didn't belong to anybody. People just threw it there. Somehow, though, that seemed a bit tacky.

Back upstairs.

Down again on the elevator; this time, with her purse.

Then—

Ten yards away, at the base of the waterfall, she saw Connor—with another woman; tall, blond, in her thirties, attractive. They were laughing. The woman reached out and touched his shoulder.

Connor turned.

There was eye contact as he saw her.

A wave of anger swept through Anne's insides.

Control yourself.

Forcing a smile, she waved and walked in the opposite direction, across the patio to the newsstand.

Stay poised.

She could feel Connor watching.

Not looking back, Anne paid for the newspaper.

Back across the patio.

Take the elevator upstairs.

In the office, she gave Hans Werner his newspaper, then returned to her cubicle and resumed indexing documents.

Let Ned Connor fuck around if he wants. He needs me more than I need him.

Crude oil production for the month of May: Saudi Arabia, 29.5 million metric tons; Algeria, 3.7 million metric tons; Indonesia, 7.9 million metric tons . . .

Does it have to be right in the building where I work, less than a week after we've been in bed together?

Iran, 12.8 million metric tons; Iraq, 6.9 million metric tons . . .

The telephone rang.

It was Muller, summoning Anne to his office. Four stacks of documents lay on his desk. "Please collate these," he told her.

Wonderful. She'd always wanted to be a secretary.

Four-thirty . . . Five o'clock . . . At 5:35 she left for home, wondering whether Connor would show up.

He was nowhere in sight.

I wouldn't expect him; not if he's got something better lined up for tonight.

Get hold of yourself. It's not that important.

But I feel used, goddammit.

And she wanted to confront Connor. Now; not tomorrow, or whenever he chose to pop up.

Upstairs, in her apartment, she was still furious. Where was his telephone number? Collins Communications; she'd put the card somewhere. There it was, on her desk.

Anne picked up the telephone and dialed.

"Collins Communications," a voice answered.

"This is Anne Rhodes. Tell Ned Connor I want to see him tonight."

Then she hung up.

And waited.

Seven o'clock.

Eight.

Just after eight-thirty, the apartment intercom buzzed. Anne went to the kitchen and picked up the receiver.

"Mr. Connor is here to see you," the doorman announced.

Moments later, the doorbell sounded.

Make him wait, Anne told herself. Let him stand in the corridor for a while before I answer. But then she got worried. Maybe he'd think she was in trouble and do something macho-stupid like kick the door down or shoot off the lock.

So she opened the door.

Connor was there. "Is everything all right?"

"Of course; things are fine, absolutely wonderful. I was just curious about the woman I saw you with this afternoon."

Connor's face registered disbelief. "You made me fly all the way back from Maryland to New York for that?"

"Tell me about her."

"This is circus material."

"What's her name?"

"You're throwing a temper tantrum."

"No, I'm not."

"Yes, you are. You're angry because we slept together last week and then, after you couldn't wait to get rid of me on Saturday, I didn't come back and beg for more."

"You arrogant smug son of a bitch."

"And if it makes you happier, the woman you saw me with this afternoon is an NSA agent covering your ass."

"I don't believe you."

"Then that's a problem, isn't it? Maybe I should go back to the White House, and ask the President to call on someone in a green dress at his next press conference. Listen, you. Three hours ago, we lost another agent. One of our men was killed in Rio. Now pull yourself together, and stop this shit."

Anne fell silent.

"I'm sorry," Connor said, moderating his voice. "I lost my temper. It's been a rough week."

Anne wasn't sure what to do or say. "How was he killed?" she asked at last.

"The boiler in the basement of his house exploded. Maybe it was an accident, but we think not."

Another death. First Harney; now this. And for all Anne knew, there were a dozen others. What did that say about her own security? If push came to shove, could they really protect her?

Before she could ask, Connor was talking. "Anne, I know you're scared. And believe me; we're doing the best we can to protect you. I'll take the blame for our sleeping together. It was unprofessional of me, and I shouldn't have done it. But we need you; we need you desperately. There's too much at stake for you to bail out now."

"I just don't know what to do."

"Trust me. That's all I ask. The lives of millions of people are at stake." There was an awkward silence, just for a moment. "Now, please; don't take this the wrong way, but I've got to go. There's a roomful of people waiting for me in Maryland."

It was ten o'clock.

Connor left.

Was the woman he'd been with really an agent? I don't know, Anne told herself. I'm not sure of anything anymore.

Maybe she should go outdoors for a walk. Not tonight. She was too frightened to go out on the street. But bad things could happen at home too. That's where Michael Harney and someone in Brazil had been murdered.

What have I gotten myself into? What can I do? I'm lonely and scared and confused and need help.

Who can I turn to?

Someone, help.

Trembling, Anne picked up the telephone.

I don't know why I'm doing this.

She dialed.

Yes I do.

Ring.

Please, be in.

Ring.

Answer the phone; please.

Ring.

Be there.

On the fourth ring, a man answered. "Hello?"

"David, it's Anne. I'm in trouble. I need you."

Chapter 11

Telephone conversation between Anne Rhodes and an adult male identified as David Akers—The call was placed by Ms. Rhodes on Friday, June 23, at 10:17 P.M.—Recorded and transcribed by A. B. Hahn

AKERS: Hello?

RHODES: David, it's Anne. I'm in trouble. I need you.

AKERS: Where are you?

RHODES: At home.

AKERS: What's the matter?

RHODES: I can't talk on the phone. David, I'm scared. I don't know what to do.

AKERS: Hold yourself together. I'll be right over.

RHODES: I'm frightened.

AKERS: Let me get off the phone. I'll be there soon.

(The conversation ended at 10:18 P.M.)

Conversation between Anne Rhodes and an adult male identified as David Akers—The conversation began with Mr. Akers's arrival at 221 Central Park West, Apartment 4-B, on Friday, June 23, at 10:36 P.M.—Recorded and transcribed by L. A. Wakula

RHODES: I'm glad you're here.

AKERS: Are you all right?

RHODES: David, I'm scared. I've gotten myself into something bizarre, and I don't know what to do.

AKERS: What's happened?

RHODES: I'll tell you, but you can't tell anyone.

AKERS: Lawyer-client privilege, I promise.

RHODES: David, I'm serious.

AKERS: *(unintelligible due to street noise)*

RHODES: That's not the point. You'll think I'm crazy.

AKERS: I already do, but I happen to love you.

175

(Continued on next page)

◆ ◆ ◆

Fort Meade, Maryland. It was one A.M.

The men in the ninth-floor command room were exhausted. Connor had been awake for forty hours. No one anticipated leaving soon.

A courier entered with two more pages of transcript.

Connor took them, and read the pages to himself. "She's spilling the beans," he told the others.

"How much?"

"Everything. Matthes. The bombs. It's not unexpected."

"What do we do?"

"Nothing. All it means for the moment is, one more person to look after."

The courier returned with pages five through seven.

RHODES: I'm scared. David, say something.

AKERS: I don't know what to say. First you call after months of not speaking to me, and then you tell me you're saving the world from nuclear annihilation.

RHODES: But it's real; I've seen things happen. Michael Harney. The blue dress at the President's press conference. You think I'm crazy.

AKERS: No, I believe you.

Connor read on.

"The plot thickens," he announced. "They're getting affectionate."

"What does that mean?"

"It means they're getting ready to go to bed together."

RHODES: I look awful.

AKERS: I think you look wonderful.

RHODES: David, I've missed you. It's been like a death in the family without you.

"Hey, Ned," one of the others interrupted. "Are you getting jealous?"

"She's good in the sack. More power to him."

Transcript pages eight, nine, and ten:

RHODES: That feels good.

AKERS: We're good together; we really are.

RHODES: I don't think two people can have better chemistry than we do.

AKERS: Does this mean we're a couple again?

RHODES: A couple of nuts. David, you turn me on. You satisfy me completely.

AKERS: Do you know what I like most about making love with you? Lying here, after we've come, just being inside you. These past few months, when

I thought about never making love
with you again, I couldn't stand it.

"Ned, are you sure you're not jealous?"

This time, Connor's response was slower in coming. "There are more important things to worry about."

"What if Akers talks?"

"Don't worry. I'll see that he doesn't."

PART THREE

In the union of love, I have seen the prefiguring vision of the heaven that saints and poets have imagined. This is what I sought, and though it might seem too good for human life, this is what at last I have found.

—Bertrand Russell

Chapter 12

Another morning after.

The same kitchen table in the same apartment; but it seemed like light-years from the Saturday morning one week earlier when Anne had sat opposite Ned Connor making awkward conversation, wishing he'd go home. Now it was David across the table. Dark brown hair curled over his forehead; streaks of sleep shadowed his eyes. Reaching out, he touched Anne's hand, and their fingers locked together. "That feels good," she said. At times like this, everything they'd fought about seemed unimportant, and the traumas of their respective pasts seemed far away.

David Akers was the product of a middle-class upbringing in the suburbs of Chicago. His father owned a small furniture store; his mother taught fourth grade. They'd gotten married in their thirties, had two children because they were supposed to, and lived an existence that on the surface seemed normal in every way.

When David was eight, his sister died. "In an accident," was all his parents told him. One day, she'd been there; the next, she was gone. "My father told me not to talk about it," David recalled years later. "He said talking about it would make my mother cry." So no one talked; no one cried. And David grew up wondering if he too might disappear someday with no trace of his existence left behind.

Growing up was an exercise in family pathologies colliding. Emotionally, David was on his own. There was none of the all-enveloping love important to a child. He learned early on not to make waves. For his birthday, three months after his sister died, his parents took him out to dinner. He'd wanted a party, but felt too guilty to ask. When it was time for dessert, he ordered pie à la mode—cherry pie with chocolate ice cream.

"Cherry pie doesn't go with chocolate ice cream," his mother told him. "Order it with vanilla."

David wanted chocolate.

"But I just told you, cherry and chocolate don't go together."

"But I want it with chocolate."

Mother was starting to get upset.

Don't make waves. Smile. Eat the vanilla ice cream.

Once, when David's sister was still alive, his father had taken the family to the movies. They got to the theater, and there were no children's prices; it was an evening show. His father tried to talk the ticket seller into letting David and his sister in for half price, but she refused, so they went home.

Do what's proper, David's father always told him. But what he really meant was, do what looks right. Outside of an occasional birthday or holiday, David hadn't seen his parents for twenty years. They were a damaged family. He'd known that much growing up, but it had been his own little secret, not to be shared. And there'd been no one around to ask for help, because no one else seemed to know or care.

Meanwhile, in another family, in another home, Anne was battling demons of her own. Probably she'd never stopped loving her father. At least, that was the assumption she made based on her unwillingness to ever truly confront him for the things he did wrong. Through it all, she was solicitous of his feelings. She didn't want to hurt him; but God, she hated his fucking around.

"It came to a head my first year of college." That was what she told Amanda, although she never got around to telling anyone else the sordid details of what had happened. "All the freshmen were assigned roommates, and mine was a slut. Her name was Irene, and if I ever need a role model for a whore, Irene will be the one. She slept with everyone. There was a peddler, a Vietnam veteran, who used to hang out on campus with a big case full of cheap jewelry. Joe was his name, and when the weather turned warm, he'd wear a tank top to show off the tattoos on his arms. One night, I came home and found Joe and Irene in bed together. He had body lice; I'm not kidding. He had body lice that I could see from ten feet away, and they were fucking. She was in bed with a dozen different guys in the two months before I moved out. She wasn't even good-looking; just available.''

After Anne and Irene had been living together for a month, Anne's father came to visit.

''I didn't know what to expect at the time. There'd been trouble at home, and my parents were on the verge of splitting. Before my father arrived, I went to Irene and told her, 'Irene, I want to discuss something with you, and I'm afraid that if I don't tell you exactly what I mean you might misunderstand me. So let me put it to you as directly as possible: Don't fuck around with my father.' The last night of his visit, I made plans for the two of us to go to a concert. Instead, he went out with Irene. She didn't come back until nine the next morning.''

For Anne, the remedy for life's deprivations was to reach out to the world, to explode on stage. David's reaction was to structure his existence, to be ordered and precise, to withdraw from others. No one ever saw his pain. He covered it well, with a ready smile and bright, alive eyes. Before Anne, he'd had the requisite number of affairs and crushes, but he'd never been in love or in a relationship without one foot out the door.

And then, one day on the street, he met Anne. They went out; the chemistry was good. She liked his friends, and he liked hers. They were compatible in bed, and shared certain values. Except Anne felt life, and David didn't. She wanted intimacy; he didn't know what intimacy was. And so, there came ''the speech'': ''David, I like you, but [there was always a 'but'] . . . You're a wonderful person, but [that word again] . . . I'm not sure how to say this, but . . . I don't want to get too involved.''

And as always, David accepted his role. Anne became someone to go out with, while he resumed searching for someone who fit his formula for love. The pattern was familiar; he'd followed it before. Always, one foot out the door.

Except then Anne fell in love with him. Neither of them knew when or why. Maybe it started in bed, where they made love to each other in a way neither of them had ever made love before. Maybe it grew out of little everyday things or from the overpowering chemistry between them. But whatever it was, both of them felt it.

Then came the explosion; the other woman; Anne rewriting history to serve her ends, forgetting how she'd pushed David away and never really drawn him back. David, his self-image and happiness tied to one woman, trying to justify everything he'd done and hold on to Anne.

Soon, an ugly battle was raging.

"You knew fucking around was the one thing I wouldn't tolerate. I told you about my father. I told you about my husband. David, you knew."

"I didn't love you when I slept with her. I didn't understand until I faced up to losing you. And since then, I've wanted to be with you, but you're so self-righteous, you'd rather hurt me than be happy together."

"What makes you think I could ever be happy with you?"

"You love me; that's a start."

"How in the world could I possibly love you? You don't know the first thing about love."

"And you do?"

"More than you. I've had relationships. I've been married."

"Yeah, and your marriage worked out just fine. It made you an expert on the Marquis de Sade."

How many times had they fought with each other? Sometimes it seemed as though that was all there was.

"David, you'll never change. You're still doing things you shouldn't do."

"Like what?"

"I don't want to talk about it."

"You're a lunatic; do you know that? I'm trying to build a relationship between us, and you're banging me over the head with blind items from a gossip column."

"I gave you three years of my life and you betrayed me."

"And now you're playing the role of martyr. Except you should stop with this shit that you're perfect, because you're not."

Why did they love each other? David had asked himself that question a thousand times. And invariably what he came up with was, Anne was as smart, as exciting and creative as any woman he'd known. She'd opened him up to being alive. He felt good about himself when things were right between them. And in the end, there was the chemistry. They both felt it. Each time Anne looked at David and tried to understand why she loved him, the chemistry was her beginning and end. Sandwiched in between, she could appreciate his warmth, his humor, his body, and so on. They had good times together. She got bored easily, but was never bored with him. He was this, and he was that but, stripped of all varnish, her feelings could be summed up by telling David, ''I love you because you're you.''

After breakfast, Anne and David went for a walk, following Riverside Drive north to Grant's Tomb. Along the way, they stopped for a soda, watched part of a softball game, and stood by as a trio of children tried unsuccessfully to fly a kite. As they walked, they talked—about her job and his, the past few months, mostly about what it had been like without each other. ''I've missed you a lot,'' David said. ''I haven't missed the fighting, but I've missed you.''

Late in the day, they bought a pound of shrimp and the other ingredients necessary for shrimp creole. Then they headed toward his apartment, stopping on the way for vanilla ice cream. David always kept a jar of homemade fudge sauce in the refrigerator, and Anne was in the mood. For months after they'd met, she'd asked for the recipe and he'd always refused. Then, on their first Christmas together, along with a half-dozen other gifts, he'd given her a jar with a label that read:

Fudge Sauce Supreme

1. Melt three tablespoons of butter and one ounce of unsweetened chocolate.
2. Blend in a quarter cup of unsweetened cocoa and three-quarters of a cup of sugar.
3. Stir in a half cup of heavy cream.
4. Bring to a rolling boil for ten seconds.

Very simple; and superb. If nothing else, they were compatible in the kitchen.

At David's apartment, they fixed dinner, ate, listened to Mozart, and made love. A perfect evening; absolutely wonderful. Lying in bed, locked in David's arms, Anne realized that, for an entire day, she'd forgotten Christoph Matthes, Leo Muller, and everything else that had been tormenting her. All her fears seemed far away.

"Why are we so good in bed together?"

"I think it's because you have large breasts."

"Is that all your highly educated lawyer's mind can come up with?"

"Also, your flat stomach, narrow hips, and shapely legs. God, I love your body."

Anne moved closer, resting her head on his chest. "I like being with you. This autumn, could we take a trip together? London or Paris, someplace romantic."

"We could do it now."

"I don't think so. I promised Connor I'd stay at The Hawthorne Group through August." Again, she moved, changing position against the contours of his body. "I guess I'm a pain in the ass to fall in love with."

"That's all right. Two years ago, I went to my twentieth-anniversary high school reunion. One of my old classmates is a Mafia kingpin. Another is on five years probation for armed robbery. Why shouldn't I be in love with an NSA operative."

The next morning, Sunday, there was intermittent rain. After breakfast, Anne worked at the *New York Times* crossword puzzle, while David readied for a meeting with several witnesses due at his apartment in midafternoon.

"The trial starts tomorrow," he told her, "and you're welcome to stay for the preparation session. Not that you'd find the Environmental Protection Act exciting, but the quality of life would be better if you were here."

"Thanks, but I'd only be in the way."

Early in the afternoon, Anne left. Out on the street, a homeless woman with an Irish face was asleep on the sidewalk. A block farther on, a Hispanic man was accosting passersby, asking for money to combat AIDS.

From behind, a hand clamped down on Anne's shoulder.

She jumped.

"Hello," said Ned Connor.

"You scared me."

"Sorry about that. Where have you been?"

There was no point in lying. Connor had found her on the street. Presumably, he knew about her weekend.

"I've been with David."

"And?"

"I told him about the plot."

The agent's eyes narrowed. "You had no right to do that."

Anne could feel herself getting angry. "Look; for a million dollars, I said I'd risk my life. I didn't promise not to go back to my boyfriend."

"But you promised to keep certain information confidential. I think you're forgetting what's involved."

"To the contrary, I know exactly what's involved.

Michael Harney is dead. They're killing infiltrators in Brazil, and I could be next.''

"Maybe, except three deaths, even a thousand deaths, are nothing compared to what will happen if Matthes prevails. Do you have any idea what one bomb can do?''

"We've been through that before. Stop lecturing me.''

"Anne, I haven't even started yet. What in God's name do you want us to do? Shut down the operation? Call back our agents? Let Christoph Matthes do what he wants? Now I'm asking you, and I need a straight answer. Are you with us or not?''

"I never said I wasn't.''

"I know, but lately your actions have been suspect.''

"I gave you my word, I'll see this through.''

As he'd done before, in the Metropolitan Museum of Art, Connor measured her intently with his eyes. "All right; then I've got a new job for you. There's something we need from The Hawthorne Group's computer system.''

"I'm no good with computers.''

"This is simple; you don't have to be good. We need a copy of Christoph Matthes's distribution list to find out if there's been a change in who gets what.''

"I don't know how to do that.''

"I'm about to tell you. Everything you'll need is in the electronic mail. Michael Harney figured out the system. Just call up one of Matthes's memos on your desk computer, and hit keys T, M, N, and F in that order.''

"And then what?''

"Unless things have changed, his distribution list will appear on the screen; not by name but by initials. L-O-M will be Leo Muller. E-L-N is Ernst Neumann. There'll be initials you don't recognize, because the distribution encompasses all branch offices. Do it soon. I'll be in touch before the week is over."

They stood on the street, facing each other. Anne wondered if Connor really needed the data, or was asking as a way to measure her commitment. He's the director. All I am is an actress in the drama. Let him guide things the way he wants.

"All right," she said. "I'll do my best."

"That's all we want. That, and one thing more. One of the conditions of your employment was silence. You've breached that condition; you've broken our contract. But we need you; there's no alternative to keeping you on the job. So I'll simply warn you, and I mean this very seriously, if David Akers talks, no matter what else happens, you don't get paid. Let me repeat; if Akers talks, no money."

"He won't talk."

"For everyone's sake, I hope you're right."

For the rest of the day, Anne read and did laundry. Around nine o'clock, she telephoned David, but he was still preparing witnesses and couldn't talk. Trial hours were crazy; she knew that from past experience. Normally, David was in the office from nine-thirty until seven, but during trials, midnight hours were common.

The next day at work, she decided to call up the distribution list as soon as possible to get it over with. The opportunity came during a midmorning lull. Alone in her cubicle, Anne brought a memo onto the screen and hit keys T, M, N, and F. Instantaneously, the memo disappeared and was replaced by columns headed LIMITED, CONFIDENTIAL, and GENESIS.

She started with GENESIS. That was the shortest:

JEB
PRB
LOM
NAK

LOM was Muller; she didn't know the others. Committing the initials to memory, she turned the computer off, wrote the initials down, and put the paper in her purse.

The CONFIDENTIAL distribution recipients were next. Four sets of initials were all she could handle at once:

BTW
HOS
JAT
JOH

Footsteps sounded. She turned the machine off, and waited until whoever it was had passed.

Now it was safe. Again, bright green letters appeared on the screen:

PLS
SLW
DAB
LYJ

Starting and stopping, working it in with other chores, Anne finished the task by late afternoon. Then she went home, expecting a meeting with Connor along the way, but there was no sign of him. In her apartment, she decided it didn't make sense to keep the list in her purse. Bringing it to the office each day, waiting for the agent to appear, would be inviting trouble. She should hide it, but where? Under the mattress; maybe in a book. Better yet, inside the sleeve of a record jacket. *The King and I* struck her as appropriate. Removing the album from her record shelf, she looked at the cover photo of Yul Brynner and Gertrude Lawrence, then inserted the list between record and sleeve. Probably she was being unduly cautious, but there was no reason to take unnecessary chances.

If I didn't believe in taking chances, I wouldn't be stuck in the middle of this mess.

David called just before she went to bed.

"The trial has started. I'm still at the office. Lawyers are greedy, stupid, and incompetent. The judge is a political hack. I'll be here past midnight. In my next life, I'm coming back as a rock star. Good night."

Tuesday, at The Hawthorne Group, work was mundane. Energy statistics, crude oil invoices. At lunch, Graham Hayes reported on a woman he'd gone to business school with at Harvard. "She was five foot seven, weighed a hundred pounds, and talked incessantly about how fat she was. Finally, I suggested she might be anorectic, and she denied it completely, saying she often pigged out on carrots."

At day's end, Anne went window-shopping in the Trump Tower atrium, then stopped on the fifth-floor terrace for cappuccino. Afterward, walking home, she wondered what she'd do with her million dollars when August 24 rolled around. Probably her lifestyle wouldn't change—but for sure, she'd get a different job.

The homeless man across the street from her apartment was singing loudly when she reached home. Several days earlier, the doorman had given him five dollars to find a new location, but the man had simply taken the money, gone away, and come back an hour later with a bottle of wine.

In the lobby, Anne checked for mail. There were the usual form letters, bills, and a magazine. Plus a letter from David; she recognized his handwriting.

Why was David sending her a letter?

Part pleased, a bit apprehensive, she opened the envelope on the elevator going upstairs. It was a puzzle, an acrostic or whatever they were called, painstakingly typed on a manual typewriter:

$$\overline{1}\ \overline{2}\ :\ \overline{3}\ \overline{4}\ \overline{5}\ \overline{6}\ \overline{7}\ \overline{8}\ \overline{9}\ \overline{10}\ \overline{11}\ \overline{12}\ \overline{13}\ \overline{14}$$

$$\overline{15}\ \overline{16}\ \overline{17}\ \overline{18}\ :\ \overline{19}\ \overline{20}\ \overline{21}\ \overline{22}\ \overline{23}\ \overline{24}\ \overline{25}\ \overline{26}\ \overline{27}\ \overline{28}\ \overline{29}\ \overline{30}$$

$$\overline{31}\ \overline{32}\ \overline{33}\ \overline{34}\ \overline{35}\ \overline{36}\ \overline{37}\ \overline{38}$$

$$\overline{39}\ \overline{40}\ \overline{41}\ \overline{42}\ \overline{43}$$

$\overline{30}\ \overline{42}\ \overline{18}\ \overline{13}$	ten-cent piece
$\overline{1}\ \overline{21}\ \overline{37}\ \overline{36}$	Helen's home
$\overline{31}\ \overline{34}\ \overline{40}\ \overline{24}$	terrible Russian ruler
$\overline{5}\ \overline{11}\ \overline{15}\ \overline{9}\ \overline{32}\ \overline{35}$	lottery of sorts
$\overline{7}\ \overline{19}$	Ma's counterpart

$\overline{28}\ \overline{14}\ \overline{23}\ \overline{43}$ excessively dry

$\overline{3}\ \overline{27}$ _____You Like It

$\overline{26}\ \overline{26}\ \overline{8}\ \overline{20}$ pre-kiss prince

$\overline{10}\ \overline{33}\ \overline{38}\ \overline{29}\ \overline{4}$ injury to the body

$\overline{22}\ \overline{12}$ hat without the "h"

$\overline{41}\ \overline{6}\ \overline{25}\ \overline{39}\ \overline{2}\ \overline{17}$ Early George Bush view of Reaganomics

All right; whatever David had in mind, she was game.

Let's see. "Ten-cent piece"—four letters; that was a dime.

"Helen's home" was Troy, and "terrible Russian ruler" was Ivan.

"Lottery of sorts"—I'll come back to that one.

"Ma's counterpart" was Pa.

"Excessively dry"—four letters; arid.

"*As* You Like It"—now we're into Shakespeare.

"Pre-kiss prince"—four letters again; I don't know.

"Injury to the body"—scar? No. Pain? No.

"Hat without the 'h' "—that would be at.

"Early George Bush view of Reaganomics"—I don't know.

Let's see what it looks like with what I've figured out so far:

```
T    A                        T E R
2 2 : 3 4 5 6 7 8 9 10 11 12 13 14
      M  A    R A I N      S A    D
15 16 17 18 : 19 20 21 22 23 24 25 26 27 28 29 30
```

195

$$\underset{31}{I} \quad \underset{32}{} \quad \underset{33}{V} \quad \underset{34}{} \quad \underset{35}{} \quad \underset{36}{Y} \quad \underset{37}{O} \quad \underset{38}{}$$

$$\underset{39}{} \quad \underset{40}{A} \quad \underset{41}{} \quad \underset{42}{I} \quad \underset{43}{D}$$

Now I'm making progress. If I fill in the end, it's "I love you, David." God, he's sweet. That means that "early George Bush view of Reaganomics" starts with a V—voodoo. "Injury to the body" is blank-O-U followed by two blanks—wound. "Prekiss prince"? Fantastic! That's frog. Moments later, the puzzle was complete:

$$\underset{2}{T} \underset{2}{O} : \underset{3}{A} \quad \underset{4}{D} \underset{5}{R} \underset{6}{O} \underset{7}{P} \quad \underset{8}{O} \underset{9}{F} \quad \underset{10}{W} \underset{11}{A} \underset{12}{T} \underset{13}{E} \underset{14}{R}$$

$$\underset{15}{F} \underset{16}{R} \underset{17}{O} \underset{18}{M} : \underset{19}{A} \quad \underset{20}{G} \underset{21}{R} \underset{22}{A} \underset{23}{I} \underset{24}{N} \quad \underset{25}{O} \underset{26}{F} \quad \underset{27}{S} \underset{28}{A} \underset{29}{N} \underset{30}{D}$$

$$\underset{31}{I} \quad \underset{32}{L} \underset{33}{O} \underset{34}{V} \underset{35}{E} \quad \underset{36}{Y} \underset{37}{O} \underset{38}{U}$$

$$\underset{39}{D} \underset{40}{A} \underset{41}{V} \underset{42}{I} \underset{43}{D}$$

What a sweetheart!

◆ ◆ ◆

Midweek saw a flurry of activity at The Hawthorne Group, sparked by gyrations in the spot price of oil. Wednesday was particularly chaotic. For most of the day, Leo Muller, Eric Winslow, Ernst Neumann, and the others sat glued to their computers charting the flow of data. No one was allowed to leave the office. Anne had never experienced a more tense atmosphere. Then, around four P.M., the market stabilized, and by the day's end, those in the know were smiling. In the course of seven hours, Christoph Matthes had turned a profit of $80 to $90 million. Lingering longer than she normally did, Anne stopped at the reception desk on her way out to chat with Mort Gordon.

"My belt buckle feels like a tourniquet," he told her. "I guess it's time to let my pants out a bit."

"Or bite the bullet and go on a diet."

"I've tried that already. Dieting, watching my cholesterol level, margarine instead of butter, no ice cream or cake. Except I always wind up watching television, and I can't watch television without beer and pretzels."

The office was calm for the rest of the week. Friday evening, Connor appeared while Anne was walking home, asked for the distribution list, and waited downstairs while she went up to her apartment to get it. After he'd gone, she changed clothes, watched the news on television, and went over to Amanda and Howard's for dinner with David.

Susan and Ellen were at the movies. Jessica mercifully had fallen asleep. It was an evening marked by fond reminiscences. Howard recounted how he and Amanda met: "I was at a party, and the same time I saw her, this other guy, a tall blond Wasp in a blue blazer with gray slacks, saw her too. He looked like a prick, but some women, I'm told, find this type appealing. We converged on Amanda, and in that instant, she saw us both and turned toward me. Then she said hello."

"What did you say back?" David queried.

"Something clever like, 'My name is Howard.'

I've always been good with witty rejoinders. Anyway, the Wasp hovered nearby for most of the evening. Once, he came back and forced his way into the conversation, and Amanda left to go to the ladies' room. That left me and the Wasp together, which neither of us wanted, but he seemed willing to endure me on the theory that Amanda would come back and he'd have a chance to impress her. Meanwhile, I had no desire to give him an opening, so I wandered off to get a drink. That meant we were on opposite sides of the room, and I started worrying that, when Amanda came back, maybe she'd go over to him. Fortunately, she didn't.''

Amanda in turn recounted the day she met Howard's mother: ''This woman was something. In no way did she consider me good enough for her son. You name it, and it was wrong with me. I'd been divorced; I had two children; my breeding was poor; I was a political liberal. Once, I don't know why, I tried to appease her by suggesting some women belonged in the kitchen. All she did was pat me on the hand and say, 'No, dear; the maid and butler belong in the kitchen.' ''

Jessica woke up around ten o'clock, and climbed out of her crib to join the party. Susan and Ellen got home from the movies a half-hour later.

''Where do eggs come from?'' Ellen demanded.

''Chickens,'' David offered weakly.

''Wrong; guess again.''

''The supermarket?''

''No; one last try.''

''I don't know; I give up.''

''Eggs come from eggplants.''

Around midnight, the party ended.

"You and David belong together," Amanda said as she kissed Anne good night. "There's a sparkle in your eyes that's not there when you're apart."

"And congratulations," Howard added, saying goodbye to David. "You've engineered the greatest comeback since the Resurrection."

Out on the street, it was raining lightly. Walking home, David brought Anne up to date on his trial. One of the other side's witnesses was lying. Another had told a few half-truths, but no whole ones. Most likely, the case would go to the jury in two weeks.

Upstairs, in his apartment, they got ready for bed. Anne brushed her teeth and put in her diaphragm. Then it was David's turn to use the bathroom.

"Do you want some music?" Anne called out.

"Sure. Put on whatever you like that's romantic."

The stereo and records were on a wall unit beside the telephone. A slip of paper caught Anne's eye:

Kimberly
755-0400

Something inside her twisted up.

In the bathroom, the sound of running water stopped.

David emerged.

"Who's Kimberly?" she demanded.

"Who?"

"Kimberly. Is that another one of the women you're friends with?"

"I don't know what you're talking about."

Then he saw the slip of paper, the smoking pistol.

"Oh, Christ! That's the Kimberly Hotel on Fiftieth Street. One of our witnesses is staying there."

"Which one?"

"A heterosexual male marketing manager named Anthony Fraoli."

"I was asking; that's all. There's no need to be defensive."

It was starting again. David had forgotten what it was like. Years before, the first time Anne had slept over at his apartment, in the morning with coffee, he'd given her his robe. He rarely wore it; it had been in the closet for years. Anne had put it on, held a strand of hair to the light, and proclaimed, "Oh, how nice! A bathrobe with someone else's long blond hair."

But that had been then. Now was now.

"Anne, I'm not seeing other women."

"Maybe not, but with your history, I have a right to ask."

"Your tone of voice wasn't asking; it was accusing. Now before this gets out of hand, what would you like to listen to on the stereo?"

"Acid rock; something angry."

David put on a record.

And then they made love.

And as always, in bed they were perfect together.

But that was only reality.

◆ ◆ ◆

The black car moved slowly down the Taconic State Parkway, through the Hudson Valley under cover of night. Every few miles, the driver passed another dead animal by the side of the road. Raccoons, skunks, rats, squirrels. On nights when it rained, the death toll was particularly high.

The rain bothered him. It was difficult to drive in the dark with one eye, and the streaked windshield coupled with raindrops glistening in the glare of headlights made it harder. Some acts, though, required darkness. That had been explained to him before he became foreman.

He didn't feel like listening to the radio. There was no one to talk with; maybe that was good. He could concentrate on the road; hum a song if he got bored. Once or twice, he thought back to Vietnam, even though twenty years had passed since he'd come home from Saigon.

Just beyond Millwood, he turned onto Route 133, followed the highway to Ossining, and drove south onto Route 9.

Briarcliff Manor.

Scarborough.

At the north end of Philips Manor, he turned onto Sleepy Hollow Road, its asphalt surface slick with rain. There were woods on one side, ramshackle homes on the other. He drove past a barn, several houses, and fields. Stone walls; dark underbrush. The road narrowed to one lane, rose, curved, and fell as woods closed in from either side. Finally, the car came to a halt at a chain-link fence by a rutted dirt road. Ignoring the rain, the foreman got out, unlocked the gate, and opened it wide. A brook clogged with leaves flowed nearby. Wild daisies, dandelions, and goldenrod bloomed unseen in the night. Easing his car onto the dirt road, he killed the lights. Then he relocked the gate and began to walk.

The road was muddy. He'd been here many times.

An old Victorian house loomed ahead. Its walls were peeling and overgrown by vines. The windows were broken, with discolored lace curtains on one side, torn screens on the other. The roof tiles were loose, but had kept their design. A copper weather vane, green with age, listed to the right.

Reaching the house, the foreman took a key from his pocket, unlocked the front door, and stepped inside. Only then did he take the flashlight from his belt and switch it on.

Through the foyer; past a winding oak staircase; down the hallway over a scarred parquet floor. Into the dining room where glorious dinners had once been served. In the pantry, another key unlocked a heavily padlocked door. Down a flight of narrow creaking stairs. In the basement, stone walls sloped to an unevenly cut stone floor. The air was musty, dank, and warm.

In a corner, the foreman saw the bomb. The one that would be held back when the others were shipped; the one that had already been wired to explode. Encased in lead six inches thick, it looked like a steamer trunk with a box the size of a cable-television channel selector on top. The box was a detonator. Each Friday at noon, it was reprogrammed by a radio signal sent from a transmitter somewhere in upstate New York. And each Friday, an hour later, a countdown began. The bomb would explode precisely 168 hours after programming unless and until it was reprogrammed again.

Within that framework, the foreman's job was simple. Every Friday at midnight, twelve hours after reprogramming, eleven hours after each new countdown began, he was to visually inspect the bomb.

Once a week, without touching it, he examined the red-on-black digital timer to confirm that the mechanism was functioning properly.

155 hrs: 59 min: 48 sec.

155 hrs: 59 min: 47 sec.

All was well.

Slowly, the foreman climbed back upstairs. All that remained was one telephone call. As per instructions, he would drive to a pay phone, dial, and wait for someone to answer. There would be no voice. The receiver would simply be picked up at the other end of the line, and the foreman would utter one of two phrases—"On time" or "Off," by however many hours, minutes, and seconds.

Retracing his steps, the foreman moved back to the car. Through the gate, out again onto Sleepy Hollow Road. Past the same landmarks he'd skirted before.

At Route 9, he turned south.

Sleepy Hollow Manor.

Archville.

Finally, north of Tarrytown, he came to a stop, pulling his car to the side of the road. The rain was still falling. Exiting from his car, the foreman walked toward a solitary telephone booth, inserted a quarter, and made his call. Then, head down, he crossed the road to a small stone building marked by a sign that read: OLD DUTCH CHURCH OF SLEEPY HOLLOW, 1685.

It was a simple structure. He'd been inside many times. Three rows of pews painted washed-out blue. The artifacts were pewter; the walls hundreds of years old. But what held him most was the adjacent cemetery, where three centuries of history lay underground. Faded headstones weathered by wind, rain, and snow. Sandstone, fieldstone, granite, slate, marble, and brownstone markers.

Jacob Buckhout, 1759–1812, dead at age fifty-three. Jane Hammon Buckhout was buried beside him, dead at eighty, a widow for thirty-seven years. Silas Bingham, born 1715, died 1803. Susan Lloyd Bingham, born 1720, died 1807. Row after row. Sixteen hundred marked graves in all. Seventy soldiers from the Revolutionary War. Scores more from later battles. Who were these people? There was no way for him to know. All he knew was, coming to this place gave him a sense of time and belonging. And God willing, despite his sins, maybe someday it would save his soul.

Chapter 13

Another Saturday.

Anne woke up in David's bed, and part of her wanted to be alone with him, part of her wanted to be home alone. He hadn't done anything to make her angry. Last night, the Kimberly Hotel; that hadn't been his fault. Still, with so many women floating around, she didn't know what to think or do.

David lay on the far side of the bed, eyes closed, still sleeping. He'd never known how much he hurt her; how beaten and devalued he'd made her feel.

If only she could let go of her anger. That was what Amanda had told her. Let go of your anger. Concentrate on the positive. David has so many good qualities. There's so much potential for the two of you.

The telephone rang.

David stirred, and opened one eye.

Ring.

He squinted and looked at the clock. 8:45 A.M.

Ring.

He picked up the receiver. "Hello . . . I'm asleep; I'll call you later."

Then he hung up, closed his eyes, and drifted off, leaving Anne to wonder, who was it? And why was he, or was it she, calling at that hour? Maybe she'd never be able to trust him the way she wanted to. In bed, they were close to perfect together. Why couldn't that carry over to the rest of their lives?

They woke up officially at ten o'clock, and Anne read the newspaper while David went jogging. Then they had brunch, and he kept her company while she shopped for pantyhose. Lemonade at the Lincoln Center Fountain Cafe; more errands. Early in the evening, they decided to go to an Off Broadway show. Getting to the theater was vintage New York. At the entrance to the subway kiosk, all four turnstiles had been jammed by token-suckers. On the platform, waiting for the train, amplified rock music was blaring. When the subway arrived, there weren't enough seats because two men were stretched out asleep over a space large enough for ten people. Midway through the ride, a panhandler entered from the next car and announced, "Ladies and gentlemen, I'm not a criminal; I don't rob nobody. I'm collecting money for poor children. Poor children, they need your help."

The theater was several blocks from the Sheridan Square subway station. Walking along Christopher Street, Anne and David passed a transvestite selling crack. At the box office, they were told only obstructed-view seats were available, and were about to leave when another patron came in to try to sell his pair of orchestra tickets.

As for the play, it was well written but badly cast. Anne was more talented than the lead actress, and would have been better in the role. Afterward, David took her to an Italian restaurant for dinner.

"Do you miss acting?" he asked, as they touched glasses over a bottle of wine.

"Not as much as I thought I would. I got tired of auditions where I was a little too short, a little too tall, a little too dark, a little too light. And the sexual come-ons drove me crazy. Producers who wanted to sleep with everyone; directors who thought they owned you offstage as well as on. I'm glad I did it, but that part of my life is done."

They spent the night at Anne's apartment, and Sunday morning, had brunch with Mark Dunlop, one of David's partners. Mark spent the meal talking about court cases he was involved with. Anne was bored; so was David. Sometimes she wondered how David, Mark, and Shelly could work together; they were so different in personality and temperament from each other.

After brunch, Mark went to the office. "Sunday clean-up," he explained as he left. Anne and David went for a walk; first down Broadway, then along Central Park South. Several times, Anne wondered if they were being followed. Probably they were; not by Connor but by one of his flunkies. As they neared the Plaza, a tall shapely redhead approached.

David's gait seemed to stiffen.

The redhead drew closer and smiled in his direction. "Hi," she said.

"How are you?" he answered.

"Pretty good."

She was younger than Anne, with shoulder-length hair and a toothpaste-ad smile.

David kept walking. "Take care," he said.

No introduction. Nothing.

"Who was that?" Anne asked when they were past the redhead.

"Someone I went out with last month."

"Does she have a name?"

David didn't answer.

"I mean, most people have names, but since you didn't introduce us, I thought maybe she didn't."

"I didn't know introducing you was important."

"It wouldn't be, except everywhere we go, there are women you went out with. I'm not saying you shouldn't have gone out while we were split. What bothers me is, whether you're still seeing that woman."

"You're starting again."

"Not really. All I'm doing is reacting like any normal person would. It's not unreasonable for me to wonder who she is, how you broke up. Is she still a friend? Do you have coffee with her once a month? Or is it lunch? Or dinner?"

"Can I say something?"

"David, you don't have to. I'll say it for you. There are too many women I know nothing about. What does this one do for a living? Is she a manicurist? A model? She was wearing a watch, so I assume she's smart enough to tell time, but I doubt very much that she's a rocket scientist. And there are diseases around. Did you wear a condom when you slept together? And how many—"

"You're assuming we slept together," David interrupted.

"Of course you slept together. It was written all over your face when she passed; and hers too."

"Anne, I have no desire to fuck around, but I'm not about to stop talking with half the people on this planet simply because they're women. I don't want to rule out having lunch with clients and lawyers I do business with or saying hello to neighbors."

"By 'neighbors,' I assume you're referring to your pal across the hall."

"Gail Kramer?"

"That's right; the one who looks like a cow the farmer forgot to milk. As I recall, you were bedfellows once."

"We've been through this before. That was seven years ago."

"I know, and there's no problem now; she's just a friend. She's nice, she's smart, she has an MBA from Columbia. Anyway, that's what you tell me. The fact that her tits look like bookends for an encyclopedia is irrelevant to your friendship."

"Gail Kramer lives across the hall, and we have coffee together now and then. If that bothers you, I'll stop, but don't make it out to be more than it is. Don't make it sound like I can't be trusted. And before this inquisition gets too one-sided, I should remind you that last year, while you and I were together, you had your own little rendezvous."

"Only after I found out about you."

"Why do you always have to be right?"

"I don't have to be. I just am. At least, I am with you."

"Anne, look at me."

209

"I don't want to look at you."

"Look at me, goddammit, because what I'm about to say is important."

They stopped on the sidewalk, facing each other. "What is it?"

"I want you to love me. And I want you to stop punishing me for things I used to do."

"David, what do you want from me?"

"I just told you. I want you to feel the way I do—that the idea of our not spending the rest of our lives together is unbearable."

And then she was crying. She didn't know where the tears came from; just that they were there.

"Why are you crying?"

"I don't know. I want to believe in you; really, I do."

"Then trust me."

"I want to. My life is better when I'm with you."

The next day at work was relatively slow. Several secretaries took the day off to fashion a four-day Fourth of July weekend, but Muller and the other executives were there. At lunch, Graham Hayes continued the saga of his anorectic Harvard Business School classmate: "She had a pet poodle, and whenever she traveled, she took the dog with her. That, to me, was a mark of insanity."

As Hayes talked, Anne glanced toward the top of the bookshelf, wondering if the antenna she'd planted was still there. Probably it was; otherwise Connor would have told her.

During the afternoon, she spent a lot of time thinking about David. Did he really love her? I don't know. Did she love him? I think I do. Was it possible they'd actually get married and have children? In less than a month, she'd be forty years old.

Walking home from work, Anne was aware of being followed. Some guy in a blue suit who looked like a cop stayed close behind but didn't bother her. Actually, in a way, it made her feel secure. With the NSA on her trail, at least she wouldn't be mugged.

That night, she saw David, and all was calm. The next morning, the Fourth of July, dawned sunny and bright. After a quiet day, Anne and David joined Amanda, Howard, and the children for an early-evening picnic, then crossed Manhattan to the East River in anticipation of the annual Macy's fireworks. "My foot hurts," Jessica announced as they walked. Amanda checked, and found a picture hook lodged in the toe of her shoe. Ellen was eating chocolate chip cookies at a speed sufficient to cause Susan to remark, "They'd go faster if you put them in your mouth two at a time."

At the fireworks, Anne saw Connor, watching. He was about twenty yards away, leaning against a lamppost, looking in her direction. Part of her was surprised she could see him at all, given the crush of people pressed between them. Then, slowly, he began to walk toward her, threading his way through the mass of humanity at the river's edge.

Fireworks lit up the nighttime sky. Red, green, blue, and gold. The sound of explosions filled the air, like machine guns mixed with cannon fire.

Connor drew closer.

Anne leaned toward David. "That man over there; the one in the striped shirt. Do you see who I mean?"

David looked in the direction she was indicating. "There are a thousand people wearing stripes."

Very deliberately, the agent reached into his pocket.

"Straight ahead, coming through the crowd. That's Ned Connor."

He was almost beside her, five yards away. Another volley of fireworks exploded. "Oohs" and "ahs" sounded in delight. Jessica stared transfixed toward the sky.

The agent's hand emerged from his pocket, clutching a roll of cherry Lifesavers. Now he was at Anne's shoulder. "I'll call you tonight; be at home," he whispered.

It was after eleven when David walked Anne back to her apartment. Both of them had to get up early the next morning; David for his trial, Anne for the office. Would you like to come up, she started to ask. Then she decided not to offer.

"Will you be all right?" David queried at the door.

She nodded. "All Connor said he'd do is call."

"I think he's an asshole, the way he follows you around."

"He's only trying to do his job."

"That's what he says. I think there's something more involved."

Anne braced for the next question: Did you sleep with him?

But it didn't come. Instead, David reached out, put his arms around her, and kissed her good night. "Tell Connor I admire the work our intelligence network did in Iran, Lebanon, and Vietnam. And the Bay of Pigs was a high point too."

Anne went upstairs.

212

Minutes later, Connor called. "There's something else we need from you," he told her.

"What now?"

"The ribbon cartridge from the office Telex. Over the weekend, Matthes telexed some data from headquarters in Brussels to the New York office. If we get the ribbon, we can re-create the message."

"How am I supposed to get the ribbon?"

"The same way anybody else would. Take it out of the printer. Sometime this week, when you're in the equipment room, get clumsy and spill coffee on the cartridge so it has to be replaced. You know where the supply cabinets are; changing ribbons is part of your job."

"But bringing them home isn't."

"It won't be dangerous if you do it right."

"And if I do it wrong?"

"You won't."

So much for that issue; on to the next. "Ned, what was the reason for the theatrics tonight?"

"I'm not sure what you mean."

"Yes, you are. Why did you come over to me at the fireworks? It would have been just as easy for you to telephone without that."

"I just wanted to remind you to keep your priorities in order. Sometimes, I'm not sure we can trust you."

Anne could feel her fear-level rising. She wished August 24 had come and gone. She wanted everything about The Hawthorne Group to be over.

When the work week resumed, the office was at full strength again. For most of Wednesday morning, Anne processed medical insurance forms. Then Muller gave her a pile of documents to enter in the image-processing file system. None of her chores took her near the Telex. Better to wait another day before removing the cartridge. There was always the danger someone would change the ribbon before she got to it, but she didn't want to tip her hand either. Tip her hand—that was a euphemism for saying if she got caught she could wind up dead like Michael Harney.

That night, at home, there was another letter in the mail from David; this time, a poem:

In Honor of Donald Trump and Those Who Work in His Tower

Trumpty-Dumpty sat on a wall
Admiring his tower and chic shopping mall.
But in the near future I fear for the worst
He'll have eaten up all of Manhattan and burst.

Clever. She called David at the office, where he was working late, to thank him, then telephoned Amanda to chat. Jessica was throwing a temper tantrum because she wasn't allowed to crayon on the wall. Ellen was throwing things in general because Susan had socked her in the arm. Howard was mad because Susan had developed the habit of blowing her nose into her table napkin at dinner. "I'll call you back when the kids are grown," Amanda promised.

The following morning, when Anne arrived at the office, she went into the equipment room. Kurt Weber was at the paper shredder. Leaning against the Telex with a cup of coffee in her hand, Anne asked if he'd seen the Macy's fireworks two nights before.

He hadn't.

"They were wonderful."

Weber said that was nice.

Following several more minutes of conversation, Anne turned to leave and bumped into the Telex. A swirl of coffee tumbled down, staining the ribbon and turning the paper brown.

"Shit," she muttered. "I'll get some paper towels."

Weber kept feeding documents into the shredder. Anne wiped the Telex dry, tore off as much of the paper roll as had been stained, and decided out loud to change the ribbon. Weber asked if she needed help, and when she didn't, he was happy to be oblivious to it all.

For the rest of the morning, she invoiced documents, with the ribbon cartridge tucked in her purse. At one point, she thought about calling Connor from the lobby, but decided that reporting her achievement could wait. Around noon, she had lunch in conference room B. Then Muller summoned her to his office.

"Please, sit down."

Anne did as instructed.

Muller handed her a nine-by-twelve-inch manila envelope.

"I'd like you to take this to Mr. Matthes's apartment."

"Pardon?"

"Mr. Matthes has an apartment on the sixty-first floor. On occasion, he works there instead of in the office. The entrance to the residential portion of Trump Tower is on Fifty-sixth Street. That is all."

Envelope in hand, Anne went back to her cubicle,

picked up her pocketbook, and went downstairs. She wondered if Matthes would actually be in his apartment, and whether she should deliver the envelope in person or leave it downstairs. Maybe she should open it; it wasn't sealed. But what if she got caught?

Then she remembered the Telex ribbon cartridge. She didn't want it in her purse. Get hold of yourself; Matthes isn't going to search you in his apartment. But what if he did? Walking through the bronze Trump Tower portal out onto Fifth Avenue, Anne felt the unmistakable signs of panic. Get rid of the cartridge. Do it now.

There was a mailbox on the corner of 56th Street and Fifth Avenue.

It's amazing how much faith we have in our postal delivery system, David had once told her. We put a letter in a box on the street, and assume it will be delivered wherever we want by total strangers.

Even if Matthes's henchmen were following, the ribbon cartridge would be safe in a mailbox. They wouldn't be able to get it out and learn what it was.

Anne stopped at the corner, opened the mailbox, pulled the cartridge from her purse, and dropped it down. No address or postage, but that would be Connor's problem. There was a pay telephone across the street. How much time did she have? Enough. Rummaging through her purse, she found a quarter, crossed Fifth Avenue to the phone, and dialed Collins Communications. On the second ring, a man answered.

"This is Anne Rhodes. Tell Ned Connor, if he wants his Telex ribbon, it's in a mailbox on the corner of Fifth Avenue and Fifty-sixth Street."

Then she hung up, took a deep breath, and began to shake. Pull yourself together. Get hold of yourself.

The entrance to the residential portion of Trump Tower led to a small marble-floored lobby. Two uniformed doormen and a concierge stood nearby. Like most Trump Tower security personnel, they were well built and pleasant-looking, between the ages of twenty-five and forty.

"Can I help you, madam?"

"I have an envelope for Christoph Matthes."

"Your name?"

"Anne Rhodes."

After calling upstairs on the house intercom for clearance, the concierge ushered her by. The elevator was noiseless. On the sixty-first floor, Anne got off, and rang the bell to Matthes's apartment.

Matthes himself answered the door.

"We meet again. Come in, Miss Rhodes."

The foyer was small, with a rose-colored marble floor, a gilt-edged mirror on the north wall, and a Baccarat crystal chandelier. Matthes looked the same as when she'd seen him at the office. Impeccably dressed, intense with dark melancholy eyes.

Anne handed him the envelope.

"Would you care for tea?"

She might as well be a good spy.

"Thank you; that would be nice."

Matthes gave instructions to a maid who appeared on signal, then led Anne to the living room. "Have a seat, please."

The room was large, with a thick white carpet and black leather sofa flanked by lacquered end tables. One wall was glass, overlooking Central Park. There were Steuben bowls, a small museum-quality painting by Paul Klee, objets d'art from around the world. But no plants, no photographs of people, nothing personal or alive.

Anne sat on the sofa. The maid returned with tea and scones.

"I've been reading a rather interesting book lately," Matthes said, taking a seat adjacent to Anne. "It's about a boy found in the jungles of India. When discovered, he had claw-length fingernails, walked on his knees and forearms, and was presumed to have been raised by a pack of wolves. The authorities placed him in a home where he learned to bathe and dress himself, but never to speak. He died at the approximate age of nine."

"That's horrible."

"I would agree. Perhaps he should have been left in the wild, but that is my own point of view, and I have little expertise in these matters. You see, the burdens of society do not interest me. My life revolves around the accumulation of wealth. I am a businessman, concerned only with utilizing all available means for conducting business on profitable terms."

"Why are you telling me this?"

"Because you have a quality that demands attention. Perhaps that is why you were successful on stage."

Through an open door, Anne could see the bedroom, with its thick black carpet, round bed, and white satin spread. What did Christoph Matthes want from her? It wasn't sexual; at least she didn't think it was. A whore for my country? No way, José.

As she surveyed the room, Matthes continued

talking. "You must understand, becoming a scientist is an act of commitment to the pursuit of knowledge. Scientific discoveries are made not because they are good or useful, but because it is possible to know. Becoming an evangelist requires a belief in proselytizing and, above all, God. I, on the other hand, am devoted to wealth. I learned long ago that every home, every industry, every mode of transportation and communication, is controlled by energy; that those who control energy control the wealth of the world."

In the adjacent study, a telephone rang.

The maid appeared. "For you, sir. Mr. Potter, calling from London."

Matthes stood up and left the room. With minimal effort, Anne could hear his end of the conversation. "I believe so . . . Yes, that would be appropriate. Fifty thousand, no more . . . No, we don't play those games in that part of the world. If it was promised, it will be done . . . Very good; thank you."

Then he came back and stood by the sofa, indicating by his stance that tea was over. "I'm afraid our discussion must prematurely end. Perhaps it can be continued another time."

The office seemed quieter than normal when Anne returned. Most of the executives were behind closed doors. The entire support staff was quietly engaged, without the small talk usually heard. For the next few hours, Anne indexed documents, trying to understand what if anything Matthes wanted from her. Then, at four-thirty, Harry Ragin left for a dental appointment, and she took over at the reception desk for the final hour.

Gordon came in at five-thirty sharp, and let out a sneeze that sounded like a volcano.

"That should kill all the germs," she told him.

They had their usual five-minute conversation about life, liberty, and the pursuit of happiness. Then she left, anticipating a rendezvous with Connor, who appeared on Central Park South in the back seat of a surveillance car.

"Would you like a ride?"

Anne got in.

"We found the Telex ribbon," he announced as the car entered Central Park. "Why a mailbox?"

"I'm sorry; I panicked."

"We figured as much; although I have to admit, the mailbox was secure."

"Would you like to know why I panicked?"

"Given the fact that you entered the residential portion of Trump Tower at one-twelve P.M. and left seventeen minutes later, I assume it had something to do with Matthes."

For the next half-hour, Connor debriefed her in the car, beginning with a physical description of Matthes's apartment. The foyer, living room, and as much as she'd seen of the bedroom and study. Connor took notes, jotting down details on a thin white pad. Furniture; Mr. Potter calling from London; even what kind of tea and scones were served.

"Why do you think he invited me to his apartment?"

"Maybe he needed an envelope delivered. More likely, he wanted you in particular to bring it."

"Why me?"

"I don't know. It could be as simple as your being an attractive woman. Matthes has never been married, and oddly enough, we're not sure of his sexual orientation, but we know he surrounds himself with good-looking people.''

When the debriefing was done, Connor dropped Anne off at her apartment, leaving her to wonder what ugly twists of fate Christoph Matthes had experienced in life to make him the way he was. Perhaps he had suffered as a child. Certainly he deserved to suffer now.

That night, she slept poorly, plagued by fears that wouldn't subside. Seven more weeks and it would all be over; but seven weeks could be a very long time.

The next day at The Hawthorne Group, she had trouble concentrating. Thank God it was Friday; she needed some time off. Index documents, conform spreadsheets. At lunch, Ernst Neumann pontificated about the oil depletion allowance being an integral part of America's tax structure. As he talked, Anne indulged in some numerical calculations. It was July 7. July had thirty-one days, which meant August 24 was forty-eight days away. Thirty-four workdays. Thirty-four more days at The Hawthorne Group. And then she'd be rich—if she was still alive.

After lunch, David telephoned with the first good news she'd heard in a while. ''The trial is over.''

''I thought you had another week to go.''

''So did I, but the bad guys folded. They settled this morning for four million dollars, which means this weekend you and I are having a celebration.''

The celebration, they decided, would come on Saturday. ''And I'll cook tonight,'' Anne promised. If she left work at 5:30 and stopped to market, she'd be home by 6:30, maybe 6:45. Add on another hour to get ready. "Why don't you come at eight," she offered.

Then it was back to indexing documents and organizing files until quitting time. On the way home, she stopped to buy filet of sole, champagne, and the makings of a salad. In her apartment, after changing clothes, she decided to poach the sole in white wine with mushrooms. Butter, salt, a pinch of pepper, lemon juice, cream. Just before eight, David telephoned to say he'd be late, which threw her schedule off slightly, but there were no major culinary problems. At eight-thirty, he arrived and Anne met him at the door.

"Congratulations!" she offered. "What have you done to celebrate so far?"

"Exciting things like doing the laundry."

"Is that why you were late; waiting for the laundry?"

There was an awkward moment. At least, that's how it seemed. Sometimes Anne thought she knew him too well.

"Not exactly."

"What kept you?" Ordinarily, she wouldn't have asked, but something in David's voice suggested a problem.

"Gail Kramer called. She was going out and they're redoing the plumbing in her bathroom, so she wanted to come over to take a shower."

"And?"

"I let her."

Anne could feel her blood pressure rising.

"That's nice. Did you watch while she was in the shower?"

"What kind of stupid question is that?"

"I don't think it's stupid at all. There are eighty families who live in your building. Why did she have to come over to your apartment?"

"Probably because I live across the hall."

"David, come off it. No one is as innocent as you pretend you are. I've seen Gail Kramer, and she's a provocative woman. You introduced us once, and do you remember what she said? If there's such a thing as reincarnation, she wanted to come back as a football, so she could have all those big husky men chasing after her."

"That was a joke."

"Was it? Coming from Gail the Whale, I wasn't sure."

"You're acting silly."

"No, I'm not. You're the one who's slipping and sliding all over. I don't have old boyfriends hanging around, coming over to my apartment on Friday nights to take a shower. Trust me! That's what you said last Sunday afternoon, when we walked into that redhead on Central Park South. So I trusted you, and this is what happens."

"You're blowing this all out of proportion. If you'll sit down and—"

"I don't want to sit down. It's done; you were wrong."

"I want you to see my point of view."

"Then you haven't really changed at all."

"All right. I was wrong. Okay? I know the problem, and I shouldn't have let her come over to take a shower."

"David, you don't understand. The problem is you."

"Look, I just apologized and said I was wrong. In

fact, if it makes you happier, I'll admit to making a quarter of a million mistakes in this relationship; but you contribute to the problems we have too."

"How?"

"By never forgiving me for things I've done wrong. By always telling me what you won't give, and never what you will. By acting like you're the only person in the world with problems. You're very good at spotting flaws in other people, but not so good at seeing them in yourself."

In the kitchen, a bell-timer sounded.

"Dinner is ready," Anne said.

"How can you possibly eat now?"

"It's easy; I'm hungry."

"And you can digest food with your stomach tied in knots?"

She shrugged. "I'll try."

So they ate. Poached filet of sole, salad, and champagne, by candlelight. Dinner was a way of retreating from battle. At least, that was how it seemed to David. The conversation was stilted, but it got them by.

Afterward, they washed the dishes together.

"How late do you plan on staying?" Anne asked.

"I don't know. I was hoping to spend the night."

"Not after Gail Kramer's shower. When I heard that, I promised myself we wouldn't make love tonight."

"There's always the morning."

"David, I'm furious."

"So what else is new? Every relationship you've ever had has ended in self-righteous anger."

"You deserve it."

"I'm not talking about me; I'm talking about you. You sermonize a lot about trust and love, but there are miles between what you preach and practice."

"Is that so?"

"You'd better believe it. So stop telling me how untrustworthy I am and how wonderful you are. I'm just as good as you are. Not better, but just as good."

The telephone rang. Casting a last dirty look in David's direction, Anne crossed the room and picked up the receiver.

"Hello? . . . No, I have company now . . . That's all right. I'll call you tomorrow."

Then she hung up, and returned to the fray.

"Who was that?" David demanded.

"None of your business."

"That's nice. Every time my phone rings, you go crazy. Your phone rings, and you won't even tell me who it was."

"Let's stop, all right? I don't want to fight anymore." The phone rang again. "Shit!"

Once again, she picked up the receiver. "Hello? . . . No, I'm fine. I just happen to be busy at the moment. Goodbye!"

"People," she muttered. Then she turned back toward David. "Now what do you want?"

"I want you to understand how rejecting you've been. I want you to let go of the mistakes in our past. And most of all, I want you to love me."

Holding her ground, Anne shook her head. "I don't know. Once, I thought we'd spend our lives together. But now, after everything that's gone wrong, maybe it's too late."

◆ ◆ ◆

Friday night, Fort Meade, Maryland. By now, the men were used to their routine. Each new piece of data that came in was indexed, cross-referenced, and analyzed to shreds. Memoranda were exchanged between each intelligence agency, and once a week the agency heads met. Then it was back to the drawing board; more data analysis, endless options.

"It's getting to me," one of the agents said. "When this thing started, I was sure we'd win. Now . . ." His voice trailed off. "Matthes is a smart bastard."

A courier entered the room, and handed several transcript pages to Connor.

"More soap-opera drama," a third agent muttered. "First she loves him; then she doesn't. Then she loves him; after that, who knows?"

Connor shrugged. "You read the file. She's jealous and insecure."

"Yeah, but Akers didn't do anything to deserve the beating he's getting."

Turning away from the conversation, Connor read the pages to himself:

AKERS: I want you to understand how re-
            jecting you've been. I want you to
            let go of the mistakes in our past.
            And most of all, I want you to love
            me.

RHODES: I don't know. Once, I thought we'd
            spend our lives together. But now,
            after everything that's gone wrong,
            maybe it's too late.

AKERS: You say that like some sort of Buddhist mantra. Too late; too late. All too late means is you're punishing me for what I was instead of who I am now. You're saying you're unwilling to let go of the past.

"Matthes is too smart to transport his bombs on military vessels," one of the agents said. "They'll be on old cargo ships that carry refurbished machinery or bananas."

"So what do we do? Blockade every third-world country forever?"

"Let's go over the broad picture again. We lost in Iran because we expected Khomeini to behave like a rational person. We screwed up in Vietnam because we didn't understand Hanoi's thinking. At least with Matthes, the motivation is clear. Financial gain, pure and simple . . ."

AKERS: You seem to think those things were self-evident, and they weren't.

RHODES: To any normal person they would have been.

AKERS: Stop with that normal shit. You never once talked to me about marriage or babies or any of those things on a serious level.

RHODES: That's because you didn't want to.

"Some things are easy if you risk the consequences. To get rid of Qaddafi, you destroy Libya's oil wells. Give Iran enough weapons, and the Iranians will take care of Iraq. But the way Matthes has this set up, with everything compartmentalized . . ."

AKERS: Didn't you ever make a mistake?

RHODES: I sure did. I wasted three years of my life with you, and believe me, I won't make that mistake again. In six months, I'll be living with someone, and whoever it is, it won't be you.

"Syria and Iraq are building weapons installations. The other countries aren't, which means some of the bombs will be stockpiled under the worst possible conditions."

"If they're stockpiled. Don't forget; they could use them . . ."

AKERS: I love you. And unless you love me, I can't go on seeing you.

RHODES: You don't know the meaning of love.

AKERS: Why do you have to talk like that? Why do you always downgrade the good things we shared?

RHODES: Maybe they weren't all that good.

AKERS: If that's how you feel, I'd better go.

228

"Another thing I'd like to do is bomb Switzerland. Do you have any idea how much of Matthes's money flows through nice clean numbered Swiss bank accounts? Switzerland might be the worst country in the world. Hey, Ned. Why don't you join the conversation?"

◆ ◆ ◆

Midnight.

Slowly, Anne rolled back the covers of her bed. Two weeks. That's how long her reunion with David had lasted. Two weeks, and now it was done.

With or without him, she'd pull her life together. So why was she crying? It had ended the only way it could. David was gone; this time for good.

Chapter 14

Alone again, Anne felt like a woman withdrawing from an addictive relationship, trying to convince herself that it never should have been.

Anger, sadness, despair, pain. There were so many emotions. We weren't really a couple; at least, not at the end. We were two people papering over our differences, when we could have poured six inches of concrete on top and the differences would have remained.

Flashbacks. Too many women. Pick a month. Last February; Valentine's Day.

Anne had suggested dinner at a Mexican restaurant.

"I had Mexican food for lunch," David told her.

"Who with?"

"Caroline Logan."

"Who's Caroline Logan?"

"One of the lawyers on the Dow Chemical litigation."

"Why did you have lunch with her?"

"For the same reason I had lunch with Larry Mason yesterday. I was hungry."

"But why her? What does she look like?"

"Here we go again."

"No, David. Here you go again. Because without ever having seen Caroline Logan, I'm sure she's one of the better-looking women lawyers around."

Alone in her apartment, Anne stared at the wall, cursed, and slowly sipped a cup of coffee.

Come September, I'll be a millionaire. Maybe someone will marry me for my money.

All day Saturday, she stayed indoors. Once or twice, the telephone rang. She took a nap, cleaned the kitchen cabinets, and in the process, dropped a bottle of catsup on the floor. The shattered glass looked like it was swimming in blood. Methodically, she cleaned it up, and went on to other household chores.

Sunday morning she took a walk. Someone had given the homeless man across the street a radio, which he wanted to sell for five dollars.

"Lady, it's a good radio. Listen to how good it works."

Anne wasn't interested. All she wanted was to be left alone, but there was quiet desperation in the man's voice. For the first time ever, she gave him a dollar.

In Central Park, she watched the joggers.

She read.

Watched television.

And finally, telephoned Amanda.

"David and I have broken up."

"Not again."

"Leave it alone, all right?"

Amanda wouldn't leave it alone. Instead, she began talking about psychotherapy—how it had helped her, and maybe Anne could benefit from it too. Except what Amanda didn't know was it would be a hell of a first session, when Anne tried to convince a psychiatrist that she wasn't delusional; that truly, she was saving the world from nuclear annihilation.

Sunday night, walking barefoot through the kitchen, she stepped on a sliver of glass from the catsup bottle. David's revenge, she called it, since at the time she stepped she was thinking about David. Soon after she'd bandaged the wound, Connor called and was a pain in the ass. He didn't seem to want anything. Rather, he was calling just to be friendly, but she wasn't in a friendly mood.

"What would you think of me if we met at a party for the first time?"

"Ned, what difference does it make?"

"I was curious; that's all."

That night, asleep, she was aware of her dreams. A miniature lion had grabbed hold of her foot and was biting her heel. The pain increased; Anne wanted to scream. The lion was David. She didn't know why, but she was sure David was tormenting her in her dream.

The work week began. Documents, invoices, Graham Hayes telling stories over lunch in conference room B. "Yesterday morning, our daughter came into the bedroom," he revealed. "She's three, and quite proud of being able to operate the television, but my wife and I were worried about what she was watching. As Melinda described it, a naked man was standing on something with another man screaming. We thought maybe one of the public-access channels was showing porn at an inappropriate time, but it turned out to be Jimmy Swaggart in front of a crucifix.''

That night, the lion came again.

Kick it, it's your dream. Destroy the lion before its teeth sink in.

Anne reached down, picked up the lion, and punted it like a football player up toward the sky. Round and round and higher it spiraled, until finally it disappeared from view.

One night later, there was another lion in her dreams. Six feet long with monstrous claws, growling, not at all tame. Kick me, the lion seemed to say. We'll see what happens if you do.

At the end of the week, Connor invited Anne to dinner. ''Nothing special,'' he told her on the telephone. ''I just figured, it's been a while.''

Anne had nothing better to do. For variety's sake, they chose an Italian restaurant on the East Side.

''I hear you and David broke up,'' the agent announced as they were seated at a table in the corner.

''I don't think that's any of your business.''

A waiter came, and they ordered wine.

A loose end was dangling.

''Ned, how did you know David and I broke up?''

''Osmosis.''

''No, I'm serious. How did you know David and I split?''

''The same way I knew you bought a nectarine on the way to Tower Records in June.''

233

"That was different. You knew about the nectarine by following me on the street."

"That's right, and we haven't seen you and David together for a week."

The waiter returned and Anne let it drop. Dinner was ninety dollars for two. Connor paid; then they took a walk down Fifth Avenue, talking mostly about Christoph Matthes.

"Why don't you just put a bullet in his head?" Anne asked.

"We'd love to, but there's no way of knowing what his death would trigger."

"I still don't see how he gets away with it all."

"It's a corrupt world. Every major corporation on the planet makes blackmail payments to terrorist organizations. Most heads of state can be bought and sold. Matthes is just particularly well connected— with terrorists, with diplomats, with businessmen and government leaders. Every time we do a political or economic study, his name comes up in one of our computers."

"David—"

"My name is Ned. Remember?"

"I'm sorry. My mind was somewhere else."

"So I gather."

He said it with irony, not hurt or anger; and for a moment, Anne wondered if she and Connor might become lovers again. In some ways, she liked him, but his strength was in distance and exercising control. He was part mentor, part protector, part friend, with a touch of adversary thrown in. She wondered what he saw when he looked in the mirror each morning. At times, he seemed trapped behind a self-constructed facade. But the reason she'd gone to bed with him before was to punish David, and she wouldn't make that mistake again.

He walked her home and said good night. Across the street, the homeless man was asleep, his radio playing.

Upstairs in her apartment, Anne got ready for bed. She brushed her teeth, took off her clothes, and stood in front of the bedroom mirror, naked. Men liked her body. When she gained weight, it was well distributed; not just on her stomach and hips. If anything, a disproportionate amount found its way to her breasts.

"Very few people have a body as good as yours," David once told her.

"You'd better believe it," she'd answered.

"Why can't you just take the compliment graciously?"

"Why can't you stop comparing me to other women?"

It didn't matter who was right; not anymore.

I hate you, David.

Was that really what she meant? Or was it, David, I'm furious at you because we screwed it up and I love you.

That night, she had so many dreams it was like spending eight hours in a front-row seat at the movies.

The weekend was quiet. David didn't call. She'd miss him for a while, but in time she'd get used to his being gone.

The new work week began with rain. Each minute at the office seemed like five. Monday afternoon, Anne screwed up a clerical assignment, and earned a look of astonishment from Muller. The look, she knew, wasn't true astonishment. Rather, it was designed to humiliate and shame.

Walking home, she fought the temptation to jam her umbrella into the wheel-spokes of a bicyclist who rode perilously close by. Tuesday and Wednesday brought more of the same. Graham Hayes's lunchroom patter wasn't charming, funny, or otherwise meritorious. Filling out a health insurance form on Thursday reminded her that her fortieth birthday was eight days off. Gazing out the reception-area window, Anne couldn't help but think, one bomb and all the buildings she was looking at would be rubble. She was drifting, so much so that Connor was a welcome sight when he appeared in a surveillance car at Columbus Circle on her way home.

Anne got in back. There was small talk about what was and wasn't happening at the office. Then Connor said simply, "We have a problem."

"I thought we already had a problem; or doesn't nuclear annihilation count?"

Ignoring her comment, the agent went on. "How much, if anything, do you know about cryptology?"

"I was in a play once—Breaking the Code."

"That and a token will get you on the subway, so why don't I enlighten you for about two minutes."

The car entered Central Park, their normal route away from midtown traffic. Anne stared out the window at a horse-drawn carriage, and as she did, Connor began. "Codes involve substituting whole words and symbols for one another. In a cipher, a letter or number stands for a single letter or number, not a whole word. In a complex cipher, a symbol stands for different letters or numbers depending on variables such as the number of times it appears, whether it comes after a vowel or consonant, and so on. In other words, the first time F appears in a cipher, it could stand for R; and the second time it appears, it could stand for S. Also, you have what are called multiple ciphers, in which symbols have to be translated two or more times. For example, C-P-P-N can become E-L-O-B, which becomes ANNE. Are you with me so far?"

"I think so."

"All right; let's go on. Once upon a time, codes were fashioned and decoded with paper and pencil. Then, in the 1930s, mathematical calculating machines came into vogue. Now it's computers. Matthes sends messages with a fifty-six-bit key. That means his code has seventy quadrillion possible combinations. We, in turn, have a computer that utilizes a million search chips, with each chip capable of testing a million solutions per second. That means, when we intercept one of Matthes's coded messages, under normal circumstances the entire range of possible keys can be searched in less than twenty hours."

Anne's eyes were starting to glaze over.

"I'm almost done. Forget the numbers; the concept I'm getting to is this. Normal circumstances don't apply. Matthes uses one key to encrypt his messages when he sends them from Brussels, and a different key to decrypt them when they're received in New York. That means we're dealing with seventy quadrillion times seventy quadrillion, and brute-force computer use without more won't decode his system. Six months ago, Michael Harney uncovered Matthes's decrypt system. That is, he found a message from Brussels that had been encrypted and ciphered at Matthes's end, but not yet deciphered at the New York receiving station. That plus our satellite intercepts enabled us, in layman's terms, to break the code. Now Matthes has changed the code. That means we're back to square one again, with August twenty-fourth on the horizon.''

"Ned, there's no way I can deal with codes."

"I don't expect you to; I can't either. But we have to get a man into the New York office at night. Our people have spent months studying The Hawthorne Group's intrusion-security system. And with all its cameras and computer access cards, it can still be beaten with help from the night receptionist. My question is, what's your reading on Mort Gordon?''

Anne took a breath, and let it out slowly. "I don't know. I like him, but I'd have thought you people know more about him than I do."

Connor looked out the car window at the park. "Probably we do, but we're not sure how to judge him. Gordon grew up in Pennsylvania, spent two years in the army, and after that, disappeared from view. For the past six years, he's been a security guard and night watchman. Harney told us he wasn't a bad sort; that when the chips were down, we might be able to trust him. If you'd turned us down, we'd have approached him for help. The feeling, though, was that you were safer, smarter, and more predictable.''

"Thanks; I've always wanted to be thought of as predictable."

"Substitute reliable if it makes you feel better. The important thing is, we need Gordon's help, and probably he trusts you more than he'd trust us."

An hour later, Connor dropped Anne off on the

street just outside her apartment. For the rest of the evening, she watched television and read. At one point, her mind wandered, and she began to create a board game—Genetic Dice—as a counterpart to Amanda's earlier-created Divorce. The idea would be to have a superstar baby. Obstacles would include finding the right man, sterility, infertility, birth defects, AIDS, and nuclear radiation. Around the time she went to sleep, she imagined Connor and Michael Harney discussing her reliability two months earlier, not unlike the manner in which she and Connor had discussed Mort Gordon.

Work the next day was better than usual. Hans Werner's anniversary was coming up, and he sent Anne to Bloomingdale's to buy a present for his wife. Along the way, she bought lingerie for herself, and stopped for a Popsicle outside F. A. O. Schwarz. Muller was out of town on business, which always made the office seem brighter. Gordon came in just before five-thirty, and Anne stopped by his desk in the reception area on her way out.

They chatted. Anne recounted her two hours shopping, and Gordon reciprocated with a story about his aunt. "She always made pot roast when I came for dinner. Actually, I hate pot roast; it was my brother who liked it. And each time I went, right up until she died, she'd tell me, 'Mort, I made your favorite meal for supper.' "

"Mort, what time do you get off work?"

"Two in the morning."

"How would you like to have a drink afterward?"

Just for a moment, his eyes seemed to narrow. "Sure. You pick the place, and I'll be there at two-thirty."

"How about Stella's? It's a pub on Eighth Avenue I used to go to when I was acting."

"Fine by me. By the way; what's up?"

"What do you mean?"

"I mean, I know my limitations, and girls like you don't ask guys like me for drinks unless something is up."

"Mort, I'll tell you when we get together tonight."

But first, the evening had to pass. Home alone, Anne waited.

At seven o'clock, she made a salad for dinner.

Eight P.M. This is crazy.

Eight-thirty. Violent images flashed through her thoughts. Iraqi mobs—"Death to the Great Satan." Michael Harney's lifeless body.

Pull yourself together. It's only stage fright. Remember opening night, your first Broadway performance.

An hour before showtime, the producer had come into Anne's dressing room, put his arm around her, and told her, "I thought about you while I was masturbating in the shower this morning." That had given her three pieces of information. One, the producer masturbated. Two, at least some of the time, he did it in the shower. And three, he wanted to go to bed with her; probably after the cast party that night.

Why am I remembering this?

The telephone rang.

Wrong number.

At nine o'clock, she turned on the radio. WCBS-FM. Frank Ifield was singing "I Remember You":

"I remember too a distant bell
And stars that fell
Like rain out of the blue-ooh-ooh-ooh."

Two weeks had gone by, and she hadn't heard from David. No calls; no letters.

"I like being with you," he'd told her once.

"I like being with you too, when you're good."

"Why did you have to add, when I'm good? It's looking for trouble."

"David, don't start."

"I didn't start; you started. You were reminding me that, whatever I do, no mistake is forgotten."

"When my life is through
And the angels ask me to recall
The thrill of them all,
Then I will tell them I remember you."

Anne turned the radio off. The song reminded her of David, and he was the last person she wanted to think about.

Nine-thirty. So who else was there to think about? Her father, Amanda, Shakespeare, Connor.

She wanted a drink. Just one; something to get her through until midnight. Then from midnight until two—the thought was fragmented, but roughly what it amounted to was, at midnight she'd want another drink, which wasn't much of an idea, since the last thing she wanted was to show up high for her meeting with Gordon.

Ten o'clock. She was alone; that's what she felt. She had Amanda and Howard, but they belonged first to each other. And she had friends and acquaintances, and herself. But there was a hole in her life, where she'd made room for David.

I'm not bitter.

Yes, you are, a voice inside answered.

Eleven P.M. Pull yourself together. It's just another performance tonight.

Finally, two o'clock came, and she went downstairs. Connor's driver was parked at the curb. Anne got in back; the first time she'd been in the car without Connor. It was cold for July. Wordlessly, the driver steered down Central Park West, then over to Broadway, and eventually, Eighth Avenue. At 2:20, the car came to a halt.

Anne got out, glanced at her watch, and went inside Stella's Pub. Part restaurant, part bar, it was a hangout for actors and other night people. She hadn't liked it much when she was acting, but it was a place where people could talk at two-thirty in the morning.

The headwaiter led her to a booth in back. Across the room, Connor was at a table, sitting next to a man she vaguely recognized.

Another waiter came, and Anne ordered a beer. Then she looked up and saw Gordon approaching.

So far, so good.

He waved and joined her.

"Hello, beautiful."

"Hello, Paul Sorvino."

Off to the side, a redheaded woman was singing, backed by a bass, drums, and piano. The room was smoky and dimly lit. Gordon flagged down the waiter, asked for a beer, and as an afterthought, added a request for fries.

"Nice place," he said, turning back to Anne.

"I'm glad you like it."

"Yeah; I should keep it in mind. Getting off work at two in the morning, there's not many places I'm likely to go."

More small talk, mostly about the office.

Anne waited until they were served.

"Leo Muller is strange," Gordon was saying. "One night, a week ago, I was making the rounds. You know, checking things out. It was ten o'clock. I check all the doors to make sure they're locked, so I checked Muller's and it was open. Then I saw, he was sitting at his desk in the dark. Not sleeping; just sitting there, wide awake with his eyes open and the lights off. I gotta tell you; it was weird."

"Mort; how good are you at judging character?"

"Pretty good, I guess."

"How do you rate mine?"

"Good, real good."

Anne leaned forward, elbows on the table. "I need your help."

"Like I said at the office, I figured something was up."

"I know, but this is serious. There's two more people; I'd like them to join us."

Gordon looked around. "How much trouble is this likely to cause?"

"I hope none."

"That doesn't sound reassuring."

"Mort; I'm trying to be honest. These guys can explain things better than I can."

Now was as good a time as any. Looking across the room, Anne nodded to Connor and beckoned him forward. The agent stood up, and leaving his companion, crossed to the booth where Anne and Gordon were sitting.

"Ned, this is Mort Gordon."

The two men shook hands.

"I apologize for approaching you in this manner," Connor began, "but several things have happened and we need your help."

"I'm listening."

"Fair enough. I'll make it short. I'm employed by the Federal Drug Enforcement Administration. Six months ago, we got a tip that Michael Harney was laundering money for an international cocaine cartel. We started an investigation, but before we could act, he shot himself. Now we think he had a partner; someone he worked with at The Hawthorne Group. Miss Rhodes has agreed to assist us in gathering information, but we also need your help."

"What sort of help do you have in mind?"

"As you're aware, security at The Hawthorne Group is tight. Miss Rhodes has been helpful during the day, but we need access to certain areas of the office at night."

"You gotta be kidding."

"Does this sound like a joke?"

"What it sounds like is, you should get a warrant and search the place like any other cop. How do I know you're not some kind of industrial spy?"

Raising his hand, Connor signaled across the room. The man he'd been sitting with rose and joined them.

"Mort, this is Detective Frank Burka of the New York City Police Department. Do you remember him?"

Gordon took a long look. "Yeah, you're the guy

who came to the office asking questions after Harney died."

Connor went on as Burka remained silent. "That's right. And if you need more proof regarding our credentials, we'll arrange for you to meet the police commissioner. That's how high this thing goes."

Gordon looked around, as though expecting more cops. "Just what kind of help do you guys want?"

"We have to get a man inside the office, and give him an hour to look around. Doing it openly would tip our hand. That means we want to come in at night. As far as locks and other security are concerned, we can beat the system."

"What's in it for me?"

"Help us out, and we'll pay you for your help."

Gordon turned toward Anne. "How well do you know these guys?"

"Well enough," she answered.

For the first time, the man who'd been introduced as Detective Burka spoke. "You have to understand, this is an important investigation. Dozens of drug enforcement officials are involved. We're not asking you to go out on a limb; just look the other way while we come in for an hour."

"I don't know. You guys are gonna have to do something more to convince me you're legit."

"And if we do?"

"Then I'd want to know what happens next."

"You tell us," Connor countered. "What goes on in the office each night?"

"All right. Probably, I shouldn't be talking right now, but let's say I'm a curious sort."

The agents waited.

"Most people leave the office by nine o'clock.

Sometimes one or two of the executives stays later, but almost always, everyone is gone by eleven. I sit at the reception desk, and walk around to make sure the doors are locked. The office has cameras that tape what happens. Each tape runs for twenty-four hours. The last thing I do before I go home is go into the control room and change the tapes."

"What happens when you change the tapes?"

"Nothing. All I do is take the old tapes out, put new ones in, and leave the old tapes on Muller's desk."

"How do you get into Muller's office if the door is locked?"

"My computer card lets me in at two A.M. for five minutes five nights a week."

"Then what happens?"

"Usually, I go to the bathroom and take a leak. Then I go home, and no one else comes into the office until morning."

Connor sat silent, pondering the data.

Gordon finished his beer, and put his mug down on the table. "Penetration; that's what you guys call this, isn't it? Putting someone inside the other side's operation."

"That's right. Except before we tell you anything more, you have to promise you'll keep this quiet. That means, you talk to no one except Detective Burka and myself."

"I'm not sure I want to hear more," Gordon countered. "You guys may or may not be on the level. And if you are, you mentioned something about money."

"Money and our credentials can be taken care of later. The first thing is, you don't talk; and that includes not talking about this to Miss Rhodes again, in or out of the office."

"Don't worry; I'm not a talker. And besides, I like my job. If I talked and Muller found out I was working with you guys, he'd fire me."

No he wouldn't, Anne thought. If Muller finds out, he'll put a bullet in your head.

◆ ◆ ◆

Four A.M.

New York Harbor, the finest natural seaport in the world. Six hundred fifty miles of navigable waterfront carved from the earth by glacial erosion.

The launch moved slowly through the murky water, with waves expanding from either side. The Statue of Liberty loomed ahead, its torch raised upward toward the nighttime sky.

"One sees New York best from the water," Leo Muller told the boatman.

The motor droned beneath their words. The skyline was a mix of old and new. Wall Street skyscrapers; rusting burned-out rotting piers; the World Trade Center and the Woolworth Building; old factories and high-tech lofts; Ellis Island, Battery Park City.

Thirty-four days, Muller told himself.

It was best to see now what it would be like on August 24, at four in the morning when the bombs were exchanged. Less than an hour would be needed to transfer the cargo and send it out to sea; but meticulous preparation was required.

The harbor was ideal, fronting Manhattan, Brooklyn, and parts of New Jersey. Thousands of ships came and went each week. Concealing the weapons would be an easy task. The thirteen-kiloton bomb that destroyed Hiroshima had been ten and a half feet long and twenty-nine inches in diameter, weighing 9,700 pounds. But the technology of death had evolved since then. Matthes's weapons were a mere two and a half feet in length and eighteen inches wide, with an explosive yield of one hundred kilotons.

"We were lying there, very tense," Isidor Rabi wrote once of the first atomic bomb test at Alamogordo in 1945. "There were just a few streaks of gold in the east; you could see your neighbor very dimly. Suddenly there was an enormous flash of light, the brightest light that I think anyone has ever seen. It blasted, it pounced, it bore its way right through you. It was a vision which was seen with more than the eye. It was seen to last forever. Finally it was over, diminishing, and we looked toward the place where the bomb had been. There was an enormous ball of fire which grew and grew and rolled as it grew; it went up into the air in yellow flashes and into scarlet and green. A new thing had been born; a new control; a new understanding which man had acquired over nature."

"I am sure," wrote George Kistiakowsky, another witness to the explosion, "that at the end of the world, in the last millisecond of the earth's existence, the last man will see what we have just seen."

The launch moved forward at a speed of ten knots, its bow slapping against the tide. There was, of course, no certainty that any of Matthes's weapons would ever be detonated. Hopefully, they would simply be diplomatically used to restructure the world's balance of power. Still, gazing at the shadow of buildings in the night, Muller understood how vulnerable everything was. In the event of a blast, any target city would be destroyed. Hundreds of square miles would be rendered uninhabitable for decades. Millions upon millions of people would die.

Play the game. Wealth is worth. Live to the fullest while alive.

Besides, the third world would be capable of developing nuclear weapons on its own within ten to twenty years. This was simply accelerating the inevitable in exchange for unimaginable riches while there was still time.

Chapter 15

After their meeting with Mort Gordon, Connor and Burka drove Anne home. It was four A.M. when she got back to her apartment, and almost dawn when her eyes closed. She slept until noon, then did some errands, and Saturday night went to a party given by a couple who lived down the hall. Once or twice, she thought about Gordon. She could probably trust him, but she wasn't sure.

Monday at the office, there was a five-minute fire drill. Contrary to New York City ordinances and regulations, Leo Muller refused to leave his desk, which led to words with a fire marshal. Otherwise, the day was routine. A catered lunch; spreadsheets monitoring the spot price of oil; everything functioning the way it should, from computer printouts to the paper shredder whirring.

At five-thirty, on her way out of the office, Anne stopped to chat with Gordon. There was no reference to Friday's late-night encounter. Just normal conversation; nothing out of the ordinary.

She went home, changed clothes, and had drinks with a friend. Then she returned home again, made a sandwich for dinner, and began reading various magazines.

Amanda and Howard telephoned midway through the evening to invite her for dinner on her birthday, Friday.

July 28. The big four-oh.

"We'll have a cake," Howard promised. "And Jessica is rehearsing to sing 'Happy Birthday.' "

The next few days were quiet at the office.

Wednesday it rained.

Thursday, Anne had dinner with Connor.

"Gordon is on board," the agent told her. "At first, he wasn't sure he could trust us, but a trip to police headquarters and five thousand dollars gave him confidence in our honor."

"Salaries are going down."

Connor shrugged. "You signed on for three months. Gordon we need for about an hour."

"How soon is he letting you into the office?"

"You know our motto—Sooner rather than later. Besides, August twenty-fourth is coming."

That night, again, Anne was aware of her dreams. Nude photos of her littered a bright green lawn. David was standing there, looking down. A voice intoned, "The rubber swan is mine."

"I don't love you, David."

"Yes, you do," he answered.

A tall blond woman came into view, dressed in black, wearing aviator glasses.

"The glasses look good," Anne snapped. "They cover up the bags under her eyes."

What she really thought was, she'd never seen a more beautiful woman before.

The woman reached out and put her arms around David.

"She touches everyone," he explained. "It's nothing personal."

Then the alarm clock buzzed, and Anne lay in bed, eyes closed, realizing it was her birthday. She was forty years old.

If the day was special, nothing at work showed it. Muller and Ernst Neumann were more brusque than usual. Hans Werner asked her to conform forty pages of an account ledger. Lunch was ordinary, which didn't matter, but a cupcake with a candle would have been nice.

Gordon came in a few minutes early, and Anne sat with him in conference room B over coffee. He was in a good mood; at least it seemed that way, although possibly he was a trifle nervous. For a while, they talked about theater and acting. "What I'd like about being an actor," he said, "would be everyone in the audience applauding for me when the show was over."

"That's part of it," she told him, "but there's a lot more."

Walking home, Anne thought about David, and wondered if he'd send a birthday card. Rhodes, stop picking at your goddamn scab.

When she reached her apartment, the mailbox was empty.

You lose, David. And maybe I lose too, but that's another story.

Dinner with Amanda and Howard was a joy. Amanda had spent most of the day in the kitchen preparing a meal that would have done Julia Child proud. Jessica sang "Happy Birthday" as promised, and confided in Anne, "Mommy bought you a zambooli."

"What's a zambooli?"

"What Mommy bought."

The "zambooli" turned out to be a replica of a Tiffany lamp, so designated because, as Amanda explained, "Jessica can't keep a secret." Thus, when they'd gone shopping for a present, Amanda told Jessica they were getting a zambooli.

Howard was in good spirits throughout the evening, and recounted battles he'd had with his mother. "She's a truly nasty woman," he observed. "In fact, even when she tries to be nice, things turn out wrong. I had a weight problem when I was young. I still do, but I'm less self-conscious about it now. Once, when I was twelve, we were in a restaurant, and she told me not to look at the right side of the menu. What she meant was, I shouldn't worry about what things cost, but desserts were listed on the right and I thought she meant I shouldn't order any because I was fat."

Around eleven, Anne went home. It was getting late, and David might call. Not that she expected him to, but it was her birthday, after all.

In her apartment, she felt terribly alone. She turned the television on. There wasn't much of interest to choose from. Finally she settled on HBO, where a blond comedienne named Anita Wise was performing:

My psychiatrist moonlights as a stand-up comic [*chuckles from audience*]. I caught his act at a club last week, and his entire routine was about me [*laughter*]. Now he pays me ninety dollars an hour and complains if I stop in the middle of a story when our time is up [*more laughter*].

Anne turned off the television. She wasn't in the mood. Maybe she should find a place to put the Tiffany lamp. Living room or bedroom—that was the first question. The best place might be the night table next to her bed.

Rearrange a few things.

That looks good.

Now the lamp from the bedroom could go on the end table adjacent to the fireplace. And there was still that space on the mantelpiece, where the vase David once gave her had been.

Where was it now? In a shoebox in the bedroom closet.

Anne wanted some music. WCBS-FM. Jimmy Webb's "MacArthur Park" was playing:

"There will be another song for me
    For I will sing it.
    There will be another dream for me
    Someone will bring it."

So who could she count on to bring her next dream? Not Ned Connor; that was for sure. The night they'd slept together, even then she'd asked

254

herself, why am I in bed with this man when I love David?

>"But after all the loves of my life,
>   After all the loves of my life,
>   You'll still be the one."

The song depressed her.

Who do I love more than anyone else in the world? David. Will I ever forgive him? I don't know.

On impulse, Anne went to the closet, took the shoebox off the top shelf, and set it down on the floor.

I shouldn't do this.

Carefully, she unwrapped the vase. She'd forgotten how truly stunning it was.

It belonged on the mantelpiece.

Why? Just because.

In the background, The Platters were singing:

>"So I chaffed them and I gaily laughed
>   To think they could doubt my love.
>   Yet today my love has flown away
>   I am without my love . . ."

"Smoke Gets In Your Eyes"—another reminder of an up-and-down past, which had become an unhappy present without enough love.

Returning to the living room, Anne set the vase on the mantel above the fireplace. What was it David had told her once? Either you're perfect, or I'm much more tolerant than you are. She wasn't perfect; not by a long shot. She wasn't even any better than he was.

"So I smile and say,
When a lovely flame dies,
Smoke gets in your eyes."

She'd die someday; so would David. And until then, really, they belonged together. All she had to do was pick up the telephone.

And dial.

And hope it wasn't too late, because there was always the chance he'd had enough already and would tell her no.

I shouldn't do this.

Yes, I should.

She dialed.

Four rings.

David answered. "Hello?"

"David, it's Anne." And then she spoke the most difficult words she'd ever spoken. "I apologize; I was wrong."

◆ ◆ ◆

It hadn't been a good day for Gordon. First, construction workers outside his bedroom window had jackhammered him awake after he'd been asleep for five hours. Then he'd gone to the dentist for a checkup, and two large cavities had to be filled. He'd arrived at work early, passed some time with Anne over a cup of coffee in conference room B, and tried to act as naturally as possible. But then she'd left, the novocaine had worn off, and his mouth had begun to hurt like hell.

Now he was frightened. Not panicked, because he'd known what was coming, but definitely scared.

Five minutes earlier, at 2:01 A.M., the electricity had gone off on the twenty-third floor of Trump Tower. Moments later, as arranged, Gordon opened the door to the public corridor, and three men carrying metal equipment cases had come inside.

"You stay here," Connor ordered.

Gordon had waited in the reception area, and the three men disappeared from view.

The computer age. With all the marvels of modern technology, it was remarkable what blowing a fifty-cent fuse could do. Kill some lights, overload a circuit, and computer security was still vulnerable to the human spy.

Forty-five minutes. That was how long the men wanted. Gordon wished he were more certain that they were good guys instead of bad.

Chapter 16

Saturday morning; nine o'clock. Anne lay in bed next to David with her eyes still shut, the night before echoing in her mind.

"David, I was wrong." That's what she'd told him. And after that came a montage of thoughts, back and forth, some good, some bad.

From David: "I'm tired of always feeling like I'm on probation . . . Last month, you weren't seeing me to rebuild the relationship. You were looking for problems, putting nails in our coffin . . . Every time you talked about someone else, for me or for you, you degraded me and what we had . . . Whenever I opened up to you, you took what I told you and fashioned it into ammunition."

And Anne: "I know I have faults; we both have faults. But I won't disappoint you again, I promise . . . It would be a tragedy if we never saw Paris together . . . I want to spend my life with you.''

And in the end, they'd gone to bed together, resolving that this time things between them would be right.

Anne didn't notice until morning that sometime during the night, the chain on her locket had broken.

◆ ◆ ◆

MEMORANDUM

To: The Director of the NSA
From: E. N. Connor

Penetration of The Hawthorne Group's New York office proceeded early this morning as planned. Entry was achieved at 0203 hours by the undersigned, Joseph Shields, and Arthur Nissen. William Baker remained in the public corridor for security purposes. It is believed that The Hawthorne Group's computerized security system recorded our time and entry and departure. However, the synchronized overhead surveillance cameras were temporarily out of order as the result of an NSA-induced power failure, which blocked the flow of electricity to the twenty-third floor.

Departure occurred at 0247 hours. During the intervening forty-four minutes, copies were made of available documents, tapes, and computer programs. Preliminary indications are that the mission was successful, and that within twenty-four hours, we will again have the capacity to decrypt messages transmitted from The Hawthorne Group's headquarters in Belgium.

The operation was facilitated by the night receptionist, who has been provided with a plausible explanation of events for use when questioned by his superiors. For his services, we have paid him five thousand dollars in cash (an amount sufficiently small to forgo taxes). The receptionist has been advised and has agreed not to discuss or refer to the intrusion in any way with any person including Ms. Rhodes. No further contact with him is planned.

◆ ◆ ◆

Gordon was tired, and scared. In a way, it was like basic training in the army, when they'd sent him slithering through a field on his stomach with machine guns firing bullets three feet above the ground. Keep calm, stay low, and everything would be all right. Still, he wished Matthes would let him go home.

Electric power had been restored to the twenty-third floor of Trump Tower at 2:45 A.M. Thereafter, as per instructions in the office manual, Gordon had telephoned Leo Muller at home. Muller arrived an hour later, listened to what had transpired, and telephoned Christoph Matthes in Belgium. Ten hours later, at 2:00 P.M., Matthes was at Trump Tower on the twenty-third floor. By then, Gordon had been awake for twenty-seven hours. Now it was thirty, too many of which had been spent sitting, waiting, answering questions, and wondering how much longer the interrogation would go on. He'd never been in Matthes's office before. Most definitely, he wished he weren't there now.

"Tell me again," Matthes prodded. "From the beginning, precisely what occurred."

"Yes, sir. Where would you like me to start?"

"Wherever you wish."

"Okay. The last guy to leave the office was Eric Winslow. He left around nine-thirty. The cleaning woman was gone by then. I sat at the reception desk, and read some magazines, and walked around to make sure all the doors were locked. Just before two, I took the tapes out of the cameras and went to put them on Mr. Muller's desk. That's when the lights went out."

Muller sat motionless.

"Go on," Matthes urged.

"Okay; so when the lights went out, I found my way back to the reception area. Then I opened the door to the outside corridor to see if it was dark out there too. It was, so I closed the door and waited. Finally, around three, the lights came back on. When that happened, I put fresh tapes into the video cameras and telephoned Mr. Muller."

"When you opened the door to the public corridor, did it occur to you that an intruder might be present?"

"No, sir."

Matthes waited, indicating that a more elaborate response was required.

"I mean, this is a secure building, right? There

was no reason I should expect trouble. And there wasn't any."

"Did anyone other than yourself enter the office?"

"No way."

"Why didn't you telephone Mr. Muller when the lights went out?"

"I did."

"To the contrary, you waited almost an hour."

"That's because the office was dark. There was no flashlight, and before I could call, I had to look in the office directory for Mr. Muller's home telephone number."

"When did you put fresh tapes in the cameras?"

"A little before three, when the lights came back."

"So there was a period of about an hour when the cameras were not operative. Is that correct?"

"Yes, sir."

"And during that period, you opened the door to the public corridor once?"

"Yes."

"Perhaps, then, you could explain to me why the computer entry system—which is battery operated—indicated the door was opened once at two oh-three A.M., and then again at two forty-seven."

"That's the second time I opened it."

"Mr. Gordon, you just told me, the door was only opened once."

"I know, but after the lights came on again, I looked out into the corridor to make sure everything was okay there too."

"Why didn't you put fresh tapes in the video cameras at one fifty-five when you removed the old ones? It would have been much easier that way than returning to the cameras after placing the old tapes on Mr. Muller's desk.''

"I don't know. I guess I just didn't think of it."

"You usually do. In fact, I believe in all other instances when you've changed the tapes, they've run sequentially without a break of more than a minute. Here, even if the power failure hadn't occurred, approximately five minutes would have been lost."

"I don't know," Gordon repeated. "Like I said, I guess I just didn't think of it."

"Very well, then, I believe that answers my questions. Mr. Muller will make certain you are provided with a flashlight for future use. As for now, you must be tired. Please accept my apologies for keeping you for so long without sleep. You may go now."

Gordon left.

Only then, alone with Muller, did Christoph Matthes rise from his desk.

"He's lying, you know," Muller offered.

"I'm afraid that's right. Watch him, closely."

PART FOUR

Not far from this village, perhaps about two miles, there is a little valley among high hills, which is one of the quietest places in the whole world. A small brook glides through it, with just murmur enough to lull one to repose; and the occasional whistle of a quail or tapping of a woodpecker is almost the only sound that ever breaks in upon the uniform tranquility. If ever I should wish for a retreat whither I might steal from the world and its distractions and dream quietly away the remnant of a troubled life, I know of none more promising than this little valley. From the listless repose of the place and the peculiar character of its inhabitants, this sequestered glen has long been known by the name of Sleepy Hollow.

—Washington Irving

Chapter 17

The first week of August was oppressively humid, with temperatures in the nineties and occasional rain. Throughout the city, commuters trudged from one indoor air-conditioned sanctuary to another. Even at The Hawthorne Group, the atmosphere seemed charged, with Leo Muller more remote than ever.

Two days after Anne and David reunited, David flew to Chicago for a trial. Meanwhile, Amanda voiced delight at the reconciliation, and Howard predicted, "You'll be the happiest neurotic couple we know." Ned Connor surfaced briefly in mid-week to report on the break-in of The Hawthorne Group offices. For once, the NSA had gotten lucky. Its computer experts had broken Matthes's code.

David's trial recessed for the weekend, and he

flew back to New York, arriving Friday night at Anne's apartment. Saturday afternoon, they played Scrabble together, stretched out on the living room floor.

"C-H-A-F-F-E-D," she announced, spreading seven letters across the board.

"How in the world did you come up with 'chaffed'?"

"I've been listening to the radio—'Smoke Gets In Your Eyes.' "

The next day she took a photo of David that had been in her scrapbook and put it on her dresser. A whole weekend; no fighting. And the chemistry between them was still there.

On Monday, the oppressive humidity broke, and walking to work was less of a chore. Also, Muller was out of town on business, which to Anne's way of thinking improved working conditions considerably. Gordon came into the office early, and began reminiscing about a baseball game from years before.

"I was in high school," he recalled. "Eleventh grade. This kid named Bill Jackson was a real fucker—the kind of guy who's never happy unless he's picking on someone. Always asking in front of girls, how come I never went out on dates; stuff like that. Anyway, Jackson had a team in the Babe Ruth League, and some friends and me got together to challenge them. We were winning by one run in the ninth inning, and I gotta tell you, I was nervous. It's like, we were three outs away from the game being over, and if we won, we had bragging rights for the rest of the year."

"What happened?"

"We got two outs. Then they loaded the bases, which was partly my fault because I dropped a pop-up. Then Jackson came up and hit this shot to left field that could have crossed the Grand Canyon. I mean, he walloped it. Our left fielder was a guy named Pete Francisi, an Italian kid. And Pete hated Jackson on account of Jackson was always making fun of Pete's parents and the way they dressed. Anyway, Pete took off after the ball the moment it was hit. No one thought he had a chance, but he ran it down, dove, and somehow the ball stuck in his glove."

Before Anne could offer appropriate congratulations, Gordon glanced at the bare spot at the base of her neck. "I just noticed; don't you usually wear a locket or something?"

"The chain broke; I haven't had time to get it fixed."

Kurt Weber walked by and waved good night.

"Listen," Gordon told her, ignoring Weber. "A long time ago, when my parents died, someone gave me my grandmother's gold necklace. I'll bring it in, and you can keep it."

"Mort, I couldn't take something like that."

"Why not? It would go nice with the locket, and I know my limitations. I'll never have a real girl-friend or get married. And I'll feel good, knowing someone I like is wearing it."

"Why don't you think about it?"

"Thinking is easy. The hard part will be finding it. But I'll bring it in sometime soon. I promise."

Walking home from the office, Anne varied her

route, following Fifth Avenue to 72nd Street before crossing the park. The paths were filled with bike riders and joggers. Along the way, she thought about David, wondering if they'd ever get married.

The homeless man across the street from her apartment seemed drunk or on drugs, in another dimension, when she passed. At times, Anne had to remind herself he was human, that being homeless was a tragic curse. Just for a moment, she wondered what it did to her soul when she passed people like him on a daily basis without caring. Then, before she could finish the thought, she saw Ned Connor in a car parked at the curb.

The agent waved.

Anne stopped, and he got out of the car. By now she had learned to read his face.

Something was wrong.

"Let's take a walk," he suggested.

Together, they moved up Central Park West, stopping at a bench a few blocks north. Gesturing for Anne to take a seat, Connor waited until an elderly man with a cane passed, then sat down on the bench beside her. "A couple of things have happened," he said. "The way we read it, there's nothing to worry about, but it's important for you to be kept up to date."

Anne waited.

"This past weekend," Connor continued, "Matthes conducted a security sweep of the office. Probably, it was occasioned by last week's power failure. Whatever the reason, he found two of our bugs. One was a miniature camera in the copier. The other was the relay antenna you planted on the bookshelf. Obviously, Matthes knows he's being watched. And just as obviously, there's no way of tying it to you. All I'm suggesting is that you be particularly careful and not discuss any of this with Gordon.''

"What do you mean, be particularly careful?"

"I just told you. Talk with Gordon, but keep it casual. He was on duty the night we broke in, so I wouldn't be surprised if they're having him watched.''

A young man passed, dribbling a basketball on the sidewalk, threading his way through shards of glass. A bent beer-can tab glistened in the sun.

"How much danger is there for Mort?"

"Don't worry about Gordon. He knows how to take care of himself.''

Once again, Anne felt herself getting frightened.

"That's all for now,'' Connor told her. "I'll walk you back to your apartment if you'd like.''

The late-afternoon sun was nearing the horizon. A gentle breeze blew overhead.

They stood up and began walking south, along the park.

The agent whistled.

Nine notes, not quite to himself.

Silently, Anne matched the notes with their lyrics: "So I chaffed them and I gaily laughed.''

And then she stopped.

"Ned, what made you whistle that?"

"I don't know. I guess I like it.''

Anne's mind was a jumble of thoughts. Listening to the radio alone in her apartment. Playing Scrabble with David, just the two of them in her apartment.

Her first day of work, when she'd come home and somehow her apartment had seemed violated.

Her words came tumbling out. "You bastard; you've bugged my apartment."

"What?"

"Don't deny it. Don't lie to me, Ned. If you lie to me now, I'll walk off the job so fast you won't know what happened."

There was no response.

"You son of a bitch."

"Anne, don't get excited."

"Don't get excited! You goddamn fucking son of a bitch. You've been listening to everything I've done for months."

"It was done to protect you."

"Protect me, bullshit. How dare you listen in on my life. It's—Oh, my God. You've got it all, don't you? Right down to the two of us in bed together."

"You didn't do anything to be ashamed of."

"That's not the point. What have you got? Transcripts? Tapes? There must be some record of your heroic conquest. And David? You've got the two of us in bed together too; something to play at your next office party."

"Anne, certain things are essential in this business. Information is—"

"Don't start that crap, you sadistic bastard."

"Control yourself. There are people watching."

Anne stopped short and looked around. A young woman, walking a dog, stood nearby. A middle-aged man sat on a bench, staring.

"Ned, you have ten minutes to get those bugs out of my apartment."

"Be reasonable."

"And if you don't, I'm quitting The Hawthorne Group tomorrow."

"I don't believe you."

"Oh, no? Then call my bluff, and see what your boss thinks when you walk in and tell him you've lost your contact."

For a moment, they stood facing each other.

Then Connor folded. "All right; let's go upstairs and I'll take the bugs out."

Anne led him into the lobby of her building, to the elevator, then up to the fourth floor. Inside her apartment, he walked to the bedroom, and unscrewed the mouthpiece on the telephone receiver. A small metallic device was wired inside.

"That's it," he said. "That and one more in the telephone in the kitchen. They're electronic transmitters capable of picking up everything in the apartment."

"Take them out."

"All right, if that's what you want."

"Now."

Connor did as instructed. Both telephones.

"Now, get out of my apartment."

"Anne—"

"I said, get out!"

"Listen for a minute."

"I don't want to listen. You should be in one of those mental hospitals where they let people out on day passes to do their job. Now get out."

"You know I'll be back."

"Unless I quit."

"You won't do that. There's only seventeen days

left, and we need your help. Look, I didn't organize the world, and sometimes I fuck up. For what it's worth, I apologize; I'm sorry."

"Send me a letter."

Connor shrugged. "All right, if that's the way you want it. The bugs are gone. You're on your own."

Then he left.

And Anne called David in Chicago. As she was telling him what had happened, she got scared all over again, because she realized she was dragging him into the middle of this whole bloody mess, and she'd never forgive herself if something happened to David.

◆ ◆ ◆

Brussels. The Hawthorne Group headquarters.

Christoph Matthes sat at his desk as Leo Muller finished speaking. Neither man was afraid of facts; reality was always dealt with promptly.

Here, the facts augured poorly for Mort Gordon. First, there were the incongruities surrounding the power failure. Contrary to normal operating procedure, Gordon had waited an hour before replacing the tapes in the surveillance monitoring system. Moreover, the door to the public corridor had been opened, not once but twice. Thus, outside parties might have been allowed to enter the office and move about freely.

Then there was Matthes's own security sweep of the office, conducted shortly after the power failure. Two surveillance devices had been uncovered—a miniature camera in the equipment-room copier and a relay antenna in conference room B. That had further increased suspicion; so much so that a microphone and camera were installed in the reception area to monitor Gordon's conduct. Nothing abnormal had been observed. Gordon seemed to be friendlier with Anne Rhodes than with the other employees, but their conversations were of little consequence. Then came the evidence which to Matthes was conclusive.

"We've run a check on Mr. Gordon's financial condition," Muller reported. "Several of our inquiries were through normal channels. Others were less formally put to friends at various banks."

"And?"

"Three days after the power failure, Mr. Gordon opened a new account with five thousand dollars in cash."

Matthes sat silent, digesting the data. Finally, almost impassively, he spoke. "I suppose then, the issue is how to deal with Mr. Gordon. We can watch him further in the hope of gathering additional information, or dispose of him now inasmuch as his presence is dangerous."

Muller waited.

Matthes went on in a calm monotonal voice. "When you return to New York, I would like you to arrange for Mr. Gordon's death. And perhaps it would be wise to look a little more closely at Miss Rhodes."

◆ ◆ ◆

Fort Meade, Maryland.

A half-dozen National Security Agency personnel

sat conversing around the room. Empty soda cans and Styrofoam cups lay scattered on desktops. Paper plates; the remains of sandwiches.

"It's ironic," one of the agents was saying. "Just when the superpowers are cutting nuclear arsenals, the third-world atomic buildup starts."

"The best thing about Hiroshima and Nagasaki," said another, "is they proved to the world that nuclear holocausts are for real."

The door opened, and Connor walked in.

"Hey, Ned. I hear you fucked up this afternoon. It's in one of the transcripts. Take a look."

Connor glanced in the direction of the speaker, then reached for the pages and scanned the last part:

RHODES: Take them out.

CONNOR: All right, if that's what you want.

RHODES: Now.

CONNOR: Okay. I said I'd do it.

(At this point, the transmitter located in the subject's bedroom became nonoperative.)

RHODES: Now the other one.

CONNOR: Anne—

RHODES: Don't talk; just do it.

(All transmissions from the subject's apartment ceased.)

"So what happens next?" one of the agents prodded.

Laying the pages down on a desk, Connor rubbed

his eyes and looked at his watch. August 7; eleven o'clock. "Time's running out," he said at last. "And there are people more important than Anne Rhodes to worry about."

"Which means what?"

"Judging from the latest batch of cables, Leo Muller has more authority than we thought. I think it's time we played hardball with Muller."

Chapter 18

L eo Muller was back in New York the day after the listening devices were removed from Anne's apartment. He looked tired, as though he'd traveled all night, but his demeanor was the same as always. Cold, aloof, methodical, proper. Midway through the morning, he called Anne to his office, and gave her a stack of documents to index. That kept her busy for the rest of the day, segregating invoices by price, product, and date. Most of the documents related to petroleum drawn from wells in Qatar and Bahrain. Tiny spots on a map of the Persian Gulf; each one smaller than the state of Vermont, oil-rich beyond a sultan's dreams.

At 5:35 P.M., Anne finished her work and passed through the reception area on her way out of the office. Gordon was bleeding. That was the first thing she noticed—a trickle of blood running down his cheek, stopping short of his jaw where the smear turned brown.

"I cut myself shaving," he explained when she asked. "I thought the blood stopped when I took a shower, but I was wrong."

At Anne's suggestion, he went to the men's room and washed up while she sat at the reception desk. Then he returned, reclaimed his chair, and asked if she had time for another high school story.

"That guy, Bill Jackson, the one I told you about yesterday. Once, at a school assembly, there was a contest. Anybody who wanted could come down and do push-ups, and whoever did the most would win a prize. Anyway, ten or twelve guys volunteered. Most of them did thirty, maybe thirty-five push-ups. Then Jackson's turn came, and he did fifty-nine, which is a lot. I mean, I worked in a quarry on weekends and after school, so I was strong, and I don't think I'd ever done more than forty. But there was nothing in the world I wanted more than to beat Jackson in front of everybody, so I figured what the heck, I'd give it a try. Anyway, I was the last guy. And when I went onto the floor, I remember Jackson made some crack about my having a potbelly, and all the kids started to laugh. It got to me; it made me mad, and I started off faster than I should. The first twenty push-ups I did real fast, and by thirty I could feel my arms getting tired. Somehow, I got up to forty-five, and I didn't have any strength left, but the kids were counting. You know, with each push-up, they'd shout forty-six, forty-seven, forty-eight. So I got up to fifty, and there was no way I could do ten more. Maybe if I was lucky, if I gave it everything, I could get to fifty-two, and then when I got to fifty-two, I told myself, fifty-three, do one more.''

Anne waited.

''Fifty-four. Fifty-five. And I gotta tell you, people were going crazy. It was the first time in my life I heard people cheering for me. Like I was the underdog, and everyone was rooting for me. At fifty-six, I knew I was finished. I just hung there. No way was I getting up to sixty. I never prayed to God before but I was praying then, and that gave me something and I got to fifty-seven. Fifty-eight, I don't know how I did it. I was out of it by then. My arms were limp, like spaghetti. There was pain like I never felt before. Two more was impossible, and then I realized, one more was all I needed to tie Jackson. That push-up, number fifty-nine, lasted forever. People were screaming; it was pandemonium. And then I did sixty. I'll be honest, I don't remember sixty on account of I passed out afterward.''

The telephone rang, and Gordon picked up the receiver.

It's a strange world, Anne thought as she waited. A strange world, but it's the only one we've got.

Gordon was on the phone for about a minute. Then he hung up, and turned back to face her. ''Anyway, that was my moment of high school glory. And before I forget, I found the necklace I told you about yesterday. It was in a sock in my bureau. I'll try to remember to bring it in tomorrow.''

''You don't have to.''

''I know, but I want you to have it. You know, it's funny, thinking about high school. I don't think anyone in the world except me remembers those push-ups."

"Hey, Mort?"

"Yeah?"

"I'll bet Jackson remembers."

Gordon smiled. "Good night, beautiful."

"Good night, Paul Sorvino."

♦ ♦ ♦

David had returned to Chicago for his trial, so Anne spent the evening at home alone. Amanda called, and they talked about the children—particularly Susan, whose vocabulary of the moment seemed to consist of "gross," "boss," "yucky," "no way," "don't sweat it," and "so funny I forgot to laugh."

Afterward, Anne turned on the radio. Country music from the Grand Old Opry:

"Last week I got fired
    My wife and I had a fight.
    My shrink is sleepin' with my girlfriend,
    And my dog don't treat me right."

Shrinks in Tennessee; the world was changing. And all the while, Anne mused, a dozen schmucks working for the NSA were sitting around monitoring her sex life.

David telephoned before she went to bed to report that his trial was going nicely. Every time he tried a case, he focused on one or more of the jurors. It gave him an idea of how the case was going, and hopefully during deliberations there'd be someone in the jury room pleading his case. This time, he seemed to have three strong allies—particularly juror number two, a housewife with long brown hair, wheelchair-bound from an automobile accident years before.

That night, again, Anne was aware of her dreams. "What good are dead leaves?" a voice demanded. "They feed the earth, and look pretty on trees."

"Autumn colors; you're a romantic, aren't you? When you strike at a king, kill him, or don't strike at all."

At 6:30 A.M., the telephone rang. Half asleep, Anne reached for the receiver. Whoever it was had better have a reason for calling at that hour.

It was Connor.

"I have to see you."

"Ned, it's six-thirty."

"I know; this is important." The urgency in his voice said it wasn't a game. "I'm in a phone booth across the street. Get ready, and I'll be there in an hour."

She wasn't sure she wanted him in her apartment—not after the bugging—but before she could say no, Connor hung up. What to do? If she showered and dressed quickly, she could meet him downstairs.

At 7:25, Anne was waiting in the lobby. Five minutes later, Connor approached.

Their eyes met.

"I'd rather do this upstairs," he told her.

"And I'd rather not."

The agent shrugged. "All right; let's go someplace where we can talk."

"Coffee?"

282

He shook his head. "Someplace without people."

Before Anne could answer, Connor gestured for her to walk. Down Central Park West, just a block, into a playground enclosed by a cast-iron fence. Slides, swings, a jungle gym, and sandbox. In a matter of hours, it would be teeming with children, but for the moment, except for the two of them, it was deserted.

They sat on a bench opposite the swings.

"I'm not sure how to begin," Connor started. "I know you're angry, and I apologized once but that's not enough. The bugs in your apartment were there to monitor what you were doing. It wasn't a matter of prurient interest. We did it because of the stakes involved. You're waiting for August twenty-fourth, because that's when you get paid. We're dreading that date, because if August twenty-fourth comes and the bombs are shipped, a nuclear holocaust will confront us all. But regardless, you trusted me and I didn't return the favor. I don't like the way we left things, and I'm sorry."

There was no mistaking the sincerity in his voice, but his eyes suggested something more.

"We screw up sometimes," Connor continued, a rueful smile crossing his lips. "I've said that before, and it's painfully true. Last month, one of our agents was supposed to bug a telephone, and wound up bugging an apartment intercom instead. All we got on tape were deliveries: 'Chinese food and pizza coming up.'"

A homeless man carrying a large plastic bag stumbled into the playground and began rummaging through the trash. Two soda cans, a beer bottle.

Anne watched for a moment, then turned back toward the agent.

"There's something you're not telling me."

Connor nodded, then spoke four words: "Mort Gordon is dead."

Anne's senses numbed. She started to shake.

"I wanted you to hear it from me first," the agent said. "Right now, we're not sure how it happened. He was found on the street this morning at three o'clock, shot once in the heart with his wallet missing. Maybe it was a robbery; that's how tragedies happen. But we can't discount the probability that it was Matthes."

Anne said nothing, and continued to shake.

"I know how frightening this must be for you. But you're a courageous woman and you have to understand, if the bombs go off, all of us will be dead. That's why you have to keep doing what you're doing. This might be the hardest thing you'll ever do, but I want you to go to the office this morning like nothing has happened. Wait for someone to tell you about Gordon. Be shocked, grieve, do whatever you want. But don't let on that you know something more."

"I can't do it."

"Yes, you can. Anne, I believe in you."

Then her tears came, accompanied by soft choked sobs.

Connor sat and waited while she cried. A long time, until finally she dried her eyes.

And then Anne surprised him.

She looked at her watch. "It's eight-thirty. I'd better be going to the office."

"Are you all right?"

"I'll be fine, but I want you to promise me something. And Ned, I mean it; no false promises."

"Anything you want."

"When this is over, whatever it takes, I want you to kill Christoph Matthes."

Chapter 19

Anne had been through the ritual before, ten weeks earlier when Michael Harney died. One by one, as The Hawthorne Group employees arrived, they were told to report to conference room B. At nine-fifteen, Leo Muller entered the room. His face was grave, his demeanor sad, as he told them of "the second great tragedy to strike in our midst."

Mort Gordon, Muller explained, had left the office shortly after 2:00 A.M. On the street, he'd been confronted and shot to death. His wallet was stolen; robbery was the presumed motive. The police reported no witnesses to the crime.

Anne listened with the others. There was shock; several secretaries began to cry. At the end of his remarks, Muller announced that Gordon's closest relative was an aunt in Pennsylvania, and that most likely the body would be buried in Altoona. The Hawthorne Group would pay burial expenses, and assist in tying up loose ends. Then it was back to documents and computer files.

That night, rather than be alone, Anne had dinner with Amanda and Howard. She told them as much as she could about Gordon, but stopped short of revealing essential truths. Partly, that was because she'd pledged silence. And in part it was because she felt responsible for involving Gordon with Connor. If she told Amanda what she knew, and something happened . . .

Anne refused to finish the thought.

The rest of the week passed slowly at work. Thursday, on her way home from the office, Anne saw Connor sitting on a bench across the street from the St. Moritz. He waved as she approached, and stood up as she passed.

"How are you doing?"

"Not well," she answered.

"I wanted to make sure you were all right." Anne kept walking with the agent at her side. "You're still angry at me, aren't you?"

"Ned, what do you expect? You intrude; you lie; I'm scared half to death."

"I'm sorry. No one feels worse about Gordon than I do."

"I didn't know you had room for feelings."

"Feelings are facts, and I'm as vulnerable as the next person. But you have to remember the stakes involved."

"We've been through that, and I'm still scared."

"It doesn't matter. You have to maintain self-control. Anne, I'm not going to say this isn't dangerous. But think of the cause. Two million, five million, ten million lives. One bomb in New York City would equal the holocaust; genocide against millions of people simply because they're Americans. Control your fear. We need you for two weeks more."

At Columbus Circle, there were dozens of magazines on the sidewalk, spread out for sale by a homeless woman. *Time, Newsweek, Sports Illustrated, Playboy, Penthouse.* Neatly arranged; fifty cents each, except for the "adult" magazines, which were a dollar.

Anne and Connor walked in silence until finally the agent spoke.

"Last night, the CIA introduced a computer virus into The Hawthorne Group's computer network. It started in Japan and spread through Asia. By the time Matthes caught it, there was considerable damage."

"Does it make a difference?"

"In the long run, probably not; but we're doing everything we can to keep him off balance."

"Will you stop him?"

Connor shrugged. "I don't know. It's getting close. Sometimes I think we'd be better off if we had better people. In Israel, the cream of the crop goes to work for the Mossad. Here in the United States, the best and brightest become doctors, corporate executives, scientists, and lawyers. Very few Phi Beta Kappas become spies. Intelligence work requires close attention to detail. Care and vigilance are crucial to what we do. So what does government service get as an example? For eight years, we had a president who couldn't concentrate on any issue for more than half an hour, forgot the names of cabinet officials, and fell asleep at an audience with the Pope. He said he didn't remember when he learned American weapons were being traded for hostages; and if you take him at his word, he was unperturbed that illegal aid was funneled to the Contras in Nicaragua without his knowledge. Will we stop Matthes? I don't know.''

The homeless man across the street from Anne's apartment had a new shopping bag to hold his belongings. Connor reached into his pocket for some change, gave the man a quarter, and walked Anne to the awning. She said good night, went upstairs, and spent most of the evening thinking about Gordon. She wished David were there to comfort her. She wanted him back from his trial in Chicago. She felt isolated and lonely and, most of all, scared. Throughout her life, there'd been a constant assumption. She could screw up, do things wrong, but always there would be time to change. Now she realized that at any moment she could die. A bomb, a car accident, a bullet in the brain.

David's trial ended on Friday, and he flew back to New York in time for dinner. Saturday he and Anne went on a picnic with Amanda, Howard, and progeny. For most of the afternoon, Susan seemed bent on tormenting Ellen; then was surprised when Ellen flew into a rage.

''Ellen is the dumbest person I know. I don't lose my temper like she does.''

''No,'' Howard countered. ''You just make everybody else lose theirs.''

Anne couldn't stop thinking about Gordon. That

night, she tossed and turned in bed. "I'm sorry," she told David in the early hours of the morning.

"Do you want to talk about it?"

"Actually, I want to sleep, but I can't."

Sunday morning, reading the newspaper, she found herself looking at the obituaries. It depressed her to see people survived by a brother or sister or nephew but no children.

"David, I'm scared. I keep thinking about Mort Gordon and Michael Harney and what will happen if I die."

"You'll be all right."

"I want a will."

"Nothing is going to happen to you."

"You're a lawyer. Draw me a will. Please! I'll feel better if you do."

Resigned, David reached for a pad. "All right; tell me what you want, and I'll do it later at the office."

"I don't know. Where do I begin?"

"How much do you have in liquid assets?"

"Not much; maybe ten thousand dollars."

"And the apartment?"

"I own it outright; no mortgage."

"What's it worth?"

"Maybe three hundred thousand."

"What about life insurance, trust funds, other sources of income?"

"Just my job."

"Personal belongings—furniture, jewelry, things like that?"

"Only what's in the apartment."

"Okay; now we come to who gets what. What do you want done with your personal belongings?"

Anne sat silent, disconcerted by the thought. "I don't know."

"Take your time. You can think about it during the week, and let me know."

She shook her head. "I want Amanda to have my jewelry. Everything else, I want divided among my friends, including you."

"And the apartment?"

"Sell it."

"All right; next question. What do you want done with the rest of your assets? And remember, we're talking about a lot of money once the apartment is sold."

They worked out a formula, establishing a college trust fund for Susan, Ellen, and Jessica, with the remainder divided between Amanda and David. Then they went to an afternoon movie, and spent Sunday night at David's apartment.

"I feel like I belong with you," Anne said as they lay in bed beneath the covers.

"Me too."

"David, if I give you a key to my apartment, will you give me a key to yours?"

"Sure."

"That way, it would be easier to spend time together."

"I'd like that."

"Sleep well. I really love you."

The next day, Christoph Matthes was in the office. Otherwise, the morning was largely routine. Anne went to the bank, collated documents, and worked the paper shredder while Kurt Weber was at the duplicating machine. Then, at noon, the staff was called

291

together, and Matthes addressed them in conference room B.

"I know all of you are upset about Mr. Gordon. I share your grief, and assure you that his affairs will be well taken care of." For several minutes, Matthes talked about The Hawthorne Group as a family, and closed by introducing Gordon's replacement. "Paul Schmidt will assume the duties of night receptionist. I'm sure you will give him your fullest cooperation. And as in the past, for the good of the company, you must report any unusual occurrences to Mr. Muller or myself. By my presence, I trust you understand the importance of what I have just told you."

Schmidt was a large heavyset man in his late thirties, built like a professional athlete. Anne recognized him as one of the bodyguards she'd seen in the past accompanying Matthes. When the meeting ended, it was time for lunch, and she sat with Eric Winslow, who complained that the chicken salad wasn't up to par. Then she went back to her cubicle, and found herself staring at the calendar on her desk. It was Monday, August 14. August 24 was ten days off. A week and a half more. She could hold out for that long.

The documents she was indexing were more interesting than the norm, but working with them was still a chore. A little before four, she went to the kitchen, poured a cup of coffee, and returned to her cubicle. More documents, most of them dealing with Libyan oil. She was close to finishing for the day, when Leo Muller telephoned.

"Come to my office," he instructed.

Whatever it was, it had better not keep her past five-thirty. There was a limit to how much of The Hawthorne Group she could endure.

Muller was sitting behind his desk when Anne entered. She sat on command.

"You wanted to see me?"

"I wish to give you something," Muller answered. "The night that Mort Gordon died, I had occasion to talk with him before leaving the office. I always liked Mr. Gordon, and as I'm sure you know, he was quite fond of you. During our last conversation, he mentioned a necklace, one that once belonged to his grandmother. I believe he intended for it to be worn with a particular locket." Opening the middle drawer of his desk, Muller took out a brown paper bag. "After his death, this was found in Mr. Gordon's apartment. I'm certain he would have wanted it given to you."

Anne reached for the bag. Inside, there was a gold chain. Victorian, the same era as her locket. Not too heavy, but heavy enough. The clasp, in particular, caught her eye. It was oval shaped, hollow, sealed with a decorative gold overlay.

Anne's voice wavered. "Thank you," she said.

Then, fighting back tears, she left.

That night, she joined the chain with her locket. She wanted to wear it as a remembrance of Gordon. Too many thoughts were spinning in her head. Her nerves were raw. I don't want to die.

Then, in the morning, everything changed. Anne was in the office, beside the water cooler outside conference room A. Graham Hayes had just complimented her on her blouse, when the door to Christoph Matthes's office opened.

Matthes stood there, shaken and pale. His arrogance was gone. For the first time ever, Anne saw vulnerability in his eyes. She was directly in front of him, so he addressed her first.

"The authorities just called. Leo Muller is dead."

Chapter 20

Ned Connor sat on the sofa in Anne's apartment, the first time he'd been allowed in since removing the bugs. Ten hours earlier, Anne had learned that Muller was dead. Now Connor was telling her what he knew about the accident.

"It happened last night, in upstate New York. Muller was driving on the Taconic State Parkway, when he swerved out of control and jumped a divider. There was an oil truck; they collided. Muller's body was burned beyond recognition. We confirmed his identity through dental records this morning."

"What happens next?"

"Our people in Washington are considering options."

"Will his death make a difference?"

"Maybe; maybe not."

After Connor left, Anne went to David's apartment. She felt more secure next to him in bed.

Nine more days.

The following morning, Christoph Matthes addressed the office staff. Speaking with emotion, he extolled Muller's virtues and announced that, until a successor was chosen, he personally would supervise operations in New York. The atmosphere was one of shock. Three deaths in three months; the portents were ominous.

◆ ◆ ◆

Fort Meade, Maryland. Three P.M.

The dark blue sedan turned off the highway down a well-guarded asphalt road, moving slowly until it came to a halt. Adjusting the color-coded badge on his pocket, Ned Connor got out and crossed the yard. Closed-circuit cameras peered down from above. Infrared beams traversed the grounds. For years, the NSA had utilized a security system dependent on lights aimed at photoelectric cells. If a beam was obstructed, an alarm sounded. But then an intrusion analyst discovered that mirrors could be used to divert a beam while ultimately allowing it to reach its goal, and in the process spaces could be opened, enabling a potential intruder to pass without notice. Thus, a more complex system was installed—one that measured the time it took each beam to reach its sensor.

Connor entered the building at Gatehouse 1, where a guard examined the identification photo on his badge. Then he walked down a long corridor to another checkpoint, where the magnetic coding on his credentials was processed. Directly ahead, a cut-glass mosaic of the NSA seal dominated the wall. Twenty thousand pieces of polished glass, fashioned into an eagle with a key in its talons. Two more guards; another corridor. Then he came to a bank of elevators, entered one, and descended to the subbasement level. There, with two more guards watching, the agent rested his chin on a curved metal base and stared into what looked like an ophthalmologist's eyescope. As he did, an infrared beam passed through his right eye, and the image reflected by his fovea was processed. The resulting photo of blood vessels and retinal tissue was as distinctive as a fingerprint. Seconds later, a chime sounded, indicating that the microcomputer had matched his image with one in storage. Then he proceeded down one last corridor into a room the existence of which was known to only a few people.

Leo Muller sat in a chair. He'd been without sleep for fifty-eight hours. His eyes were glazed, but still defiant. A large man known as The Inquisitor stood over him.

"So far, we've been gentle," The Inquisitor was saying. "If necessary, we'll employ a more physical form of interrogation."

Muller sat still, and said nothing.

"Silence will only bring you pain. In the end, you'll be broken; that much I promise." Then The Inquisitor looked up and saw Connor. "I'm afraid Mr. Muller is exceedingly stubborn. Perhaps more extreme measures should be taken."

The agent nodded. "Do what you want. It's been authorized at the top."

''To what degree?''

''Start slowly. If necessary, torture him.''

◆ ◆ ◆

The rest of the week was oppressive in the office. Fear and tension hung in the air. Graham Hayes did his best to be cheerful, telling anecdotes at lunch about his son and daughter, but nothing he said could lift the clouds.

Thursday, August 17.

Friday, August 18.

Friday afternoon as Anne sat in her cubicle, the mechanics of quitting dominated her thoughts. After the weekend, there'd be four days to go. So what would she do on August 24? Give notice? Stay through Friday? Walk out of the office and never come back? Probably the latter. And what if Connor asked her to stay on? He hadn't so far. And if he did, she wouldn't. As of next Thursday, she'd done her job.

Friday after work, Anne went to David's apartment, where they exchanged keys, reminisced, and drank margaritas.

''When I was a boy,'' David recalled, ''my parents used to play a game with me called Booie. Whenever we traveled by car, each of us would look for station wagons, and whoever saw one first would get a point for hollering 'booie.' ''

''When I was five,'' Anne remembered, ''I wanted to be a writer. That seemed to me like a wonderful job. Then one day, Vicki Schwartz, the neighborhood bully, told me, 'You can't be a writer; you don't even know how to read.' ''

Midway through the evening, Anne asked about her will. David assured her that it was written and in his attaché case. On request, he took it out to be read. Sitting on the sofa, Anne held it to the light:

I, ANNE RHODES, of New York County, State of New York, make, publish, and declare this to be my Last Will and Testament, hereby revoking any and all other wills and codicils heretobefore made by me.

First: I give and bequeath to my friend Amanda Otis all of my jewelry. I give and bequeath all of my other personal belongings . . .

"All right," she said when the reading was done. "What do I do now to make it official?"

A middle-aged couple lived across the hall. David knocked on their door, and asked if they'd act as witnesses. They agreed, and he guided them through the signing. Then he and Anne went back to his apartment.

"I'm glad that's over."

"Me too," she said. "And remember, if something goes wrong, Connor owes me a million dollars."

◆ ◆ ◆

Saturday morning. Five A.M.

After five days without sleep, Muller was talking. As he spoke, computers analyzed photos of his eyes taken at thirty-two frames per second. Twelve hours earlier, sodium pentathol had been injected into a vein in his arm. The drug disconnected pain centers and destroyed inhibitions. He'd begun to talk, but details and complexities were blurred. Accordingly, when the drug wore off, a new round of questions began. Thick polygraph belts were strapped to his chest and blood pressure pads tied to his arms. Voice prints were monitored.

"He knows where the bombs are," The Inquisitor told Connor. "And probably he knows how and when they'll be shipped, but he's a tough bastard. So far, he hasn't given us much."

"How do you read him?"

"I think we can break him, given enough time."

"Time is the problem. I'm afraid we'll have to bring in The Man."

Computer tapes silently turned. Polygraph needles swayed back and forth. Left alone for a moment, Muller closed his eyes; then opened them at a gentle tap on his nose.

A man in his thirties stood looking down. He was narrow-shouldered, with a thin chest, flat stomach, and small hands. Five foot ten, with an expressionless face and neatly pressed casual clothes.

"My name is irrelevant," The Man said. "You will think of me as a bad dream, but in time you will realize I'm worse than a nightmare because I'm real."

Then his hands moved, and Muller's nose exploded, split to the bone with blood pouring down.

Muller shrieked. And then, as quickly as the cry came, it was gone, and he stared at his tormentor with hate-filled eyes.

"We'll start with pain," The Man said calmly. "Then we will move to maximum pain. And if that doesn't work, we'll try mutilation. In the end, you'll tell me what I want to know.''

"I'll die first."

"But we won't let you, Mr. Muller. Dead, you are of absolutely no use to us. So why don't you spare yourself the pain and tell me what I want to know."

♦ ♦ ♦

Saturday night. Anne and David lay in bed.

"Are you sure it's all right if I don't put my diaphragm in?"

"Positive."

"And we're getting married?"

"With an autumn wedding. If people can get used to wearing contact lenses, I can get used to a wedding ring."

Anne smiled and slid into David's arms, thinking people were crazy because, with pleasure like this in the world for the taking, how could anyone choose to make bombs.

And then she realized her fears were intruding. And try as she might, she couldn't banish them from her thoughts.

"What's the matter?"

"I'm sorry; I was thinking about Matthes."

"It will be over soon."

"David, if something happens to me, if there's a heaven, I'll be waiting there for you."

"Don't talk like that. Nothing is going to happen to you."

"I'm sorry; it's what I feel. But it's important to me that you understand, I love you."

◆ ◆ ◆

Sunday morning. Ten A.M.

Leo Muller sat strapped to a chair with blood pouring from countless wounds. His head sagged; his eyes were vacant.

"Tell me about the necklace," The Man demanded.

"In the clasp . . . transmitter . . . monitor the girl."

"How long has the transmitter been in operation?"

"Gordon dead . . . insert radio . . . girl in office."

"What have you learned from monitoring Miss Rhodes?"

An ugly rattle escaped Muller's lips. His eyes grew wide. "I'm dying," he whispered.

"I'm afraid that's right."

"Help me."

"It's too late."

Connor leaned forward.

"He's dead," The Man said.

"Shit."

"I'm sorry. I thought I could push him a little more. Did we get enough?"

"Maybe," the agent answered.

"Where do we stand?"

"From what we got, there are thirteen bombs in the Hudson Valley. Twelve are scheduled for shipment on Thursday. No two are stored at the same location, and if Matthes is thwarted, the last warhead automatically detonates."

"Can you find the bombs?"

"Not now, but my guess is, Matthes will bring twelve of them together for shipment. That means our biggest problem will be number thirteen."

"What you're saying then is, we can't stop Matthes. He's got the last bomb, and unless we find it, he's safe."

Connor nodded. "I can find it, I think."

Chapter 21

Sunday in Manhattan.

Anne spent the day with David at his apartment, sheltered from the heat, isolated from the world. At least, for the moment, she felt protected. They read the newspaper, talked, listened to records. Under different circumstances, it would have been a pleasant Sunday.

Late in the afternoon, the telephone rang. David picked up the receiver. "Hello? . . . Just a minute; who's calling? . . ." Then he turned toward Anne. "It's for you; it's Connor."

Anne made a face, and took the receiver. "Ned, what do you want? . . . I can't; I'm busy . . . All right; five minutes."

She looked toward David. "He says it's urgent; he wants me for five minutes. I'll go downstairs if you don't want him in the apartment."

"Either way."

Anne turned her attention back to the telephone. "All right, you can come up . . . What difference does it make if David is here? If I see you alone, whatever you tell me, I'm telling him anyway."

Moments later, Connor was at the door. David let him in, and led him to the sofa. He'd seen the agent once before—at the Fourth of July fireworks. Connor had doubtless seen him many times. They eyed each other with studied politeness; then the agent looked at Anne and smiled.

"You're wearing your locket again."

"Yes."

"When was the chain fixed?"

"Someone gave me a new one. Ned, just say what you have to say, and make it good because all you have is four more days of my life."

"All right, try this on for size. Leo Muller is alive."

Anne's face registered shock. "I don't understand."

"That's what I wanted to talk to you about. I decided, since you're in this, you have a right to know what's happening. But we're at a crucial point, and if Matthes finds out, we could lose everything."

David shifted uncomfortably on the sofa. Ignoring his presence, Connor went on.

"Muller was arrested last week. We picked him up, put him in solitary, and staged the accident so Matthes wouldn't know what was happening. All the rest—the body, dental records, the truck—was bullshit. For the past six days, we've been questioning Muller. He's stubborn, a good soldier; but bit by bit, we're breaking him down. He knows where the bombs are; all thirteen. Shipment is scheduled for

305

this Thursday night. We're fairly certain he'll crack before then."

"And then what happens?"

"Once we know where the bombs are, we strike; a simultaneous assault against all thirteen targets. The only way we fail is if Matthes moves the bombs before we get to them."

"You make it sound easy."

"It's not. It's scary, because everything we do now is predicated on breaking Muller and getting into position for a Thursday morning strike."

"And suppose Muller doesn't break?"

"Under the circumstances, we're prepared to use extreme measures."

"What does that mean?"

"Torture."

Anne was growing increasingly nervous. "How are these things structured in Washington?"

"You don't have to know that."

"You're very good at what you do, aren't you?"

"I try."

Too many things were converging in her mind . . . Harney . . . Gordon . . . Muller . . . Hiroshima . . .

"When this is over, you'll be a hero, won't you?"

"Only if we win," Connor answered.

"And if you lose?"

"They'll give me a pretty hard time in heaven, but eventually they'll let me in."

Anne sat silent on the sofa, digesting everything she'd heard. "Is there anything else?" she asked at the end.

"I don't think so. We're going down to the wire on this one. But one way or the other, on Thursday you're done."

Two hours later, Connor was back in Maryland, recounting his visit to New York for representatives of every military intelligence organization in Washington. "That should get Matthes moving," he told them.

◆ ◆ ◆

The air was warm; dusk had fallen. Forty miles east of New York Harbor, the oil tanker *Pegasus* idled above the continental shelf. Nothing in its design distinguished the ship from a thousand other tankers built to transport petroleum. Columbus, Magellan, Balboa, the Spanish Armada. For centuries, nations rose and fell in accord with what transpired upon the oceans. Yet from the beginning of time, no ship had carried a cargo more deadly than that scheduled to be loaded into the *Pegasus*'s front hold. It was to be a small cargo. A dozen crates, each one weighing several thousand pounds. Hardly noticeable on a ship with five decks and six cargo holds— a vessel twelve hundred feet long with a deadweight of 260,000 tons.

Christoph Matthes stood on the tanker's bridge, one hundred feet above the water. Two bodyguards were at his side. The ship's captain stood close behind. Like the rest of his officers, the captain was European. The crew was Asian. The vessel flew under a Panamanian flag.

"We've had a slight change of plans," Matthes told the men around him. "Instead of August twenty-fourth, the cargo will arrive in thirty-six hours."

"Will there be any other changes?"

"Perhaps one more crate; a baker's dozen."

The captain retired to the middle deck.

Matthes looked out over the ocean. Several minutes passed; then he spoke again, addressing one of the bodyguards beside him.

"Tomorrow night, I would like you to kill David Akers. I myself will eliminate the woman."

Connor sat in an underground bunker at Andrews Air Force Base in Maryland. The walls were cinder block, painted hospital green. The men with him were the ultimate decision makers. As the director of the nation's Nuclear Emergency Search Team spoke, the others listened. For six months, NEST had combed every northern and middle Atlantic state. "We were unsuccessful," the director concluded. "Even with ultrasensitive neutron and gamma ray detectors, we were unable to locate any of the bombs."

One at a time, the men around the table spoke. The hours passed. Finally, it was Connor's turn.

"I've been living with this crisis for a long time," he began. "I've lost several friends, and made a few others. I feel like I know Christoph Matthes well, although the truth is, I've never met him. Regardless, I suppose the threshold question is whether Matthes will move all thirteen bombs. I hope he does; I think he will. His original plan was to sell twelve bombs and leave one behind as an insurance policy. But because of disinformation passed to him through Miss Rhodes, he has to be concerned we'll find number thirteen before the others are delivered;

and if we do, his insurance becomes worthless. So my guess is, Matthes will ship the insurance bomb with the others. Thirteen bombs will bring him more money than twelve. And that leads to the ultimate questions: where are the bombs, and how will they be transported? According to what we've learned so far, they're spread throughout the Hudson Valley. Matthes could fly them out on small planes or remove them by truck, but at some point he has to get them across the ocean, and most likely he'll do that by water. So why not assume he'll bring the bombs down the Hudson River? That's a guess on my part; a little like going to the beach and looking for a sliver of glass; maybe you have to step on it to find it. He could ship the bombs out of Boston Harbor or from some inlet off the coast of Maine, but my instincts say no. I think that very soon, before August twenty-fourth, a cargo of atomic bombs will be floating down the Hudson River. Our job is to find them once all the bombs are together. And then comes the dangerous part—we have to secure control before one of the bombs explodes.''

Chapter 22

Monday, August 21.

Anne arrived at the office at nine o'clock. On the surface, everything seemed normal. Most of the executives were at their desks. Kurt Weber was operating the paper shredder. Each secretary was in the appropriate cubicle.

Soon after she arrived, Ernst Neumann gave Anne a stack of documents with instructions to enter them in the image-processing file system. She went to the kitchen for a cup of coffee, then to the computer room, where she began the job. Four more days, she told herself. Less than that, if she was counting by the hour. On Thursday afternoon at 5:30 P.M., she was walking out and never coming back.

The documents dealt mostly with the purchase and sale of oil. Anne didn't have to read them as she filed, just feed them into the scanner one at a time. An hour after she started, she was interrupted by Eric Winslow, who sent her to the bank to make a deposit. Then Hans Werner borrowed her for another chore. Late in the morning, she returned to filing, and worked until one of Matthes's bodyguards appeared in the doorway.

"Mr. Matthes would like to see you," he instructed.

Whatever Matthes wanted, Anne assured herself, it was unlikely he'd shoot her on the twenty-third floor of Trump Tower. Following the bodyguard down the corridor, she took a deep breath and entered the corner office. Matthes was standing by the window, looking down at Fifth Avenue. He turned and gestured for her to sit.

"I thought perhaps you would like to have lunch with me today."

She couldn't plead other plans, because employees were on call from nine to five-thirty.

"That's lovely, but I promised Ernst Neumann I'd finish a job this—"

Before the sentence was complete, Matthes waved her off. "I'm sure Ernst won't mind if we go out for an hour or two. And should he object, I will speak to him on your behalf."

It was a command performance.

"Perhaps you would like to go now."

Anne nodded, and Matthes led her down the corridor, through the office reception area to the elevators. Two bodyguards followed as they went through the lobby, out onto Fifth Avenue, where a black limousine was parked at the curb. The lead bodyguard stepped forward to open the door. Anne got in back with Matthes beside her. Both body-guards sat in front with the driver.

Down Fifth Avenue.

West onto 51st Street.

"Where are we going?" Anne asked.

"You'll find out shortly," Matthes told her.

Between Sixth and Seventh Avenues, the limousine stopped. One of the bodyguards opened the rear door. Matthes got out. Anne followed, and looked up at the awning that stretched toward the curb. Black letters on gold: Le Bernardin.

This might not be so bad after all. Maybe Matthes was simply exercising the prerogative that powerful people have of attracting who they want into their lives.

Through the revolving door into the restaurant.

The bodyguards remained outside.

As Matthes entered, the maître d' nodded in recognition and led the way to a corner table. The room was large, unpretentious, and comfortable, with a teak ceiling and blue-gray walls. Once they were seated, the captain approached, and Matthes asked to see the wine list.

"Will you join me?" he queried, turning toward Anne.

She might as well. "Yes, thank you."

"A bottle of 1983 Haut-Brion Blanc," he instructed.

Soon after, the captain returned, opened the bottle, and poured. Matthes examined his glass for color, swirled, and tasted.

"Very good; thank you."

Then menus. Appetizers: a choice of slivers of black bass with basil and coriander; carpaccio of tuna; tartar of cured and raw salmon; seared oysters with caviar; broiled shrimp with parsley-shallot butter . . . And main courses: sea scallops with sorrel and tomatoes; sautéed filets of pompano with a parsley coulis; rouelle of salmon with fennel julienne; black sea bass with zucchini, tomatoes, and basil . . .

They ordered, and Anne surveyed the room. Most of the patrons were quite well dressed. She wished she'd had notice to prepare for the occasion. Trying to relax, she sipped her wine.

"I'm reading a book about Albert Einstein," Matthes told her. "He was a truly remarkable man."

Anne wasn't sure how to respond. The remark seemed introductory to a more elaborate thought, and as expected, Matthes went on.

"Voltaire once said that Isaac Newton was the most fortunate scientist of all time, because it was his destiny to discover the basic laws which rule the universe. However, I hold a contrary view. Newton's equations, theoretically applied, could allow the universe to run backward as well as forward in time. Thus, a fully grown tree could become a sapling and then a seed. A butterfly could turn into a caterpillar; you or I could become a child. Einstein, I believe, was more theoretically pure."

"I'm not sure I understand."

"That's quite all right. Einstein was on a level higher than us all. When he died in 1955, his brain was removed for scientific study, but the anatomists could not agree on how to dissect it. Finally it passed into the possession of a pathologist, who performed the examination, learned essentially nothing, and stored the organ on a shelf in a glass jar. It's tragic, of course, that so brilliant a man had to die, but all of us grow old and die in the end. Death is simply an obligation each of us owes in return for the gift of life.''

Good restaurant, bad company, Anne decided. The service was attentive and the food a delight, from her seared oyster appetizer to the millefeuille with green apples for dessert. But the cost was too high; not the prix fixe, but being with Matthes. Even if she could let go of her fear, they weren't having a conversation; she was listening to him pontificate.

''The pyramids of Egypt represent an extraordinary accomplishment; an entire society massed for decades to build a grave. Unlike the pyramids, which were made of limestone and granite, the pharaoh's palaces were constructed from mud bricks, which explains why none remain today . . .''

When the meal was done, Matthes signaled for the check. Anne glanced at the numbers. The wine had been $150. With food, tax, and tip, the total was $300.

''Thank you,'' she said. ''The food was wonderful.''

Then they left.

The bodyguards were standing by the limousine at the curb. As before, Anne got in back next to Matthes; the guards in front beside the driver. The car turned south onto Seventh Avenue, then east on 50th Street. Anne expected that the driver would turn again, up Sixth Avenue to 57th Street, then east and let them out in front of Trump Tower.

Except instead, the limousine kept going along 50th Street past Fifth Avenue.

Anne tensed. ''Where are we going?''

"A brief diversion," Matthes answered.

At Third Avenue, they turned north; then east once more onto 61st Street, edging through traffic to the FDR Drive. Anne could feel the fear in her stomach. For a moment, she thought she might throw up.

"Where are we going?" she asked again.

"For a short ride. I'm sure you'll enjoy it."

Traffic was heavy on the FDR Drive. No one spoke. Matthes gazed out a tinted glass window. North of Manhattan, the limousine turned onto the Bruckner Expressway, then the Bronx River Parkway, and finally, after twenty miles, onto the Taconic. At Poughkeepsie, they passed a large green sign with white block letters that read:

STATE POLICE
TROOP K HEADQUARTERS
NEXT RIGHT

Then the road narrowed to asphalt strips on either side of a metal divider, before broadening again to concrete lanes separated by a long grass stripe. Small dead animals littered the road. The wildflowers of late summer were in bloom.

"It's rather amusing," Matthes said, breaking the silence that had lasted for an hour.

He seemed to expect some sort of response.

"What's amusing?" Anne asked.

"Words; the English language. Take violets, for example. The violet is such a beautiful flower. But add one letter—a simple *n*—and 'violet' becomes 'violent.' Don't you find that amusing?"

"Not really."

315

"Oh, well; perhaps we have things other than humor in common."

She was being tested. And whatever else was happening, two things were for sure—they weren't going upstate to an orchard to pick apples; and there wasn't much Anne could do about the situation except hope, wait, and look out the window.

Small farms dotted the landscape. Bales of hay stood in the fields. The road was marked by old stone bridges, deer crossing signs, and falling rock zones. Flies and mosquitoes began to accumulate on the windshield. New York City was far behind. Two hours after leaving Manhattan, they exited from the Taconic Parkway onto Route 203.

"Where are we going?" Anne asked for the third time.

Again, Matthes didn't respond.

"Am I a prisoner?"

"A prisoner? What a silly notion, Miss Rhodes."

The limousine turned onto a badly paved road, and entered a village with small stores and aging homes.

"This is Chatham," Matthes told her. "Once, it was a thriving railroad town, but the railroad died. Now the people face economic ruin."

They drove through the town, onto a narrow dirt road. Then, suddenly, the limousine stopped.

No one spoke.

Several minutes passed.

Anne could hear a vehicle behind them, approaching on the road they'd just traveled. Then a small van came into view.

With textbook precision, the bodyguards got out of the limousine. Matthes followed. One of the guards pulled Anne from the back. The van halted; a side door opened. Seconds later, Anne, Matthes, and both guards were inside. Then the van was moving again. No one had said a word.

Finally, Anne spoke. "Why are we doing this?"

"A simple precaution in case we were followed," Matthes told her.

"I don't understand."

"I think you do."

There were no windows in the back of the van. A solitary light bulb dangled from above. Matthes stood, hunched over because the ceiling was low. Anne and the guards sat on the floor beside a wood-slatted crate with a General Electric logo printed on top.

The road was uneven. The van needed new shocks . . . Five minutes . . . Ten . . . Anne looked at her watch; 3:35 P.M. One of the bodyguards took off his jacket, revealing a shoulder holster and gun. Matthes reached into a pocket for a handkerchief, and ran it gently across his brow. Anne's blouse was wet with sweat. The second guard closed his eyes, just for a moment, then opened them again.

At 3:45, the van came to a halt. The guards got out first. Matthes and Anne followed. They were standing at the edge of the Hudson River, by a gravel pit in an abandoned railroad yard. Four men Anne had never seen before rolled a forklift to the van, and with considerable effort, began removing the crate.

And then Anne realized she was standing next to a bomb.

One of the guards led her to the river, where a rotting pier abutted the railroad yard. A tugboat and garbage scow were moored nearby. Straining, the men loaded the crate onto the scow, then covered it with a thin layer of garbage.

Matthes moved to Anne's side. "It's really rather remarkable," he told her. "Before the night is done, there will be twelve more pieces of cargo on board."

"Why have you brought me here?"

There was no answer.

"I'd like to leave."

"I'm afraid that won't be possible, Miss Rhodes. Now, please, the tugboat is preferable to the garbage scow. I would like you to join me for the journey home."

The journey home; whatever that meant. The workmen around them were finishing their job. Flanked by guards, Anne boarded the tug. It was larger than she thought a tugboat would be. Forty yards long, with an open deck encircling the cabin, galley, and bunks below. Ropes thicker than a man's fist bound it to the garbage scow. One of the crewmen—balding, heavyset, with what appeared to be a glass eye—signaled, and the engine roared. Then the link ropes tightened; the tug strained and pulled away from the pier.

"The crew has been instructed not to speak with you," Matthes said, drawing to Anne's side. "Other than that, I think you will find conditions on the boat to be to your liking."

"Why are you doing this?"

There was no response.

Play the scene the way Connor wrote it. Except Connor didn't write this one.

"What are you going to do with me?"

"Do with you, Miss Rhodes? I don't understand.

First, we lunched at Le Bernardin, and now I am taking you on a pleasant river cruise.''

''Why?''

''For entertainment. And as a precaution. Now, if you will excuse me, I have work to do. And please, don't try to leave the ship. The crewmen have been instructed to kill you if you do.''

There it was. And with what Anne knew, it was hard to believe Matthes would let her live, but maybe he would. After all, once the bombs were shipped, killing her would be an act of vengeance, nothing more. There'd be no harm to Matthes in letting her go, because Connor and God knows how many other agents knew what she knew. So why blow it? Why say what she was about to say, when nothing good could come from it at all?

''Matthes!''

He looked up, surprised at the use of his last name alone. ''Yes, Miss Rhodes?''

''Whatever happens to me, if what I've done these past few months help stop you, it will have been worth it.''

''Those are honorable sentiments, but I'm afraid you won't stop me, Miss Rhodes. You see, the scow we're towing is capable of carrying roughly six hundred tons, and each bomb weighs less than a thousand pounds. Encased in lead, covered with garbage, they will go completely unnoticed on a scow this size.''

''A lot of people will be looking for you.''

''Precisely; and by the time they come, the bombs will be gone. Now, again, I beg your forgiveness, but I have work to do.''

Minutes later, the tug docked once more, this time

at an abandoned quarry north of Alsen. The man with the glass eye led four crewmen onto land, where a large wooden crate lay surrounded by broken rocks and slag. Grunting, straining, they loaded the cargo onto the scow. Bomb number two. Eleven to go. Then again, Anne heard the roar of the engine, and the tug moved to the center of the river.

The mighty Hudson, peaceful and serene, Beautiful with a hint of wilderness—the way the world ought to be. Mountains and hills stood silhouetted against the sky, worn by erosion until they'd become rounded and smooth. An occasional sailboat drifted by, as the river curved gracefully on its voyage to the sea. Virgin forests lined the shore, interspersed with man-made scars. The late-afternoon sun cast shadows across the water. Moving downriver, the scow acquired momentum of its own. Only when the tug changed pace and direction did it yield, grudgingly, to the captain at the helm.

At a paper mill in Germantown, the third bomb came on board.

An abandoned cement plant gave birth to number four. Little was said among the crewmen as they worked. Clearly, their mission had been meticulously planned.

As dusk fell Anne left the deck and went inside. A fire extinguisher and first-aid kit were mounted on the cabin wall. Above them, a sign with red letters warned:

Federal Acts prohibit the deposit of any sludge, garbage, or refuse of any kind into any navigable water of the United States or its tributaries. Any person or persons violating these laws may be subjected to a fine of not more than $2,500 or up to one year imprisonment or both.

But nothing about shipping atomic bombs.

Most of the crew was in the galley. Anne went in and looked around. Two of the deckhands were playing cards. The rest were seated at a Formica-topped table, eating boiled beef, mashed potatoes, and carrots. The galley was cleaner than she'd thought it would be, with metal cabinets, a refrigerator, sink, and stove. Anne asked for a glass of water, and one of the crewmen gave it to her.

"Would you like coffee?"

"No, thank you," she answered.

She was scared and felt claustrophobic inside. She didn't want to be there, and went out onto the deck once more. The Kingston Bridge loomed above. The tug passed beneath it, and continued on.

Bomb number five was brought on board at Port Ewen. Number six was loaded in Eddyville as darkness fell.

"I trust you are enjoying the river, Miss Rhodes."

As the tugboat approached the Roosevelt mansion at Hyde Park, Matthes's voice interrupted Anne's thoughts.

She stared at the water and did her best to ignore him.

"You would be wise to look at me when I speak to you, my dear. If not, I won't hesitate to kill you."

She turned and looked at Matthes as ordered.

"That's better. I would hate to shoot you in a moment of pique. After all, it would be sad if your fate were determined by anger or whim."

"What do you want from me?"

"I'm not quite sure. For your own well-being, I believe caution would be advisable; although perhaps it's too late for caution now. I would also like deference, obedience, and understanding."

"Understanding of what?"

"The world as it is, rather than the fantasies you dream. You view life as an actress, but acting is an art; and like other arts, it cannot improve, it can only change. Science, by contrast, is constantly improving. Take weaponry, for example. In the beginning, there were two weapons—sticks and stones. The sticks were clubs; stones could be thrown. Then knives, spears, and slings were invented, followed by the bow and arrow. In the thirteenth century, the Chinese invented gunpowder. I could go on, but suffice it to say, splitting the atom for purposes of weaponry represents thousands of years' worth of effort and knowledge. There are those who say that nature is telling us something; that the horror of nuclear weapons requires an end to war. And perhaps they are right, but I'm not in a position to make that judgment. I can only appreciate the fact that nuclear weapons are a marvelous showcase for man's talents, the end product of enormous scientific genius and cooperation."

"You're not motivated by notions of science. You're a madman playing a game you can't win."

"Nor can you win it, Miss Rhodes."

◆ ◆ ◆

Manhattan. Eight-thirty P.M.

For the tenth time in two hours, David picked up the telephone and dialed Anne's number.

322

Ring after ring after ring.

No answer.

Stay calm; be cool. Probably, there was nothing wrong. After all, Anne went out all the time for drinks with friends. She could be at a museum, or with Connor, or having dinner with Amanda. Still, it bothered him that she hadn't called to say where she was. Exchanging keys and spending nights together didn't mean monitoring every moment of each other's time. But with three days left until August 24, given what had happened to Harney and Gordon—

The thought was intolerable. David pushed it down. But it kept coming back—the image of Anne on the floor of her bedroom, with blood seeping onto the carpet from her brain.

Use the keys. Dispel the fear.

So around nine o'clock, David took Anne's keys, rode the elevator downstairs, and went over to her apartment to make sure everything was all right.

Chapter 23

The night was clear. Countless stars shone over black domed hills. The Hudson flowed as it had for millions of years, an arm of the sea thrusting inland with the tide. At Poughkeepsie, the seventh bomb was raised from the depths of an abandoned silver mine. Number eight was loaded on board at Milton; the ninth at a bend in the river near Marlboro.

Anne stood on the deck and watched it all. South of Newburgh, the river narrowed and the Hudson highlands rose toward the sky. Tears were welling up in her eyes. Don't cry. Just get out of this alive. She could jump overboard, make an effort to swim for shore, but someone would shoot her before she got very far. Wait; let time unfold. Everything now was out of her hands.

The wind from the river was beginning to chill.

Anne left the deck and went into the galley, followed by the man with the glass eye. One of Matthes's bodyguards was playing solitaire. A deckhand was eating M&Ms. Anne watched as he poured color-coated chocolates into his hand—red, green, orange, yellow, brown. She wanted to ask if he knew what he was doing; if he understood the cargo they had on board. But Matthes had said the crew had been forbidden to talk with her, and besides, it was too late to influence them now.

At Cornwall, the tenth bomb was loaded onto the scow. Number eleven, a mile farther on. Once again, Anne went onto the deck. The motor and sound of the water were all she heard. Kerosene lamps burned on the scow. The moon rose higher, and Matthes approached as he'd done before. He looked out of place, dressed in a tailored British suit, silk shirt, and tie. And Anne despised him, hated him for what he'd done, what he was doing, and for putting her in a cage. She hated the feeling of being trapped, not being in control, being subject to his whim.

"It won't be long now," Matthes said, looking out over the water. "All that remain are two more bombs. Then we'll proceed to New York Harbor."

"What happens then?"

"The bombs will be transferred to a tanker under my command. Perhaps you will live; maybe you will die."

"I don't want to die."

"Neither do I."

"You're selling death."

"Perhaps; but the weapons trade has a long tradition. It began in Belgium at the end of the Middle Ages. Did you know that? In Liège, near where I was born. Coal and iron were in ample supply, and the local craftsmen were technologically skilled. Rivers and roads facilitated exportation. By the seventeenth century, Liège was producing one hundred thousand weapons a year."

"Is that supposed to justify what you're doing?"

Matthes shrugged, accentuating the gesture with his hands. "Perhaps you find my activities indecent because I'm engaged in the sale of a particular type of weapon. But nuclear or otherwise, all weapons are the same. The mother in Lebanon whose daughter has been killed by an American-made mortar; the eight-year-old in Iraq whose family had been wiped out by napalm dropped from a British-made plane. These people suffer just as much as the victims of any nuclear bomb."

"It's not the same."

"Perhaps not in degree—the number of people killed—but the principle is alike. No nation wishes to end the weapons trade. They simply want to control it for profit and their own geopolitical ends. Do you know which country is the world's largest manufacturer and exporter of arms? The United States. Imagine, if you will, walking through a supermarket for arms. They exist all over your beloved country. In Virginia, there is a privately owned warehouse with floor space equivalent to a suburban shopping mall. In that warehouse, at any given time, a half million instruments of death are for sale—bazookas, grenades, submachine guns, artillery shells—enough to supply a respectable army. The Americans who sell arms for profit don't care who their weapons kill. And when your government sends guns, tanks, and missiles to other countries, those weapons are used to kill people, Miss Rhodes. Forty nations supplied arms for the Iran-Iraq conflict. In Europe alone, a million jobs in the military-industrial sector were tied to that war. One hundred billion dollars worth of weaponry was sold by the powers that be to Baghdad and Tehran. So don't condemn me; it's mankind that is damaged. I'm a neutral businessman, that's all."

"You're not selling ordinary weapons. You're threatening the world with atomic bombs."

"You fail to understand; all weapons are the same. And what American scientists learned in 1945, the Soviets, British, and French learned soon after. Is there any doubt in your mind that, regardless of what I do, the third world will become nuclear-armed? What nature tells one group of men, she will tell in time to all those who are patient enough to learn."

"You're a horrible man."

"To the contrary; I'm simply a wise one. I understand that there are one billion operable handguns in the world, and that rulers have an unquenchable thirst for more. And I understand that mankind has cancer; a terminal case, if you will. In this century alone, the pathology has gone out of control in Germany, Cambodia, and Uganda. So I'll stand by my conduct as I have always stood, willing to accept the judgment of history on the merits of my cause."

◆ ◆ ◆

David opened the door, turned on the lights, and stepped into the foyer of Anne's apartment. No one was there. There was no sign of violence; no dead bodies in any of the rooms. Probably Anne would be home within the hour. She'd laugh at how he overreacted, and in a few days, they'd put The Hawthorne Group behind them. Except it was getting late and David didn't know where she was.

At nine o'clock, he telephoned Amanda. "Nothing important, I just wondered if Anne was there with you and Howard."

She wasn't.

Who else could she be with? Connor? One of her theater friends? Someone he didn't know at all?

David turned on the television, turned it off, and went to the kitchen for a glass of water. For all he knew, Anne could be trying to call him at his apartment. If that were so, sooner or later, she'd be home.

Ten o'clock.

Something was wrong. He could feel it. He wished Anne would come home. Maybe he should get in touch with Connor.

Collins Communications.

It took a couple of minutes for David to locate the New York telephone directory in one of Anne's closets. Collins Communications wasn't listed. What now? Maybe the number was somewhere in the apartment. Eventually, he found it on the desk, dialed, and a man answered.

"Hello, this is David Akers. I'd like to speak with Ned Connor."

"I'm sorry. Mr. Connor is unavailable."

"It's important."

"I'm sorry. He's unavailable."

The man hung up.

Ten-thirty. Maybe Anne had gone to a show on

Broadway, then out with a friend for something to eat afterward.

Eleven o'clock. Thank God, a key was turning in the door.

David rose from the sofa and went to the foyer to greet Anne just as the door opened.

I've been worried sick about you.

That's what he was ready to say, but what came out instead was, "Who are you?"

The man in front of him was short and heavy, with pock-marked cheeks and sunken eyes. A small scar ran to the edge of his lips. A skeleton key protruded from his grasp. And then David realized that, regardless of what had happened to Anne, his own life was about to end.

All he saw was the knife.

"I've been tracking you for twelve hours, Mr. Akers; waiting for the moment when everything seemed right."

The blade of the knife was coming toward him.

React, a voice inside screamed.

Nothing happened. David stood frozen.

The space between the two men narrowed. Slowly, the assassin raised his arm.

And then, in the doorway, there was another man; one with filthy clothes, a shaggy beard, and grimy unkempt hair. For months, David had seen him, homeless on the sidewalk, across the street from Anne's apartment. Except he wasn't moving like a homeless person anymore. He was agile, steady, and best of all, there was a gun in his hand.

The point of the knife was at David's throat.

The homeless man fired.

Blood and fragments of bone splattered. And people could talk all they wanted to about nuclear weapons, but as far as David was concerned, pistols were fantastic, and the proof of that was the assassin lying dead on the floor.

Now the homeless man was talking, not to David, but into a walkie-talkie. Everything was a blur, a jumble of sound. Too much was happening.

"Where's Anne?" David demanded.

"You'll know soon."

"Is she alive?"

Again, voices were coming over the walkie-talkie.

"I asked you a question. Is Anne alive?"

"Yes, and we're trying to keep it that way."

"What's happening?"

"Look, I don't have time for questions. I just saved your life, so cool it, please."

"Where is she?"

The homeless man's face showed a mixture of impatience and resignation. "All right; come with me, and we'll watch this together. But I'm warning you— do what you're told, and keep your mouth shut when it's over."

◆ ◆ ◆

Anne looked at her watch. It was eleven o'clock. Later than she thought; she'd lost track of time. She was tired; a physical and emotional numbness, brought on by tension, the hour, and the night air. The sweep of the river carried the tug and scow along, past the gray stone cathedrals of West Point and Highland Falls. At Peekskill, the twelfth bomb was retrieved from a quarry, where granite had been mined for the Cathedral of St. John the Divine. Then the river widened, veered west, and the highlands disappeared, replaced by low rolling hills. Occasional automobile headlights shone in the night, marking the highway that meandered near the shore. No one on board the tugboat slept. If anything, the crew seemed more alert than before.

At North Tarrytown, near Sleepy Hollow, they docked for the last time. The man with the glass eye seemed more involved than before, giving orders as the final bomb was loaded onto the scow. Anne watched, and felt anger mixed with apprehension and fear. Thirteen bombs; each one on board. She couldn't help wondering where Connor was. Would he swoop down from the sky like an eagle to save her? Did he even know where she was? And David. God willing, she'd see David again. David, who'd never questioned the risk to his own life; who'd come to her side the moment she needed help, never weighing the cost of becoming involved.

The Tappan Zee Bridge rose above, like an Erector Set structure fashioned by a giant child. Oil storage drums dotted the east bank. To the west, the cliffs of the Palisades began, an open book on the making of the land.

Then, in the distance like a faraway mountain, Anne saw the lights of Manhattan in the night. The Empire State Building with its spire turned gold, the World Trade Center shimmering like thousands of tiny sequins, the entire skyline framed by the George Washington Bridge. Standing on the deck, she stared like a tourist. The greatest city in the world. And it could all be obliterated in a matter of seconds if the commander of a tugboat and garbage scow so chose.

◆ ◆ ◆

A dark blue sedan was waiting at the curb when the homeless man and David reached the street.

"Get in back."

David did as ordered.

The homeless man got in front next to the driver. There were no introductions.

"Where's the tug?" the homeless man demanded.

"Twenty miles upriver. It should intersect with the bridge in about three hours."

The car moved north along Central Park to the nineties, then swung west onto the Henry Hudson Highway.

"Where's Anne?" David asked again.

"Your part of the bargain was to keep quiet."

As before, David fell silent. In the presence of these men, he felt like a child.

"She's on a boat with Matthes," the homeless man added, softening his voice as they drove through the night. "It's dangerous; we're doing the best we can."

The car left the highway at 158th Street, and circled through an underpass to the river's edge. Four soldiers stood at a wooden barricade, blocking the entrance to a narrow asphalt road. The driver lowered his window, flashed an identity card, and the barricade was moved aside. David could feel his heart pounding. Whatever was happening, it was nearing an end.

The sedan moved down the asphalt road, with the river on one side, trees, garbage, and underbrush on the other. Abandoned cars were strewn about;

their windshields smashed, trunks and hoods open, tires and engines missing, many of them burned. "Kids steal the cars," the driver offered. "Then they ride around and burn them for fun."

The road led into a vest-pocket park. The George Washington Bridge towered above. Four helicopters idled on the ground, surrounded by soldiers silhouetted in the night.

"What's the status of the bridge?" the homeless man asked.

"Both levels have been shut down."

"Kill the headlights."

The car pulled to a halt, and was surrounded by soldiers. The homeless man got out; David followed. Two launches were moored at the river's edge. The slapping of water against rocks was all David heard.

They began walking toward a rocky promontory beneath the bridge, where a small red lighthouse was located. Conically shaped, guarded by a wrought-iron fence, the lighthouse was maybe forty feet high. At the door, David ducked and stepped inside. The ground level was five yards wide, jammed with battery-powered lights and power lines running from a portable generator to a spiral stairway. Following the homeless man, he climbed to an open door on the landing above. There, as on the ground level, military personnel were at work. The walls were rusting with three portals, one facing west, one north, one south. Heavy machinery covered the floor.

A fireman's ladder led to a third level, eight feet in diameter with a nine-foot dome. Unlike the previous landing, this one had been constructed with wraparound windows, all of which had been removed. Only the window frames were left. Ten openings, each one a yard high and two feet wide, afforded a total view of the Hudson. The room was crammed with military personnel and electronic equipment. Infrared lights, nightscopes, radio receivers, transmitters.

Then David saw Connor. He was standing on the catwalk wearing a headset and swing microphone. Clearly, he was in his element; just as clearly, he was in charge. A shortwave radio droned in the background, emitting a monotonal male voice.

Connor turned and saw David.

"Shit," he muttered.

The homeless man stepped forward. "I thought it made sense to bring him. At least here he won't be a loose cannon."

Connor nodded and went back to transmitting data. David cast a glance at his watch. It was 12:30 A.M. The wind blowing in from the river picked up. The George Washington Bridge seemed monstrous above.

"Let's go over the numbers again," Connor was saying. "The center span of the bridge is thirty-five hundred feet between towers. Four seven six oh is the length between anchorages. Clear height is one ninety-five on the New York pierhead line, and two ten in New Jersey."

"At this point, there's nothing more Anne can do," the homeless man told David. "Matthes is on a tug coming downriver. All thirteen of the bombs are on board. Any sane person who constructs a nuclear weapon puts in dozens of safeguards and interlocks. The bombs have to be made ready before they explode, but when they go, it happens in microseconds.''

"What does that mean?"

"It means we don't know what state Matthes's bombs are in, but we have three hundred assault troops on the bridge ready to attack. Paratroopers who specialize in demolition and hand-to-hand combat; frogmen, snipers. Speed and surprise are what it's about."

"What about Anne?"

"The men have been instructed to treat her as a hostage. Five members of the team have her safety as their only goal."

Once again, David looked at his watch. Twelve forty-five A.M. "How much longer?" he asked.

"About an hour. And there's nothing you can do to help, so make yourself comfortable. It'll be over soon."

One o'clock . . . 1:05 . . . Each minute seemed to last an hour.

Connor took the headset off, stretched, and gently rubbed his eyes. David looked directly at the agent. There was eye contact, and Connor smiled.

"I'll bet they didn't teach you about this in law school," he offered.

"What do you think will happen to Anne?"

"Right now, I'm more concerned with eight million people getting blown up. But to answer your question, at the moment she's all right, and we'll keep it that way with a little luck."

"How do you know she's all right now?"

"There's a bug in her locket, in the clasp of her necklace."

"You told her you took all the bugs out last month."

"We did. This one belongs to Matthes. He put it in, and we found the frequency when we broke Muller."

David stood still, digesting the thought.

Then it hit.

"You set her up!"

Connor didn't answer.

"You knew! Last night, when you were in my apartment, you knew then that Anne had been bugged."

The agent stared stonily ahead.

"You used her to send a message to Matthes. You turned her into a Trojan horse. You goddamn—"

Before David could finish, the homeless man intervened. "Cool it!"

"Don't you know what he did?"

"I know exactly what he did, and he might be the best man we have. So shut your mouth like you're supposed to and wait."

End of conversation. David was helpless. Please, let everything be all right.

1:25 . . . 1:30 . . .

The pace of activity in the lighthouse quickened.

Upriver, David could see the lights of the tug and kerosene lamps on cornerposts of the scow.

1:35 . . . 1:40 . . .

"The target craft will intersect with the bridge at one-fifty," he heard Connor saying.

1:45 . . . 1:46 . . .

The tug and scow moved steadily down the river.

1:47 . . .

336

On the bridge above, four military trucks began rolling.

1:48 . . .

The truck converged.

1:49 . . .

David hated the moment.

And then, looking at Connor, he realized that Connor loved it. It wasn't revenge for Gordon and Harney; and it wasn't saving mankind or doing his job. It was the risk, the excitement, the confrontation and drama. Moments like this were what Ned Connor lived for.

◆ ◆ ◆

Anne stood on the deck of the tug, staring transfixed at the George Washington Bridge. She'd never seen it from the water before. It was breathtaking, surreal, a concrete and steel roadway spanning the sky. Silver-gray towers rose six hundred feet high, supported by thousands of cables and wires. It was awesome, the stuff of fantasies and dreams, fitting so perfectly into the Palisades that it seemed part of the natural environment. Anne stood there with the wind whipping through her hair.

The bridge loomed closer, then directly above, like a necklace hung by Gods on high.

Christoph Matthes moved to Anne's side. "Something is wrong," she heard him murmur. "There aren't enough cars."

Then, suddenly, they were bathed in light. Spotlights illuminated the tug and scow. Soldiers seemed

337

to be raining from the sky. Parachutes, ropes, cata-
pults. Bursts of gunfire shattered the night.

The first invaders landed on the deck.

Matthes had a gun in his hand.

Anne dove for the river.

There was a *crack*. Incredible pain. Then everything short-circuited in her brain.

Chapter 24

D redging the Hudson River took the better part of two days. In response to press inquiries, an army spokesman announced that the barrage of gunfire heard by Washington Heights residents on Monday night was part of a mock antiterrorist exercise. That satisfied the curiosity of the New York media, which turned its attention to other matters.

"We can't find the body." That was all Connor would tell David.

"What do you mean, you can't find the body?"

"Just what I said. All thirteen bombs have been recovered, but the current underneath the bridge is erratic. One of our men saw Anne go off the boat. He thinks she was shot. That's all we know."

Which meant Anne might still be alive. Maybe the NSA was holding her captive, waiting until her injuries healed; or until she agreed not to talk, because if she were alive, she'd be furious at being lied to and used.

A faint hope, but it was all David had. Then reality intervened. On Thursday, August 24, Connor and another man came to David's apartment. It wasn't clear why the other man was there. He didn't speak, other than to say hello. Most likely, he was a buffer of sorts, ready to intervene if things got out of hand.

Connor did the talking.

"We've searched for three days and still can't find the body. We assume Anne is dead. The case is closed."

"How can you not find the body?"

"It's a big river, and the currents are strange. The Atlantic Ocean pushes all the way up to Albany. She could be upstream, downstream; there's no way to know. We've done what we can. I'm afraid it's over."

"But I love her."

"I won't pretend to know how you feel. All I can say is, life goes on."

"But you don't understand. I'll never see her again." David's voice was rising. "What's wrong with you people? Don't you realize you're playing with real lives?"

"We understand completely, except this wasn't playing. It was for real, and with Anne's help, millions of people were saved."

"You don't know that anyone would have used those bombs."

"No, and back in 1939, no one knew Hitler would build Auschwitz and Dachau. But when foreign leaders talk about genocide and domination, responsible governments have to listen. Any one of a dozen countries could have used those bombs, against Israel, Western Europe, maybe even New York. We lost some lives, but millions more were saved in the bargain.''

''Anne was disposable; that's what you're saying.''

''Not disposable; she was a soldier in a war. She helped us because she thought it was right.''

''She didn't have to die.''

''Maybe not, but it happened. It's over and there's nothing more we can do. Now, if you'll bear with me, there are several things I want to discuss with you.''

The man with Connor looked at his watch in the manner of someone who had someplace to go.

Do you have theater tickets? That's what David wanted to ask, but didn't. Instead, he waited and Connor went on.

''We've decided not to go public with the story. Over the years, we've had a policy of silence on nuclear threats, which seems advisable to avoid panic. For the record, Anne was killed by a hit-and-run driver, who ran a stoplight on Monday night. The body was misidentified when it came into the morgue and cremated yesterday. That's the cover story. Also, for what it's worth, Matthes and Muller are dead. For security reasons, we couldn't bring them to trial, but justice has been done, and we'll be eliminating several of their employees later on.''

''And what about me? Do I wind up with a bullet to keep me quiet?''

"We don't operate that way. All we can do is ask for your silence?"

"And suppose I talk?"

Connor shrugged. "That's between you and your conscience."

"Conscience. You people who run the world: what do you know about conscience? All you know is terror and power and brutality and guns."

For the first time, the man with Connor intervened. "There's one thing more we have to discuss. Ned, perhaps you could tell Mr. Akers about Rosenbaum Associates."

"I'm not sure Mr. Akers is interested in that at the moment."

"I know, but it's late and we have to be going."

David waited.

"All right," Connor said, picking up where he'd left off. "One of our proprietaries is a brokerage house named Rosenbaum Associates. We've arranged for it to show a series of extremely profitable transactions on Anne's behalf. The balance in her account is one million dollars."

"It doesn't matter."

"Play it any way you want, just so the matter is discreetly handled. And if you have any questions, feel free to get in touch. The number at Collins Communications is still operative."

Then the agents left, and David was alone, remembering Anne and wondering if there was any hope. Regardless of what Connor said, no one had found the body. Or had they? It seemed that something was being held back.

Something inside told David that Anne was alive.

THE BEST IN SUSPENSE
FROM TOR

☐ ☐	50451-8	THE BEETHOVEN CONSPIRACY *Thomas Hauser*	$3.50 Canada $4.50
☐ ☐	54106-5	BLOOD OF EAGLES *Dean Ing*	$3.95 Canada $4.95
☐ ☐	58794-4	BLUE HERON *Philip Ross*	$3.50 Canada $4.50
☐ ☐	50549-2	THE CHOICE OF EDDIE FRANKS *Brian Freemantle*	$4.95 Canada $5.95
☐ ☐	50105-5	CITADEL RUN *Paul Bishop*	$4.95 Canada $5.95
☐ ☐	50581-6	DAY SEVEN *Jack M. Bickham*	$3.95 Canada $4.95
☐ ☐	50720-7	A FINE LINE *Ken Gross*	$4.50 Canada $5.50
☐ ☐	50911-0	THE HALFLIFE *Sharon Webb*	$4.95 Canada $5.95
☐ ☐	50642-1	RIDE THE LIGHTNING *John Lutz*	$3.95 Canada $4.95
☐ ☐	50906-4	WHITE FLOWER *Philip Ross*	$4.95 Canada $5.95
☐ ☐	50413-5	WITHOUT HONOR *David Hagberg*	$4.95 Canada $5.95

HIGH-TECH SUSPENSE
FROM DEAN ING